By the s

An Urgent Matter
(written under the pen-name of Alex Winchester)

A Murderer's Legacy

A Murderer's Legacy

Published by The Conrad Press Ltd. in the United Kingdom 2021

Tel: +44(0)1227 472 874
www.theconradpress.com
info@theconradpress.com

ISBN 978-1-914913-03-7

Copyright © Peter Redford, 2021

The moral right of Peter Redford to be identified as author of this work has been asserted in accordance with the Copyright, Designs and Patents Act 1988.

All rights reserved.

Printed and bound in Great Britain by Clays Ltd, Elcograf S.p.A

Typesetting and Cover Design by The Book Typesetters,
www.thebooktypesetters.com

The Conrad Press logo was designed by Maria Priestley.

A Murderer's Legacy

A Crime Thriller

PETER REDFORD

'If you want to keep a secret, you must also hide it from yourself.'

George Orwell

PART I

1

2ND NOVEMBER 2011
10.15PM

Jesús stared into the barrel of the old Colt 45 revolver. He saw it clearly enough but his brain did not register what he saw. The man in black was pointing it straight at him. Aiming right between his eyes. Years before, he would have known exactly what was about to happen. Not now. The disease had destroyed the last vestiges of rational thought. Jesús heard the voices but did not understand the words. He looked past the man in black at the flames dancing in the fireplace.

Maria stood behind Jesús' chair with both hands holding the back for support as she sobbed. She knew exactly what was going to happen. The small tight-knit community had been expecting it for the last few months but today of all days: 'The Day of the Dead'!

Upstairs, in her luxurious bedroom Jesús' French wife Thérèse had cried herself to sleep as she had done every night for the past six months. Her beauty which had originally attracted Jesús' attention was still evident in her advancing years. Long silky blonde tresses hung down just below her shoulders with no hint of grey. Her high cheek bones were still prominent and her skin had few flaws. Sparkling hazel eyes were as keen as ever and rarely missed anything of note.

Her petite nose and mouth were her best features and were what first attracted the attention of the talent scout for the premier modelling agency of her youth. She hardly used makeup because she didn't need it.

Large, glossy, framed photographs adorned the walls displaying her finest moments from international catwalks now long since forgotten. The occasional nagging pain from an injury to her hip, when she was knocked from a narrow platform by a careless model, now an uncomfortable reminder of past glory days.

Left alone in the enormous marital bed she missed her husband's reassuring presence. He currently spent his nights in a small anteroom, constantly monitored by a nurse as he slept in a sitting position in a hospital bed.

In a separate wing of the sprawling Posda hacienda his son slept peacefully, knowing that it was just a matter of time before he would take over his father's empire in its entirety. For several years Pablo had managed the burgeoning drugs trade, first started decades ago by his ancestors, that had grown at an exhaustive rate with each male heir. Pablo intended to reap the rewards and expand into new territories.

He was a slow learner and had caused Jesús many sleepless nights as he taught his protégé. As the only son it was accepted that he would take over on his father's death. However, Jesús' ill health had hastened Pablo's rise to power. It had been an arduous learning curve for Pablo but Jesús was eventually content that his son was ready. Then, as his mind slowly deserted him, Jesús passed over the baton.

Jesús' thirty-year-old daughter was sitting up in her bed watching some late night film on the television as she plucked occasionally at a large bunch of grapes. Her accommodation was the least grand. A few rooms tucked onto the side of the main building. Her mobile, which lay on the bed in front of her, kept pinging as texts came in from friends and acquaintances from all corners of the globe. At each sound she snatched it up, read the message and replied accordingly.

Isabella was a socialite who travelled the world extensively and was extremely popular due to her lavish extravagances. She easily deduced who were true friends and who were solely attracted by her wealth. Manipulating them all was second nature to her. Access to her father's yacht, houses in Paris and London and a flat in New York ensured a private refuge whenever she fancied more than a one night stand.

She invariably dropped her Spanish name and changed it depending upon the country she was in. As the apple of her father's eye, nothing had been too much for her. Private education ensured she could speak Spanish, French and English like a native. Jesús had taught her and Pablo his trade and saw in her a callousness that endeared her more to him than his son.

When it came to looks, she had inherited her mother's genes and was a natural athlete in whatever discipline she undertook. Her intelligence was incisive although modesty had overlooked her and had often led to violent arguments with Pablo and her mother. She knew she could rely on Jesús to always take her side.

The servants' quarters were about half a mile away in a generously appointed block built by Jesús' father. He had known the value of keeping his workers happy and contented. They would likely remain loyal when times required it. Each single lackey had the equivalent of a one bedroom flat and more members of a worker's immediate family would result in extra rooms. Maria's flat was the most opulent of them all.

She pleaded, 'Why tonight? Can't you wait?'

The man in black looked at her fondly. 'You knew I would be coming. It must be done. Today is a good day.'

'But Father, it isn't fair.'

'Maria my child, I think it would be better if you left the room. He won't suffer, I'll make sure.'

Sobbing loudly, she ran from the room closing the substantial oak door behind her as silently as she could. The man in black moved the gun to within a foot of Jesús' forehead.

'My dear friend. I know you can't understand me but what I do now is for your own good. You've trained your son well and he'll continue in your mould. He will become a credit to you.'

The noise from the gun resonated around the room as it ricocheted from one stone wall to another. The heavy calibre bullet left the gun at a sedentary rate compared to modern weapons. It bludgeoned its way through Jesús' temple and lodged in the middle of his brain as if worn out from its exertions. He was dead. The man in black took no chances. He aimed the gun directly at Jesús' heart and pulled the trigger. The bullet careered down the long barrel and then dragged part of Jesús' shirt along with it as it forced its way into his chest and just made it into his heart. Either bullet would have proved fatal.

Upstairs, Thérèse had woken at the sound of the first bullet. She started to cry at the sound of the second. Her life was about to change drastically and she knew it. Unlimited money would soon be a thing of the past. She had a choice to make, stay and be subservient to her son or go with whatever she could get. The nest egg that she had squirrelled away would help but she needed more. At least another two million to make it up to ten million. Any less would mean living in abject poverty.

Pablo had woken and heard the blast of the second bullet as it was expelled from the gun. His time in the limelight had finally arrived. Turning over, he checked his Browning 9mm High Power automatic was still under his pillow and then turned on a side light. He could see his bedroom door was secure and the window shutters were still firmly closed and locked with a bar across them. From now on, he knew he had to be careful. There was always someone else who fancied the crown. Smiling contentedly to himself, he extinguished the light and turned onto his side before quickly falling fast asleep.

Isabella heard both shots clearly and immediately sent a group text to her acquaintances throughout the world. She backed it up with emails to her really close friends. Flying through her mind were some serious questions. How much money will my brother allow me? Will he be as generous as Jesús? Unlikely. It didn't matter. Like her mother, she had a nest egg. Hers, however, was smaller and most of it was not yet tangible.

The servants who were still awake heard the distant retorts. In the stillness of the night the muffled sounds travelled swiftly to them. Not sufficient to awaken the sleepers but enough to let those that heard know what deed had been done.

Maria collapsed to the stone floor crying for the man she could never have. Born within three weeks of each other, they had grown up together. Each cared for the other as though they were siblings, but Jesús was born to take on the mantle of a drug lord and Maria that of a servant. He ensured she wanted for nothing and she worshipped him, looking after his every need.

The man in black came through the door and found Maria on the floor. His small, white, dog collar caught the light. He gently lifted her to her feet, 'Go home Maria.'

'I can't. I must look after him. No one else will.'

'I'll send someone to sort out…'

Maria butted in, 'No! I will do it. It is for me to do and me alone.' She went back into what she now considered the inappropriately named living room. She knew none of the family really cared and they would leave it to her. It was, she believed, going to be her final act for the friend she had loved for so many years.

The man in black walked unconcernedly away passing armed guards scattered about the compound. None dared to face him. They had all known what was going to happen and not one of them had tried to stop it. It was for the best. Allegiance changed immediately from Jesús to Pablo at the retort of the first gunshot. No one needed to be told.

'The King is dead. Long live the King.'

2

16TH NOVEMBER 2011
11AM

Gleb, a young Russian diplomat had his instructions. The ambassador had told him, 'Watch, listen and learn and don't show out.' He was the newest member of the embassy staff and was not a cultural attaché as stated in his credentials. He knew the Columbian government probably suspected he was a spy but they couldn't prove it. When they could, money would change hands and he would go home. But now he was watching.

The funeral was a lavish affair with the family suitably despondent in the neoclassical cathedral in Bogotá. Minor drug barons were there to pay homage to Pablo and let him know they were no threat. Well, not at the moment. Senior politicians from both the government and the *tolerated* opposition were in attendance to show their respects, but mainly to ensure their backhanders would continue. High-ranking police officers and military men were also there to ingratiate themselves with the family and to become known as 'helpful' if required. For a hefty fee of course.

Then there were the journalists. All knew what they were going to write the day before and some had already completed their copy ready for publication. They were not stupid enough to name names. Those who wanted to live to a ripe old age knew everyone in the first dozen rows or so would totally deny being associated with drugs even though they blatantly were. Corruption was an established way of life for many who aspired to reach the higher echelons of political life or their chosen professions.

Gleb had a photographic memory and recognised most of the important participants but now watched Isabella. He thought she was only a few years younger than him. Probably late twenties. His mind wandered. Rich, pretty and single. Just how he liked them.

Several hundred locals packed the remaining seats to witness the spectacle of a show funeral. Scattered amongst them were individuals in the pay of the Americans and British who wanted to update their records of the cartels that were operational in the country. Outside were concealed photographers who were snapping images of everyone in and out of the cathedral. People in America and Britain were watching video feeds in real time.

●

On the top floor of the Foreign Office in Whitehall, Tabitha Marchant sat behind her desk. Derek sat in a scruffy armchair reserved for visitors. He was half-turned and was fidgeting trying to get comfortable. They were both watching a live feed on a 40-inch television. Tabitha hated the room which was her office. She considered it way too small for a person of her standing. It had plenty of room though for an upright safe, a table and a selection of chairs as well as several shelving units and a display cabinet.

'For Christ's sake, stop fidgeting. Turn the chair round.'

Derek got up and struggled with the chair.

'Who else is getting this feed?'

Derek said, 'I'm not sure. I think someone in MI6. Do you want me to find out?'

'No I don't. The fewer people who know we are seeing this the better.'

•

Gleb had done his homework. He knew how the system worked. He was aware how the church would view any funeral requests and where they could be held. The donations made over the years by Jesús to the Roman Catholic establishment had guaranteed the cathedral's availability. Any dissent from the lower strata of the clergy would not be tolerated by the hierarchy who could always find a reason to justify the spectacle of a drug lord and renowned murderer being permitted a service in the country's premier cathedral. His tomb, where he was to be interred, was on a large plot which housed his parents, grandparents and great grandparents. All paternal males had met death by a bullet.

Towards the rear of the cathedral sat an olive-skinned man of some fifty years dressed in an elegant white suit and a black tie. In his buttonhole was a dark tulip. He was ignored by all those around him and drew no attention from any of the specific watchers. In his pocket was a small stiff envelope which contained a piece of paper with a phone number written on it. All his adult life he had operated as a pick-pocket in the capital but today was different. Five years previously he had sworn an oath to Jesús that he would complete a task on the day of his funeral. Now was the time. His eyes remained glued to his target.

Maria was seated several rows behind the main family with the other servants. People allegedly related to Jesús had arrived from around the world and taken precedence over her even though they hadn't clapped eyes on him for decades. She did not mind. She was grieving in her own way and was probably the only genuine mourner present.

Maria enjoyed the service. Not in a happy way, but in a way that befitted her best friend. The service did not stint on cost nor time. To many, it was way too long and mind-bogglingly boring. Some of the older members of the congregation were either asleep or dozing. They were there for networking or to confirm that their payments would continue, not to mourn the passing of a murderous competitor or a dead cash cow.

The choir enjoyed themselves singing copious hymns and were all looking forward to spending their small share of the donation made by Pablo. Not one chorister cared who they were there for as long as they were rewarded. Maria believed they sang solely for Jesús.

At the conclusion, all those invited started to traipse across the road towards the main hotel in the city to enjoy the extravagant wake. Maria hung back to talk to God. She had a lot to say about Jesús. Begging forgiveness on his behalf meant a lot to her. His sins were numerous. Murders by the dozen in the early years when he was establishing his position. Selling drugs throughout America, Britain and Europe to people who often died from overdosing. Maria was not concerned much for them if they were stupid enough to pay to take the stuff and then overdo it.

Gleb hadn't been invited to the wake, but it didn't stop him attending. He'd already bumped into Isabella leaving the cathedral and struck up a conversation. Throwing in a little sexual inuendo didn't offend her and raised his hopes for later. Now he was listening to all the conversations taking place and was quickly learning who he could bribe or blackmail for information.

Eventually Maria stood up and turned to leave the beautiful cathedral. Kneeling in the aisle was an immaculately dressed olive-skinned man. Maria grasped a pew for support. He had a closed, dark tulip in his buttonhole. Jesús' favourite flower! Some five years ago, at the first onset of his disease, Jesús had confided to her that one day an angel wearing a tulip would approach her on his behalf with a request.

He rose and smiled amiably at her and in a gentle, syrup-smooth voice said, 'Maria, I have a message from Jesús.'

She collapsed unconscious on the cathedral's stone floor.

Several of the clergy rushed forward to assist her. The olive-skinned man left the cathedral and had his photo taken by one diligent photographer who had remained at his post.

Maria was helped to her feet. She looked hurriedly about for the 'angel'. He was nowhere to be seen. Offering profuse thanks to those who had rushed to her assistance, she left the cathedral stepping out into bright sunlight. The street seemed to be populated by people in white suits, but none wore a buttonhole.

Had she dreamt it? The thought entered her mind. No. She

had seen him. As a devout Catholic she believed in angels. However, this was a real person. It was the shock of seeing a person all in white with the buttonhole and the seven uttered words in the cathedral that had caused her to faint.

Will I ever see him again and get the message? crashed through all her thoughts. Her eyes started to moisten. Fainting had stopped her hearing it. She silently cursed herself. Hailing a passing cab, she returned to her cheap hotel in the poorer part of the city foregoing the mockery of the wake.

3

16TH NOVEMBER 2011
11.30AM

As the funeral was in full swing, three nondescript men all carrying false identity papers were alighting from a rubber skiff onto a small, deserted beach near Caracas in Venezuela. The sailor piloting the craft was wearing civilian clothes which aggravated him beyond belief. Having been a member of the Royal Navy for his entire working life of thirty-five years, he was used to being in uniform and much preferred it. He watched his charges safely off the beach before he turned back out to sea and navigated easily back to his ship just out of sight over the horizon.

The three men quickly found what they were looking for. A battered, old and dirty green Land Rover that gave the appearance of having been dumped by the side of the road. To confuse the inquisitive, it bore cloned identification plates. It was splattered with mud and covered with a thin film of dust. In fact it had been there less than half an hour. Not long enough to have been stripped by the local gangs or stolen for profit. The ignition key was balanced on the rear offside tyre and the petrol gauge showed the vehicle to be full to the brim.

Five jerry cans in the back covered by a tarpaulin were full of additional fuel sufficient for what they needed and three rucksacks and a small case were concealed next to them under a separate cover. The older man of the three started the vehicle at the first turn of the key. The engine purred as he let it idle for a few seconds before blipping the throttle. Instantaneous reaction.

His younger colleague lay in the dirt as he felt under the chassis. Grasping fingers sought and found the two packages which he yanked free. Two P226 Sig Sauer automatic pistols with additional magazines were wrapped securely in one polythene bag and three satellite enabled and encrypted mobile phones were in another. They took a phone and the older and younger man took the weapons. The third man, Sebastian Parke, watched the other two with slight apprehension. They were his bodyguards.

The British Embassy staff had excelled themselves with the equipment.

The only thing the three men were not aware of however, was that attached to the vehicle's fuel tank, and directly below the jerry cans, was a small amount of PE-4 explosive with a remotely controlled detonator. A pair of friendly eyes had maintained observation on the parked vehicle to ensure the correct people collected it.

The British Embassy had also catered for any serious unforeseen problems.

The little group set off to drive the 1500 miles through Venezuela and into Columbia and to a meeting with an unknown person at a pre-determined location near Yacopi about 120 miles north of Bogotá. The older of the bodyguards was driving and his colleague was giving directions from the map on his strange-looking mobile phone. They were keeping to side roads for most of the journey to avoid unwarranted attention and to spot any tail more easily. The Land Rover bounced about as it navigated the barely made up roads.

A brand new, experimental military drone was flying many thousands of feet above them observing their progress. It was being operated by a young female naval rating who had the skill and dexterity required to ensure it remained undetected by the radar of the country it was flying over. It was packed with the latest monitoring and surveillance equipment and sported several new weapons. Other senior naval personnel scrutinised the video images it recorded and were mandated to authorise and activate the weaponry. All were ensconced in the bowels of a new British frigate which was conducting sea trials in the Caribbean and visiting British Overseas Territories.

Sebastian, the man from the Secret Intelligence Service was sitting behind the two members of the SBS. All three had been chosen because they could speak Spanish fluently. Hardly any words passed between them as each was focused on their respective role.

Sebastian was running through his mind who the informant might be. He knew that the person he was due to meet would only pass on the information they had for a payment of about two million pounds. The bodyguards knew they had to keep their principal alive at all costs and, if necessary, get him back to a country from where he could be extracted. If the wrong people got the slightest whiff of what they were up to, all hell would break loose.

As Pablo was winding up proceedings at the wake, the

three were settling down at a desolate spot for the night. Although they each had individual small tents, a night in the vehicle in a sleeping bag was no hardship. Sebastian phoned a number from memory and within seconds confirmed the rendezvous was still on. No idle chit chat on the phone. The faster the call the better. Harder to trace even though it was an encrypted call. It galvanised each man to thoroughly check his equipment. Which pocket contained which item and which bag held what paraphernalia. They had ten days to get to the meeting. There was no point in rushing.

17TH NOVEMBER 2011

Gleb was in bed. Isabella's hotel bed. He knew he was playing with fire. It was worth it. How much money can I make? Ever larger amounts swirled around in his head. When he had been posted to Columbia he never dreamt it could be so lucrative. He lay there thinking how much better life had suddenly become. He didn't know a couple of Pablo's men were waiting for him.

Maria had cried uncontrollably for several hours as the 'angel's' words flitted in and out of her brain. She had thrown her clothes onto a chair before climbing into bed. It was no use. She was tossing and turning and still crying occasionally. In the middle of the night, she gave up all further pretence of sleep and got up. Padding naked about the room, she picked her funeral clothes up from the chair to put them into her case. As she folded her jacket, she found the envelope in one of the pockets. Holding it in her hand she stared at her name written on the front in Jesús' handwriting.

She slumped into a chair trembling and then with cautious trepidation opened the envelope. Inside was a small piece of paper bearing a phone number. Should she phone straight away or wait until a reasonable hour? Maria picked up the hotel room's phone and dialled the number. On the second ring, a male voice answered.

'I have been waiting for your call. Please come to the Church of San Agustin where I will find you,' and the line went dead.

Without any further thought, Maria quickly dressed and ran down to the street to hail a taxi. She found the main door at the entrance to the church wide open and inviting and went inside. Several dim candles cast eerie shadows. No one else was visible. Kneeling, she offered a personal prayer. Then she sat patiently in a pew with the intention of waiting for however long it took.

A young priest soon approached from the side of the altar. 'Hello Maria, Jesús spoke fondly of you every time he came here. I have often wanted to meet you, but he forbade it until now.'

'I never knew he came here at all. He never said. Why didn't he tell me?' Small tears welled up in the corner of her eyes.

'He knew he was a sinner. This church was where he came to confess. He couldn't, or wouldn't, change his ways and he believed it best that no one should know. I could not break his confidence until now. We agreed his funeral would be the right time for you to know.'

'Why didn't he tell me?' and she burst into tears.

'He loved you so much. He trusted only you and that is why he has guided you here now. Many years back before he became ill, he entrusted this envelope to me. It is for you. I had expected your call straight after the funeral. But you are here now.' Then he handed Maria an envelope.

Maria held it to her breast as she cried.

'Go back to your hotel and read it in peace.'

Even at that late hour, someone was watching. They'd been sent by the dingy hotel's night-time receptionist who had a bad habit of listening to private phone conversations. He'd always been able to spot a potential financial opportunity and thought he saw one now.

The receptionist's predilections also ran to watching guests and their bedroom antics via small holes in walls with a clear view of the beds. However, he was struggling to see all of Maria's room clearly. He had one thing that could help.

Maria sat in a chair with a glass of water and a small packet of tissues beside her. Opening the envelope, she removed the sheet of paper and unfolded it.

Dearest Maria

You have been my best friend since childhood and my one true love. My wife and children were nothing compared to you. Your loyalty to me could never be fully reciprocated without me endangering your life. I could not let that happen. My brain is getting slowly worse and I have been told there is no cure. I write this letter while I still have the ability. Soon I may not even recognise you.

Do you remember the den we made in the forest as children? Of course you do. Go there and you will find a box with my final gift to you. There will be nothing that you will want for. I ask just one last favour of you.

You will find a mobile phone which is programmed to send a group message to all my disciples around the world. As my mind is destroyed, they alone will know the true identities of those that control our product's money in their respective countries. How it is laundered and the method used to forward it to the Posda estate. Please send this message for me.

Each one will respond asking for proof of the veracity of the message. They will ask for the name by which I know them. It is a form of security that I have put in place.

I have sent each of them a bible with a gospel highlighted. Within that gospel is a highlighted name. That is the name I know them by. You will find a list with the phone. Please reply to each one accordingly.

Should the true names of my disciples become known, their lives and those of their families will be put in danger. I consider their safety to be of paramount importance.

As my mind fades, I shall have to entrust Pablo with my disciples names so he can continue the family's business uninterrupted.

One word of caution Maria. Do not let this letter fall into anyone else's possession as it will endanger your life or that of your family. Destroy it immediately.

Maria, I await you where we shall be together for eternity.

Your loving friend

Jesús

Small tears dropped from Maria's cheeks onto the paper. She had no matches. It had to be burnt quickly. If Jesús said destroy it, that's what she had to do. The cathedral. So appropriate. A short taxi ride down the road. Rushing out of the hotel she soon found a cab and then the open door of the church. She ran inside. Candles burnt close to the entrance door and Maria put the paper to the flames.

The priest responsible for the safety of the cathedral overnight watched her from a distance. He knew people did strange things and decided not to intervene. The paper fluttered to the flagstone floor in its fiery death throws. Maria watched it for several seconds and satisfied that it was beyond redemption stamped out the final embers. Scooping up the ashes into a tissue, she ran crying from the church.

The night receptionist was happy. His colleague had reported back what had occurred in the Church of San Agustin. Now he was sitting in front of his laptop watching a still frame from his video recording displaying an image of Maria reading the letter. It was as though the camera was looking over her shoulder. The writing was clear. He knew it would be worth a lot of money to the right person.

His little bendy stalk with the small fisheye lens camera on the end had come through. It was a change from recording material to be used for blackmail.

As dawn broke he located which hotel the individual he wanted was staying in. He didn't need any mistakes by speaking to the wrong person. The phone was answered on the third ring and in French. It was to be his last ever phone call. He bled out behind the reception desk. The police never found his laptop or the camera on a stalk. They never found his killer. But then they were not really that bothered. He was nothing to them.

4

17TH NOVEMBER 2011
8AM

Gleb was no wimp. He had been well trained by his Russian masters. When he had crept out of Isabella's room he wasn't expecting any problems. His two potential assailants had underestimated him. They should have shot him straight away. He effortlessly disarmed one and used the liberated weapon to kill both before he bolted out of the rear of the hotel. Pablo should have sent a lot more men.

•

The trio broke camp and set off at a leisurely pace. The roads they were using were mainly uninhabited by any other traffic and often void of tarmac. No point in rushing and destroying the Land Rover's suspension. Definitely no police to stop them. They would be harassing the motorists on the main routes and tapping them for a bribe. Hardly a soul to see them. Just how they wanted it. Their security drone was always above when they were moving and could forewarn them of potential threats. Still ample time to get there.

•

18TH NOVEMBER 2011

Two days after the funeral, Pablo, his family and all their servants had returned to the sprawling hacienda some 120 miles north of Bogotá. Life for each of them had changed. Some more than others. Those corrupt officials who had ratified their backhanders had returned to their respective duties of doing nothing except enjoying a rich lifestyle. Guests from around the world had returned to their own erroneous endeavours. Within a day, Jesús was as good as forgotten by everybody except Maria.

Pablo knew what he had to do. His father had groomed him from a young age explaining how the business worked and what was required to quickly stamp his authority on those around him. As a teenager he had reluctantly been forced to kill people who were a mild threat to his father. Then he started to enjoy the dominance it gave him. The power of life or death was extraordinary, but now was different.

He knew who his main rival was. He knew how he was going to die. The bomb was in the boot of his car. It was put there while he was at the wake. As soon as he opened it, 'Goodnight.' Everyone would know he was responsible but no one could prove it. He was the main man now! Everybody would know and no one would mess with him. One substantial hit: that's probably all it would take.

For some reason, the explosion occurred two days later at 9am. It happened outside a swanky restaurant in the centre of Bogotá. They didn't even serve breakfast! What he was doing there remained a mystery. Body parts were strewn across the road and through the newly broken, plate glass window onto the tables already set for lunch. Pablo could not understand why he would have been opening the boot at that time of day. A true mystery. He didn't care. Point proved. Supremacy guaranteed.

19TH NOVEMBER 2011

Only back one day. It was too long! Maria had hardly unpacked but she had to get to the old den. She had to do his bidding. The person watching knew it would be sooner rather than later and wasn't surprised when she left her apartment before dawn. Maria was careless. Following her was easier than expected. She walked along an overgrown path making enough noise to mask any from her pursuer. After a couple of miles, at a lightning wracked tree, Maria veered off the path and went deeper into the forest.

It wasn't long before she reached the den. It was still reasonably intact. The sticks still gripped the two trees it was slung between although the roof had suffered in places. At one time it had been waterproofed with lichen and moss. No longer. Maria ducked down to get through the small entrance that hadn't been an obstacle for her as a child.

She promptly found what she was looking for. It was all wrapped securely in a waterproof liner. The box was about a foot square and of ornate inlaid woods engraved in silver with her name and the words, 'Never forget me'. Even before she opened it she was crying. It was stuffed full of high denomination American dollars.

The phone was in its original box with two batteries and a charger. With fumbling fingers, Maria slid one of the batteries into place. It was flat. So was the second. She was going to have to take it home to charge. Now she knew she would have to be careful. It was much too late. As she exited the den, she saw the person move.

'Hello Maria.'

Maria was hesitant. The den was so well hidden. Even as children, they had never divulged its location. The chance of a casual passer-by, or even a searcher finding it was practically impossible in the sprawling forest.

'Surprised to see me?'

'Yes,' was Maria's timid reply.

'What a pretty box.'

Maria could not conceal it as the person stepped towards her. The knife slid unseen by Maria into the woman's hand and the blade shot silently out and locked. As the woman closed the short distance her hand came up and the knife buried itself between Maria's ribs. Shock spread across Maria's face as the box fell to the floor. The knife had punctured her heart. Within seconds she was dead on the floor next to the box.

The killer retrieved her knife, cleaned it on some bracken and tucked it back into its sheath on her wrist. Rhetorically, she asked, 'Now, what is in this box?' As she opened it her eyes widened. Sitting on the ground she counted it all out. Over a million dollars. 'Thank you Jesús. I will never forget you,' and she laughed.

22ND NOVEMBER 2011

On the sixth day, the three men hid their Land Rover by covering it with foliage. The dirty green colour blended in well. They had eight miles further to go and knew they had several days to accomplish the trek. The older man thought a tortoise could have completed it in half the time.

They set off in line with Sebastian sandwiched in the middle carrying his small case. The older bodyguard at the back ensured they left no signs of their presence and the youngster at the front maintained a constant slow pace as he led them to the exact coordinates he had been told to find, just off to the side of a small dirt track. All three had a large rucksack carried on their back.

Sebastian sat on his small case as his compatriots scoured the immediate area. The fit younger man found a tree about fifty yards off that he knew he could climb which gave an unobstructed view over the rendezvous site. The other found a hiding place at the base of a decaying tree under deep piles of leaves within yards of the potential meet. The forest's dense green canopy above thwarted the vision of the high circling drone. There were still four days to go. Always better to be early. You never know what you might see.

Moving deeper into the jungle, they found a small clearing where they set up camp. Four days would be no problem for them sleeping under canvas. The bodyguards maintained an irregular watch on the rendezvous site just to ensure that no one arranged any surprises for them. They knew no one survives if they are careless.

On two early mornings, they were alerted to an industrial

drone that rose from the confines of Pablo's hacienda by the vigilant naval ratings monitoring their own high flying military drone. People in London were alerted and discussions and theories were proposed and considered. The three men were made aware of decisions taken by mandarins in expensive suits in plush offices. The two bodyguards discussed potential problems and tactics. Just because people in London said to do one thing did not mean they would do it. They believed their personal survival was paramount.

25TH NOVEMBER 2011

The evening of the ninth day, all three men sat together and went through what should happen at 6.30am the following morning. Then they went through what could go wrong and all the possible outcomes. None of them appeared worried. The plan was a simple one and had been agreed before they had left London nearly three weeks earlier. None saw any point in changing it whatever London decreed now.

26TH NOVEMBER 2011

At 4.30am they took up their positions. No one wanted to be caught napping by an early arrival. Sebastian busied himself preparing for his guest as the elder of the bodyguards unloaded his gun by removing the magazine. Then he racked it ejecting the round in the chamber and cocked the hammer in the process. From his rucksack he took out a strange cylindrical attachment and slid it over the slide and barrel of his firearm and secured it in place.

His partner took out of his backpack a foot square cannister and handed it to him. It clipped neatly beneath the attachment.

The senior man teased the end of a thin wire from it and connected it to a bulbous projectile about four times the size of a normal bullet with a slender long pipe at the back of it. He pushed the pipe into the barrel of the gun through the attachment until he heard a sharp click. The bulbous projectile was proud of both the barrel and the attachment. He had transformed his gun into an armed and ready, small missile launcher.

As if by way of explanation to Sebastian, he said, 'Better fully prepared than not.' The principal nodded. He had no idea what the item was for nor how it worked. All he knew was the two men were there to look after him. If they had a strange bit of kit, he knew it was for his safety and he wasn't going to question them. The younger of the bodyguards checked his phone. One word scrolled lethargically across the screen, *Green*.

An hour and a half later as the younger man was sitting on a branch in the crook of his tree, he heard his phone beep once in his earpiece. It was only just audible but sufficient to attract his attention. Glancing at it, the word had changed to *Drone*. One of the new surveillance systems from aboard the ship had seen it before it was twenty feet above the ground. Risking his partner's wrath he called out, 'Drone'. The man in his hide under the leaves swore. He knew that people on the ship would be taking direct action.

Deep in the depths of the frigate a naval officer, who looked older than both the bodyguards put together, spoke quietly to the young woman controlling the ship's own drone. Seconds later, she sent it immediately on a slowly descending loop towards the identified hostile intruder, to approach from behind. The officer with authority to use the drone's weaponry waited for it to get into position and then instructed the woman which system to use. The bodyguards knew that the hostile drone would be no match for the military one from the ship, but its downing would arouse suspicion.

The approaching rogue drone was disabled as it was still climbing some four miles away. It's Columbian operator, who was monitoring the attached camera, saw nothing untoward before he lost control and then all contact. It had been hit from behind with an electronic jamming device which had sent it spiralling to its doom. The jogger the Columbian had been tasked to follow and observe, saw it fall from the sky and laughed out loud as she jogged along the dirt track that some people referred to as a road.

The door flew open and the flustered operator ran in. Pablo dropped to the floor as he pulled his gun from its holster. Fearing death, the operator screamed. Pablo just managed to stop himself from pulling the trigger.

'What the fuck is wrong with you. I could have killed you?'
'Señor, the drone has crashed.'
'What happened?'
'It just fell from the sky,' said the operator in confusion.

'Did you see anything hit it?'

'No Señor, it just seemed to die and fall.'

Pablo considered what he had been told and what he knew. The drone was new. Bought the day before the funeral. It was an industrial sized drone which was probably way too complicated for a simple security guard to operate. He glared at the small Columbian before him who was shivering with fear. Pablo still held his Browning in his hand. The thought occurred to him the man was just incompetent. He probably couldn't fly it and didn't know what he was doing. Pablo decided he would deal with him later.

'Get a Jeep and go after her. I don't trust her an inch. I want to know where and how far she goes and if she meets anyone. Go on. Get on with it.'

The operator ran from the room shouting as he went. A couple of other security guards met him and they all jumped into an old Jeep and headed off along a dirt road. Within a mile the road forked and the Jeep slithered to a halt. None knew which way to go. She had not run in this direction before. A combined decision was made and the Jeep roared off with spinning wheels down the track which appeared to have been the main fork. After five, long, bumpy miles they realised they were on the wrong track. The target was already several miles away on the dirt side road.

She was still laughing.

5

26TH NOVEMBER 2011
6.30AM

At exactly 6.30am the woman ran into view and then just off the track to where Sebastian was waiting. He recognised her immediately.

'Good morning, I'm Sebastian, I'm English.'

'Of course you are. Only an Englishman would be wearing a suit and tie at this time of day in the middle of a jungle in Columbia.'

Ignoring the jibe, 'I have come a long way to meet you. I am led to believe that you have some information for me?'

'Oh yes. I hope you have brought a lot of money. What I have to sell will be worth at least two million English pounds.'

'I think we had better sit down. Can I offer you a cup of tea? I have some ready to be made.' Then as if to enforce the remark, he picked up a mug and said, 'Do you take milk and sugar?'

'My God!'

Sebastian assumed, quite correctly, that tea was not going to be taken by his guest. He, however, slipped a tea bag into a mug and from a billycan retrieved from the side of a small smouldering fire, poured some hot water into it. As he picked up his powdered milk container, he absently queried, 'I presume you were at the funeral the other day?'

'Obviously I was,' came the pithy reply. A brief second passed, 'I presume you had something to do with the drone that was about to follow me falling from the sky?'

Sebastian, with the speed and skill of a practiced liar replied, 'I'm sorry. I don't know anything about that.'

'Of course you don't! How many people are watching us?'

'Shall we stop this dancing and get down to business. Your people may be trying to locate you, so I think time is of the essence.'

The two talked quickly. The woman explained what her information involved and tendered a salacious titbit to whet Sebastian's appetite.

'I also hold the names of our contacts within your security service and government. That alone should be worth what I am asking. A word of caution. Any report you send back may find its way onto one of their desks.'

Sebastian for his part, put forward potential methods of payment as tempters to loosen the woman's tongue. Agreements were quickly reached and both seemed satisfied. In the distance they heard the distinctive sound of an old Jeep being driven hard.

The man in his tree hide heard the gentle single bleep from his phone. No need for him to check. He knew a warning would be scrolling across the screen, but it was obvious what was coming. Sebastian also heard the distant grumble of a Jeep being thrashed, 'Go back. Do not stop your routine. Jog every fine morning. I will be here as agreed for one week.'

The woman ran from the rendezvous site into the open and onto the dirt track. Her slight limp quickly vanishing. Before she had travelled two hundred yards the Jeep hove into view.

As they met, the vehicle stopped.

Sebastian was worried on two counts. He'd thrown his billycan's boiling water onto the embers of the fire and stood stock still behind a thick tree trunk. The leaves of the canopy cast abstract shadows from the morning's light that shielded him from a casual view. He knew that if the Jeep's occupants had any form of thermal imaging, they would all be found quite easily.

What the woman had said crept into his thoughts. Traitors! Where were they? 'How high were they? How powerful? Who could he tell? Who could he trust?' There was one person. He couldn't afford to use the phone he had in case the people who supplied it were able to listen. He needed a burner. Where from? There weren't any stores in the middle of a Columbian jungle. He'd have to be careful what he reported.

The senior man gently lifted a small aerial from the attachment on his gun and then pointed his weapon in the general direction of the Jeep as his colleague high in the tree adjusted his phone. A circle with a crosshair in it appeared on the screen overlaying an image of the Jeep. He waited.

Two men alighted from the Jeep as the driver remained alert with the vehicle still idling loudly. They held their ground in front of the woman. It was evident to the bodyguards, even at such a distance, that an argument was gathering momentum. The woman was pushed. A Columbian was slapped in reply. A fist was raised, but the toe of a trainer was delivered with ferocity and accuracy before a punch was delivered. The man dropped to the floor in sheer agony holding his groin. The Columbian left still standing seemed to be trying to calm the situation. A minute or so passed and then the woman ran on past the Jeep in a reciprocal route back towards the compound. The driver turned the engine off and joined his compatriot. Together, they helped their recovering colleague into the vehicle.

A phone was produced and the Columbian drone operator was clearly visible to the bodyguards as he gesticulated wildly with his free hand. The phone was returned to a pocket and the two standing Columbians, after a quick conversation, started to walk towards the rendezvous site one either side of the track. They were looking into the forest. The bodyguard under the leaves whispered to Sebastian who remained stock-still behind his tree.

It was only a couple of minutes before they were level with the rendezvous point. Sebastian held his breath. They walked on past. The dead embers of the fire had sent up a small cloud of steam when the water had hit it. It was lingering, held high in the treetops. The two searchers were not at all diligent and saw nothing. It didn't take them long to reappear and walk back to the Jeep. After a seven point U-turn the vehicle followed in the same direction as the jogger.

Pablo sat in his study deep in thought. The Columbian had managed to operate the drone successfully for a week or so without problems. Why has it failed now? Especially since she had run a different route to previous days. He made his decision. Time to see if one of his *new friends,* bought at considerable expense at the wake, were as good as they said they were. He snatched up his phone as he opened his little black book.

A direct line to the barracks commander. No introductions

needed. The colonel recognised the number calling in the display and knew there would be a bonus for the right outcome to any request. The problem was explained and the solution immediately forthcoming. A helicopter would be equipped with heat-seeking capabilities and dispatched. No longer than three hours before it would touch down at the hacienda. Pablo was impressed.

The naval rating listening in to Pablo's phone call reported it to his supervisor. Soon London knew. A hasty discussion was had and the decision passed back to the ship. They in turn passed it via secure text to the young bodyguard who informed the others. All in twenty-nine minutes.

Sebastian was worried. The helicopter would undoubtedly find them and the ship's drone would doubtless be seen on its radar if it got too close. Then it would likely become a diplomatic incident. That could not be permitted to happen. Decision made: the military drone was recalled to the ship. The two SBS men knew what to do. The elder man set off at a fast jog. He could get to their vehicle and drive back in time. The younger man began to pack up all their equipment. Nothing could be left to be found. Sebastian helped as best he could.

The Land Rover hurtled back to the rendezvous site and was loaded with all their gear in minutes. A final check was made and then they heard the distant clatter of an approaching helicopter. Caution was thrown to the wind. All got into the vehicle and it accelerated off in the opposite direction to the helicopter. They didn't know that it was only just landing at the compound and they had more time than they thought.

Twenty miles were added to the odometer before the helicopter lifted off. It would not be searching so far away. No jogger would run that far. The pilot had agreed with Pablo to search up to ten miles in every direction but he was pedantic and took it upon himself to double the distance. He knew he may be in for a thick envelope of gratitude. The three men thought they were safe.

6

26TH NOVEMBER 2011
11AM

They sat by a small fire over which a billycan was hanging, full of what they were led to believe was goulash. That is what it said on the packet, but none were sure when they looked at it. It was an early lunch as they had missed breakfast. The youngster poked the fire into life with a stick.

Then they heard the unmistakable clatter of a helicopter a long way off. Sebastian looked at the other two. Surely it can't be looking for them this far out. The two SBS men looked at each other in a worried manner. The elder one spoke, 'If it comes any nearer, it's going to find us. We'll have to down it. Let the ship know.'

The younger one sent a text. The ship's radar readers had already seen the helicopter arrive at the hacienda. Now they were watching its search pattern. The ship's captain replied to his text. He read the reply, 'They are saying "Go ahead" but only if we have to.'

'If it comes any closer, we'll have no choice.' He assembled his firearm with the bulbous projectile. 'I'll go over the other side of the track.'

The youngster set up his phone. Then they all waited. It was pointless to try and hide as any thermal imaging would spot them or the pilot would see the car. Either way, they would be located. Slowly the noise of the helicopter grew louder. It was searching along the track.

The pilot spotted the dying embers of the fire on his imaging display from three miles off. He knew he had found someone and using his personal mobile phone contacted Pablo. He was telling him where he was when there was a large flash from the side of the track below him and his alarm systems began warning him of an incoming missile. The youngster guided it right into an engine where it exploded and turned the helicopter into a fireball.

It was too late. Pablo heard the aircraft's automated warnings via the pilot's phone and then the explosion. Then nothing as the phone died along with the pilot. Now he knew for sure.

The hacienda suddenly became a hive of confusion and activity as Pablo shouted orders. Several Jeeps full of heavily armed men started to leave along the track to where the helicopter had come down. They were under no illusions. Pablo had sent them to kill whoever they found.

Thérèse and Isabella were having an early lunch and watched the ensuing panic unfolding. Somehow, one had steered their conversation to finance. Mainly the Posda accounts and the fact that since Jesús' death, people had become tardy payers. Then each bemoaned their allowances were on the wane. Neither told the other what they were doing about it.

Pablo was so enraged and intent on finding the culprits who had downed the helicopter he forgot why he was looking for them. A little while later, no one seemed to notice a Jeep with a female driver that was heading south towards Bogotá.

The three men threw their equipment into the Land Rover as the ship launched a drone. A senior naval officer contacted London. Images from the drone were displayed on screens in Whitehall. Mandarins prevaricated. Hawks and Doves in various departments argued the rights and wrongs of what had occurred. The three in the Land Rover didn't wait for any decision, they were travelling via a roundabout route to Ecuador. No one should be looking for them in that direction.

Sebastian was surprised when his phone rang and he didn't recognise the number shown in the display.

'Yes?'

A female voice drawled, 'You have stirred up quite a hornet's nest. I suggest you leave quickly.'

'How did you get this number?'

'My mother has a nasty habit of writing in a diary. She thinks she is the only one who knows where it is kept. I find it a fascinating read. Maybe we could come to a separate agreement. I shall be in America shortly and then in England. Should you get out of the country unscathed perhaps I could speak to you then?'

'You obviously have my number. You apparently know who I am. My organisation is always open to making a deal if what we are buying is good information,' replied Sebastian.

'The information would allow you to disable the entire Columbian drugs trade in your country.'

'It may be something that interests us.'

'It was of sufficient interest for you to travel to Columbia to speak to my mother about it…'

'Possibly.'

'… And to consider several million pounds in payment for the same information,' the caller continued.

'Your proposal is?'

'The same agreement as my mother but I would be able to give you details. Methods of deliveries, dates and places when deals are to be done. People involved from here in Columbia to the dealers on your city streets.'

'What proof do you have that you can supply this information?' Sebastian challenged.

'You know who I am. That should be sufficient.'

'Call this number in a fortnight.'

'Good luck. You may need it. There will be a lot of people looking for you,' then she hung up and removed the sim card which she threw into the jungle before placing a new one into the phone.

Her escape route had been arranged over a year ago. She was heading to a private airfield and then on to Florida. The three men hadn't had the benefit of time and couldn't rely on a British helicopter to get them out. All three knew if it was spotted on Columbian radar it would be shot down and definitely turn into a diplomatic incident. They had no choice: it was going to be a back-breaking, uncomfortable, bumpy ride.

●

At SIS headquarters at Vauxhall Cross, the section chief, Gareth Threadbolt and his deputy Barrington Webster were debating the potential value of any information already gleaned or expected.

'What are we going to learn that we don't already know or suspect?'

His deputy replied, 'It's a lot of money to find out very little and furthermore, we will have to pass on the information to 5 as it's domestic. The police liaison officer on JTAC will insist the Yard deal with it as it's national drug distribution.'

'We will be paying for information that the police probably already know, or suspect. I can't sanction that. The funeral told us nothing new. Just arrange for JTAC to be told what we know so far and leave it at that for the time being.'

'What about Sebastian?'

'Let's hope he makes it to the pickup.'

Webster didn't care either way. He made a phone call to the Foreign Office.

PART 2

7

7TH DECEMBER 2011
11AM

There were two sharp raps on the door about a second before it was thrown forcefully open and a large, six-foot-tall, slightly dishevelled man in his early fifties burst in. His suit was showing wear and was creased in odd places. Surprisingly, his shoes were clean and his tie was reasonably modern and in place. Long black hair was in need of combing and cutting and a day's stubble needed shaving. His face was showing a few faint scars and was a little red from his exertion of running up the five floors of stairs to the DAC's office. Only the tired or infirm waited for the lifts at New Scotland Yard.

DC John Whiles had made an effort. He, with several exceptionally smart officers, some in uniform, from Sussex Constabulary had seen the commissioner of the Metropolitan Police at 10am. The officers and some civilians were all being commended for invaluable work in bringing two serial murderers to justice. The chief constable from Sussex, where the crimes had been detected, was also there to pass on his thanks, but mainly to reinforce links between the two forces. Present also was the lord-lieutenant of London representing the Queen.

John had taken the Sussex officers to the ground floor to a room affectionately known as the 'Tank,' which was tucked away out of sight behind the back hall inspector's office. He was the person ultimately responsible for the security of New Scotland Yard. When he saw John and the officers from Sussex heading his way he politely reminded them of their responsibility to act with decorum. It was the only place in the building that alcohol could officially be bought or consumed other than in the restaurant. However, most desks that had a bottom drawer held a bottle of Scotch and everyone knew it.

In the past, operations had been planned in the Tank; trials had been discussed in there; officers' stupidity had been highlighted in there and the occasional informant had been debriefed in there. Arguments had developed in there as had the sporadic fist fight. Rank was left at the door. The back hall inspector was the ultimate arbiter. If he said 'Leave' one did or one might be looking for new employment whatever one's rank. It was where John bought everyone a drink.

Lunch would be taken later in the restaurant next to the canteen on the fourth floor. Only invited guests would be permitted entry today. Probably, thought John, because the top man is paying. When he had been to these shindigs before they had a habit of running on for several hours. Today he was looking forward to it, hence his effort. Whether the commissioner thought much of his sartorial endeavour did not really bother John.

The DAC's staff officer was at her desk. She glanced up at the whirlwind as he entered and said, 'Go on in, he's waiting for you.'

John walked through the open door to the inner office. The DAC looked up from his paperwork and indicated a chair facing his desk. John had a habit of practically collapsing into a chair rather than sitting down on it.

'God Oscar, you look worse each time I see you. I want you to do a job and I want to be kept up to date so I want Kelly to be your point of contact.' DCI Kelly Sylvester had followed John into the office and had shut the door behind her. She sat to one side of the desk and nodded in response to her name.

'Kelly, this is DC John Whiles. Often referred to as "Oscar" or "Black John" or any expletive you fancy. Don't worry what he looks like. He is loyal, discreet, dogged and very efficient. He has no respect for rank unless they are on his wavelength. He doesn't break the law but sails close to it. (Or he hasn't been caught.) Never try to match him drink for drink unless you want a ride in an ambulance and a stomach pump or new kidneys. Is that a fair resumé, John?'

'I bow to your knowledge.'

Kelly scrutinised John as the two men chatted. He had the dullest brown eyes of anyone she knew with eyebrows hanging over them that looked as fluffy as grey-steel wool. His face that was red and puffy when he had entered her office, seemed to have changed to a more normal colour now he was seated. His chin had a small scar across it that seemed to be disappearing by the second. His nose looked a plastic surgeon's delight. She wondered how many times it must have been broken.

As the two men gossiped about long past incidents, she came to the conclusion that he could appear serious one minute and cheeky the next. How do you deal with someone like that?

'Down to business Oscar. As you know the Met have been taking direct entrants at senior ranks for a few years now. It has worked most of the time when they have been placed in office bound non-confrontational positions. But some have, shall we say, escaped into operational positions. Most have not been a problem,' Kelly coughed, 'but one is starting to cause ructions.'

From her obvious attitude, John assumed Kelly was not in favour of the system. Larry Mortimore confirmed it by saying, 'It has had the effect of preventing a lot of good officers, who have come up through the ranks, being blocked from progressing further.'

Kelly remarked, 'Precisely.'

'What I want you to do is join the surveillance team that one of these direct entrants, a woman, has put together. They are all youngsters with less than three years' service and all have good degrees. Unusual in both counts to say the least.'

John saw a problem straight away. 'I don't have a degree and I am near retirement.'

'I can get around that. They have all done a surveillance course and most would have failed had she not intervened. The same happened on the driving course they had to complete. Worse, the vehicles she arranged for them are completely inappropriate for the work. Since its inception, her team have not had one positive result in over six months. The commissioner has sanctioned this operation. I want you to update Kelly on how her team is operating. We have to be in possession of all the facts before we can act. She has very powerful friends in very high political places. I don't need to warn you, she may suspect something is amiss when you join her team. So I am going to put someone else in with you who will know nothing of what you are there for. Any questions?'

'Loads of them.'

8

9TH DECEMBER 2011
8AM

At 7.30am John was sitting outside Chief Superintendent Glynnis Ashurst's office with his eyes closed. It was twenty minutes later when he opened them as he heard someone approaching. A woman about John's age was striding towards him in civilian clothes that were all of designer heritage. Not a dyed blonde hair on her head was out of place. She had gold-framed glasses with a hint of blue in the lenses and lipstick that was glistening as though just applied. The foundation she had used on her face was the only hitch. It looked as though it had been applied with a trowel. Probably, John thought, to fill in any unwanted crow's feet.

She totally ignored him as she tapped a code into a small keypad to the side of the door which released the lock. Pushing the door wide she went through allowing it to close on its own behind her. John had already been inside and had a good look round. Digital key locks were only useful if no unauthorised person knew the code. The maintenance team kept records of 'back doors' in, just in case of emergency. Logical when one thought about it.

At 7.55am a neatly groomed young man of twenty-three approached the door wearing an anorak over his police uniform. He glared at John and said, 'Don't you stand up when a superior officer approaches you?'

'No. There are no superior officers: just senior officers but I only stand for a few of them. Furthermore I am not psychic and don't know what rank you are as I can't see your epaulettes.'

'I am DS Phillimore.'

'Well in that case, I definitely will not be standing up.'

The young sergeant glared hard at John before he tapped the code into the pad and entered the office, forcing the door to close behind him.

At 8 o'clock exactly the door opened and DS Phillimore said, 'DC Whiles I presume. Follow me.' Then he turned and walked back into the outer office. With a wave of his hand he said, 'In there,' indicating an inner office.

Glynnis Ashurst sat behind her desk looking at a file. There were no other chairs in the room. John stood to the left so she had to turn her head slightly to see him. He knew the file she was scrutinising was supposedly his personnel file. He had already checked it was the one he and Kelly had created a few days earlier.

'Good morning ma'am.'

'This is your personnel file. I see you have a few minor commendations and have worked on surveillance teams most of your service. There is nothing exceptional in here. Do you know why you have been sent to work for me?' said Glynnis, getting straight to the point.

'I retire shortly and I presume you have a vacancy. The other teams are all up to strength.'

'If you don't pull your weight you'll be off. Understood?'

'Certainly.'

'DS Phillimore will fill you in as to how we work and what your role will be. What he says goes. No argument, no discussion. Understand?'

John acquiesced. 'Yes.'

'I have arranged a vehicle for you. Go and pick it up at Ponton Road. Do you know where that is?'

'Battersea.'

'You're dismissed.'

John strode back into the outer office and DS Phillimore said, 'I lead this team. What I say goes without question or you answer to the chief. Have you a job phone?'

'Yes.'

'Good. That's one thing I don't have to arrange. Get your vehicle and be at Lambeth Forensic Laboratory briefing room at 5am tomorrow. You will not be engaged in surveillance but observing how the team works. I do not expect to hear you at all on the radio. Clear?'

'Crystal.'

'You can chauffeur another newbie who is starting tomorrow. Just make sure you keep up. Goodbye,' and the DS continued typing up his briefing notes for the morning. John didn't understand why a DS would be wearing uniform but deemed it inappropriate to ask.

He made his way to Ponton Road and to the reception desk. Donald had been the manager there for as long as anyone could remember. He was also a clever mechanic and still put his skill to work. 'Jesus, Oscar. I thought you had retired. What do you want?'

'Hi Donald. You are older than me and you are still ticking

over. No apology for the pun. I have been sent by Glynnis Ashurst to pick up a vehicle. I understand I am expected.'

'You're not working for her! She hasn't got a clue. She ordered vehicles for her team that are the most unsuitable she could find. Wait till you see yours. A powder-blue great big Volvo.'

'Has it got a tracker?'

''Fraid so,' confirmed Donald.

'Can you whip it out?'

'Take me ten minutes. Obviously don't tell her I did it when she tries to find you. Help yourself to coffee. I'll be back in a minute.'

He went into the workshop as John poured himself a large coffee before dropping a one pound coin onto the tray of cups. Most visitors put something onto the tray. Donald and the mechanics had never had to dip in their own pockets to buy tea, coffee, or more importantly biscuits for many years.

Fifteen minutes later, Donald drove a powder-blue Volvo to a parking spot outside the reception office. 'What do you think, Oscar?'

'Not the best. Can you show me what it's got?' They both sat in the vehicle as Donald explained to John the additional equipment on the vehicle.

Soon John was driving back to his flat in Fulham. Tomorrow, he mused, is going to be fun.

9

10TH DECEMBER 2011
4.45AM

John left the Volvo in a side street at the rear of Lambeth Forensic Laboratory and walked into the main entrance. He knew one shouldn't park a surveillance vehicle on police premises. You never knew who was watching. The rest of the team had all driven in past the temporary gate man who gratefully wrote down every car number and description. They were swiftly passed on with the promise of a few pounds.

As John entered the briefing room, he saw two people he knew. The pilot of the police helicopter India 9 9 and his regular observer. He sat next to them and a third man who spoke with a foreign accent. John soon deduced he was an Israeli. He was discussing a new piece of kit he was hoping to sell to the Met. For a few brief minutes they all chatted amicably. Their helicopter was sitting on the helipad just a couple of miles up the road in Battersea.

DS Phillimore, now wearing plain clothes marched up to the lectern at exactly 5am, 'Quiet. Listen up. This will be recorded as operation Barnyard. Target 1 is Kristoffer Svendsen: or the other way around. Rather irrelevant. He is suspected to be this country's premier drug importer. It has never been proven. Just a few minor drugs convictions in the distant past. You'll find all the details on your briefing sheets along with some old photos of him and a list of his associates. We suspect that today he is meeting a contact from abroad. Possibly his main supplier. This is information from Crimestoppers and is considered by the chief to be highly accurate. You will each have a briefing sheet that I have prepared with the target's details and where I want you positioned in relation to his premises. We will use the surveillance Airwave radio channel for all communication. I will do a walk by at 6am and let you know of any sightings. We do not know where he is going other than to a meeting. Nor do we know what vehicle he will be in. India 9 9 will be in the air but I do not want you within fifteen miles of the target so you don't spook him unless I call you in. Clear?'

The crew looked at each other quizzically and then John who acknowledged by raising his eyebrows. It was obvious to them that they were not wanted or expected to take part in the operation. Before they could respond, he continued, 'DC Whiles and DC Lavington will run at the rear of the surveillance and will not become involved. You are here to observe today. Clear?'

'You won't hear a peep. Who is DC Lavington?' John enquired.

Phillimore glared at John as a young, black officer probably still young enough not to have to shave daily said, 'That's me.' He was stylishly dressed in green chinos, an open-necked patterned shirt, a plain black anorak and shoes made of leather. He was a good six feet tall and obviously fit with no excess fat. His head was as round as a snooker ball and his ears were practically welded to it. He was totally bald.

'Right. Now you are introduced I don't expect to hear or see either of you again today. Clear?' John was getting fed up with Phillimore's ridiculous question so did not deign to reply. 'Clear?' repeated Phillimore.

Lavington took up the mantle, 'Crystal.'

The officers on the team suppressed their sniggers. All enjoyed it when they saw Phillimore getting tetchy. John noticed the only people taking any notes were himself and the helicopter's observer. None of the team even had a pen or pad handy. Phillimore droned on for another ten minutes and then the briefing just seemed to grind to a halt and everyone made their way to their allotted positions.

John passed the time of day with the helicopter crew before walking with Lavington to his Volvo. He explained why he had parked where he had, which seemed logical to the young officer. They were in no hurry and still arrived within twenty-five minutes at their allotted position two miles from Target 1's house in Bromley.

It wasn't long before John knew what degree the officer had and his family background. He knew his first name was Clive and he'd been a uniform officer for two years prior to becoming a detective. When Clive tried to elicit any information from John however, he got very little in reply.

'You are very reticent about divulging your history but expect others to divulge theirs. Don't you think that is a little unfair?'

'It's just that I have very little history to divulge,' replied John.

Clive studied him as they sat quietly in the vehicle for a few minutes and said, 'Well. If I said I believe you have the pseudonyms "Oscar" and "Black John" would I be correct?'

John was surprised, 'How did you know that?'

'I didn't ask or want to be on this team. When I was told at very short notice that I would be on it, I made some enquiries. It wasn't hard to find out information on the chief superintendent, that pompous idiot Phillimore and your good self.'

'And what did you discover?'

'Our chief supt. was high up in the banking field for many years making obscene amounts of money. She has two children. One, a high-flying lawyer who she financed through university and then set up in her own chambers. The other is a university drop out and a waster who is being carried by his mother's influence with a security firm of some kind in a minor capacity. Her husband is dead after a car accident seven years back. She is a direct entrant at superintendent and was promoted to chief within three years and is apparently disliked due to her incompetence. But you know that already.'

'Interesting. Go on.'

'Phillimore is a history graduate who has no charisma and no basic intelligence. Nor has he any man-management skills of note. He was useless as a PC and took promotion as soon as he could. His supervisors were glad to be rid of him. One thing he can do well is study and retain the written word. He was promoted accordingly. Ashurst plucked him from uniform and he is currently waiting to be made a substantive DS. For your information, all the team can study well but most lack common sense. How am I doing so far?'

'I am interested in what you have next,' John declared.

Clive continued, 'You were fascinating. I found lots about your exploits in police publications, the Met intranet even the internet and from people I know. What really intrigues me is why you are here. No one seems to have made any enquiries about you from Ashurst down. That worries me. You seem to have somehow dumbed down your record. They have all accepted it at face value. No inquisitiveness. Only last week you were awarded a commissioner's commendation for tenacity and bringing two serial killers to justice. You have hidden that fact from the team. I wonder why? Then I ask again: why are you here? Why am I here?'

John asked, 'Why did you make such protracted enquiries? As you say, no one else seemed to be interested. Why were you?'

Clive looked at John for several seconds, weighing up his reply, 'I want to be a good detective. Detectives should be inquisitive. I believe you should never accept anything at face value unless it can be verified. You have been on specialist squads for decades and have an astonishing track record. It's what I want to do. I have a strong feeling I have been attached to this team to deflect any probes about you. Being black will attract more attention, good or bad.'

John thought for a few minutes. Clive waited. The silence was held without embarrassment. He came to his conclusion. Honesty was sometimes the best policy.

'You are mainly right. I have been tasked with assessing why this team has not had one successful result since it was set up by Ashurst over six months ago. How it operates and how it is run has caused concern. To shut it down without some form of assessment would leave the hierarchy open to criticism. I do not fit the criteria for joining this team but you do. I will be treated with suspicion by the chief superintendent, but because we started together it may deflect any misgivings towards me. Do not underestimate Ashurst, she has powerful friends in high places. You are held in high regard and when I leave you will too.'

Clive said, 'I presume that this conversation then is confidential?'

'Yes. One thing I will say is that you will get a posting that is more to your liking when we leave. I am impressed that you conducted enquiries similar to my own and that you have already established reliable contacts within the force.'

Just then the radio burst into life.

10

10TH DECEMBER 2011
6AM

Phillimore, without complying with radio protocol, said, 'I've just walked past and seen some lights on in the premises. Looks like we may be off shortly.'

The officer deputed to compiling a written timeline log of the day's events responded that he had understood the message. No call signs were given and first names were used except Phillimore's. He was referred to as sarge. John tutted.

'Why the tutting?' asked Clive.

'Think about it. There may be something important that someone wants to say and they are just going to drown it out. You always use call signs and ask permission to talk through the eyeball - the person who has the current view. Then there will only be one person talking at a time.'

'OK I get that,' said Clive.

Someone else broke in to say a large green Jaguar saloon car had stopped outside the address. Then several people all started to talk at the same time and the radio became a free-for-all and mainly unintelligible.

Clive sighed, 'Now I see what you mean.'

Amongst the garble, John and Clive made out the fact that Target 1 had left the address wearing a long, beige raincoat with the collar turned up and a baseball cap pulled well down. He was also wearing sunglasses. Within five yards he got into the back of the Jaguar via the door held open for him by the driver who gave a half-hearted salute. John looked at Clive.

'Now what?' asked Clive.

'Come on: think Clive. The target is forty-seven years old. It is still dark and the car is five yards maximum from his front door.'

Clive pondered the question, 'It isn't raining. It has the makings of a fine day. The sunglasses are pointless at the moment as it's still dark. The car is yards from his front door. He is trying to conceal his identity.'

'That, I agree, is a strong possibility.'

'Do you think he knows we are watching him?'

'After Phillimore's pointless walk by, I would say yes,' said John.

John and Clive followed at the back of the tail as directed. John was amazed that the team actually managed to follow the vehicle as they tended to panic if any other cars got between them and the Jaguar. It was a complete debacle. Radio chatter was often rife as they talked over each other. They stuck out like sore thumbs. After following the Jaguar through central London the vehicle drove onto the M1 to travel northbound. John realised that all the team were in a line, one after the other behind it.

At Watford Gap, the Jaguar drove up the slip road and into the petrol station forecourt and up to a pump. In the ensuing radio chatter, John deciphered that the target had left the vehicle and entered the garage shop. He now knew why the disguise. The radio chit-chat informed them that the chauffeur had put petrol into the vehicle and had gone into the shop to presumably pay. John drove into the main car park for all the service outlets and cafés and waited.

Soon the chauffeur and the target exited the garage together and got into the front of the car. It drove off the petrol forecourt and back onto the M1 northwards followed by the whole team. John looked quizzically at Clive.

Clive accepted the unsaid challenge, 'I understand. That is not the target. He has changed with someone in the garage. Probably in the toilet. The giveaway is a chauffeur would have ensured the car was full of petrol so would not have needed to stop. The target would not have got into the front passenger seat after originally getting into the back when he left home. Hence all the inappropriate clothing to disguise his features.'

'Spot on. Just what I was thinking. Let's go and park in the garage and see what happens. The team will follow that Jaguar for ages. I bet it goes a long way north.' John drove to the garage forecourt and they both noticed a large, gleaming, dark blue seven series BMW by an air line with the driver sitting behind the wheel. John nodded towards it saying, 'That looks promising.'

After ten minutes, the target appeared visible at the cash till in the garage shop. He was suited and booted without his raincoat, baseball cap or shades. He ambled out slowly as he unwrapped a bar of chocolate, dropping the wrapper on the ground as he strolled to the BMW. Insouciantly, he got into the back seat of the vehicle as the driver, who had quickly got out of his seat, held the door open for him. The whole team other than John and Clive were already many miles from the garage.

Clive recorded the details of the BMW and said, 'Do we tell Phillimore?'

'We should. Call him up and tell him.'

Clive called the eyeball and requested permission to speak to Phillimore. Before the eyeball could respond and he could tell him anything, Phillimore shouted down the radio and smartly told him to shut up and not to use the radio again. 'Now what do we do?' asked Clive.

'We follow him with India 9 9. I'll bet he goes back south.' John phoned the observer in the helicopter and told him what had occurred and Phillimore's attitude. It didn't take the 'copter's crew long to subscribe to John's request.

The foreigner from Israel in the helicopter with them was going to be able to show off what his firm's new piece of kit was able to do in an active scenario. He was extremely confident now that the Metropolitan Police would be buying it in the near future.

11

10TH DECEMBER 2011
10AM

The crew of the helicopter were quickly able, through their cameras, to identify the BMW as it was manoeuvring away from the air line and towards the exit. The Israeli salesman aimed what looked like a large torch at the car. As an invisible beam locked onto the roof of the car it emitted three loud beeps. Clipped beneath the helicopter was a smaller version of the torch which then automatically locked onto the BMW.

Inside the helicopter, a laptop with a scrolling map burst into life. Right in the centre was a mark indicating the exact location of the BMW. It mattered not where the vehicle went. The helicopter could locate it within seconds from ten miles' range. Far enough away so as not to be observed. John could follow at a distance unseen by his target and guided completely by the helicopter observer. He realised life was getting easier for surveillance officers.

At the first exit the vehicle left the motorway and went around the roundabout above it and back on to travel south towards London. Then at the M25 the vehicle joined the rush hour queues travelling towards Heathrow. Traffic was heavier but the BMW appeared to be in no rush. It carried on past the vibrant airport and then off at the slip road towards Reigate.

John accelerated along the hard shoulder as he was three miles behind his quarry. He anticipated the vehicle was soon to reach its rendezvous and wanted to be in a position to witness it. The BMW drove down Reigate Hill and into the one way system around the town and into Morrisons superstore car park in the town centre with John and Clive now seconds behind it.

John said, 'This looks like it'll be the meet. He hasn't come here to do his shopping. We have to assume there's a café and that's where it's going to be. Jump out Clive and get in there before him. Keep your eyes peeled. I'll join you when I can find a parking space.' Clive grabbed his large, over-the-shoulder, hippy-type man bag and was gone in seconds.

Both the BMW and John in the Volvo found places to park a long way from the entrance to the store. John sat still and watched the target alight and stroll towards the store's entrance. He saw the chauffeur settling down in his seat and resting a newspaper over the steering wheel.

A brief conversation with India 9 9's observer let John know they were landing at Redhill aerodrome six miles away to refuel. He remained in the Volvo for a further five minutes. He didn't want to follow Target 1 too closely and give him any cause to worry. Then he left his car and went into the store to find Clive in the café.

He was sitting at a table in the middle of the café with his mobile phone propped up on the tabletop next to an open tablet. John greeted him loudly as though it was a welcome, unexpected encounter and sat opposite him. Quietly Clive spoke to him.

'Behind you at 8 o'clock with a lone female who was here

when I came in. I'm recording video of her for lip reading but can't see her mouth clearly because she keeps putting her hand in front of her face.' There were few people in the café and none between Clive and the woman.

'I'll get coffee and have a good look,' and John was away to the servery.

When John returned to the table, he placed a cup in front of Clive and sat down with a cup of his own. 'He doesn't look happy. It looks like she is giving him a hard time. Can that video be sent to the Yard as it's recording?' asked John.

'Yes. Who to?'

'Kelly Sylvester,' and he dictated her email address from memory. 'I'll text her and tell her it's coming and she can get it lip read.'

As Clive sent the video to play to her email account, John texted her as to what he wanted. Kelly read the text and opened the video. 'Where the hell do I find a trustworthy lip reader at short notice?' She punched the keys of her keyboard with venom. Pages from the Police Intranet flashed on and off her computer's monitor. Then she stopped.

Details of a uniform PC who worked at Kenley Police Station froze on the screen. His security clearance rating belied his rank. He was on immediate call to the security services. Kelly snatched a phone and called a mobile number displayed on the monitor. It rang twice before he answered.

A text pinged back within minutes to John's mobile. '*Be careful! Dangerous female. Call as soon as you can.*' John reversed his phone so Clive could read it. Clive looked back stunned, 'How can anyone lip read what I've just sent so soon?'

John was thinking the same, 'Don't ask me.'

The conversation seemed to conclude after twenty minutes when both stood up and shook hands. It was obvious to both John and Clive that the woman was the dominant proponent of the meeting. As Svendsen left the café, the woman opened her handbag and took out a small object putting it into her jacket pocket. She walked quickly out of the café and supermarket after the target and towards the car park. Pausing at the exit to light a cigarette, she watched the target's progress. John and Clive remained seated and agreed it was her they should follow.

John phoned the observer of India 9 9 as they watched her through the café's panoramic windows. They saw her move off at a pace mirroring Svendsen's path. Some seventy-five yards away the woman slowed down as she approached the BMW. She took the item from her pocket. Then quickening her stride again she reached the car as it left its parking space and moved into the traffic lane for the exit. As the target lowered the window to see what she wanted, she held the short fuse of the cherry bomb to her cigarette and then tossed it in onto his lap.

It wasn't an excessively loud explosion. Only a fifth of a stick of dynamite. An old type of explosive but still deadly. In the confined interior of the car it was sufficient to deafen and disorientate the chauffeur who drove head on into a large four-by-four before passing out. Svendsen was dead with a hole blown in his abdomen and groin where it had landed. Then it set his clothes on fire as if for good measure.

Several people in the car park heard the explosion but concluded wrongly that it was the result of the crash and ignored it. John and Clive knew something had happened and had heard the muted distant rumble over the general hubbub of the supermarket and car park. They were too far away to see exactly what had happened to their target. The woman driving the four-by-four got out of her vehicle and walked the yard or so to the driver's side of the BMW.

Her screams brought people running.

12

10TH DECEMBER 2011
12NOON

John and Clive ran out of the supermarket and saw Svendsen's café companion leaving the car park and walking south into Bell Street. It was chaos around the crashed vehicles. Cars had stopped at odd angles blocking lanes and all other vehicles' entrances and exits. As they approached the BMW, they were thwarted from getting too close by a gaggle of people standing about. Some were shouting as others were trying to film the body inside the car on their mobile phones. A couple of elderly people were walking about dazed and someone had fainted as others were trying to see what all the fuss was about.

Clive forced his way through the throng as John ran on, out of the car park and into the street. He was just in time to see the woman getting into a silver S Class Mercedes and for it to move off south towards Gatwick. Too far away for him to see the number of the car. He called the observer of India 9 9 which was just leaving Redhill aerodrome. For them to find the car was going to prove impossible.

Clive ran out to join John in the street shouting, 'She's fucking killed him! He's got a hole in his belly about a foot wide! John: she's fucking killed him!'

As they both calmed down, the helicopter hurtled across

the sky above them heading south along the main road the Mercedes had taken. It was less than five minutes behind it, but it was too late. The vehicle had turned off into the aptly named Lonesome Lane which had a canopy of overhanging trees.

Sirens seemed to be approaching from every direction. The first to try to get into the car park was an ambulance. It didn't get far so the paramedics abandoned it at the entrance and ran in.

Wistfully, Clive said, 'They won't be able to help him.'

John was desperately waiting for the first police vehicle. It eventually arrived from the direction of Gatwick with just one occupant who abandoned it next to the ambulance. He stopped the officer as he was starting to run into the car park and identified himself before asking if he saw a Mercedes going in the opposite direction. He got short shrift in reply.

The next police vehicle had come from Leatherhead and had two occupants. As it stopped, John approached. The passenger ran off into the car park. A quick conversation and the driver said, 'Get in.'

John jumped into the vacant passenger seat leaving Clive to return to the carnage surrounding the BMW. The police car accelerated off now some ten minutes behind the Mercedes. It was a forlorn hope but worth a try. They arrived at Gatwick having seen nothing. It was then a fast run back to Reigate.

Calling Kelly, John relayed the full facts to her as she listened intently. Then she explained her text:

'I managed to find the only lip reader in the Met who has a high security clearance. He's on a constant retainer to the security services. When he opened the file, he recognised the woman who he had seen before. He gave me the warning and that is what I passed on to you. I'll brief the DAC. You are going to have to fill in Ashurst. Good luck with that. If it turns really ugly, call me,' and with that she hung up.

John and Clive stood away from the BMW as a cordon was thrown up around it. They agreed that John should tell Ashurst which pleased Clive no end. Returning to the Volvo they got in and turned the police radio to the original channel. They heard that the surveillance team were approaching Carlisle. It brought wry smiles to both their faces.

Calling up the eyeball John requested authority to speak to Phillimore. In reply, Phillimore didn't wait for permission and was livid, 'I told you in the briefing that I do not want to hear or see you. What didn't you understand?'

John could take no more, 'You pompous prat. You are not following the target but a stooge. The target is dead in a BMW in a car park in Reigate. He was murdered less than an hour ago by the person he met. If you don't believe me, listen to the BBC news channel or look on your smartphone.'

There was no reply. In fact the complete team were checking their phones for the news. As they saw mobile footage already posted online by ghouls depicting the dead man's expressionless face they realised they had been duped. The chatter erupted as each saw something new or different to debate.

As soon as they could, John and Clive left Reigate and went to Cobalt Square in Nine Elms where Ashurst had her office. When they walked in through the open outer office door they were greeted by a young female civilian secretary. Telling her they had come to see Ashurst did not seem to please her.

'She is not to be disturbed. There has been some kind of problem with an operation she is running.'

John replied, 'Correct. We are the problem. We are going to see her. Please tell her we are here.'

The young girl did not know what to do. Should she interrupt her boss against her distinct instructions by doing what the two men standing in front of her were asking. Or stop them from entering? The door to Ashurst's office was firmly closed. She made her decision.

'I am sorry but I cannot disturb her. You will have to leave.'

John brushed past her and banged on the office door. Seconds later it opened. Ashurst was beside herself. Her face was red and her eyes were like fury. Her makeup was destroyed by dried tears and her hair had adopted a wayward style of its own. The whiff of alcohol was evident. She had obviously heard from the team. Likely Phillimore himself.

'What the hell have you done? Why aren't you in Carlisle with the rest of the team?'

'The reason we are not in Carlisle is because your team led by that idiot Phillimore are following a stooge. It was obvious when the switch was made but he refused to listen. We followed the true target to the meet in Reigate where he was murdered. In the chaos that followed the murderer escaped. We have completed a timeline log and have a saved video file of the meeting all on a USB. I also recorded the briefing and radio communications, for what they were worth, up until the switch was made and they are also on the USB.' John slapped down a USB stick onto her desk. 'That's a copy for you. As members of your staff, we intend to assist Surrey and Sussex Police Major Crime Unit to investigate this murder with your blessing, which I presume we have?'

'And if I refuse?' challenged Ashurst.

'You most certainly will not. I am sure the commissioner will authorise it if you don't. I will expect your secretary to complete the paperwork within the next hour. We will be back then.'

'Who the hell do you think you are talking to?'

'Someone with no idea of how active police officers work,' and John turned and walked out of the office followed by Clive.

'Jesus John: you were pushing your luck.'

13

10TH DECEMBER 2011
6PM

John and Clive strode into the DAC's outer office to find Kelly chatting on the phone. They waited until she'd finished before John introduced Clive to her.

'Have I got you to thank for sending me to that surveillance team?'

A gruff voice from the inner office replied, 'No. You can thank me.'

Clive looked in and recognised the DAC from photos he had seen of him in the past. He had never met such a senior officer before. Now he was embarrassed.

'Shut the door, Kelly and come into my office. We'll need another chair. I presume you are Clive?' and he offered his hand. 'I am the DAC. Larry Mortimore. Sorry about what transpired today. I hope it hasn't put you off police work?'

Clive was surprised, 'No. No, not at all sir.'

'When you work with Oscar, anything can happen and usually does. I think it prudent that you fill me in with today's events. John tends to miss things out for brevity. Start from this morning's briefing until you walked into this office.'

Clive had an exceptional memory and didn't require notes. He was methodical and meticulous and needed no prompting from John. Whilst he was able to say what he had seen when he first approached the BMW, John was able to mention the silver Mercedes. He glossed over how the discussion with Ashurst went.

The DAC had a familiar trait to other senior officers who John knew, which was to rest their elbows on the armrests of their chair, steeple their hands and place their fingertips under their chin or on their lips. It seemed to help them think. Mortimore adopted the position.

At the conclusion of the recounted day's events, there was an unembarrassed silence. No one present broke it. It was for the DAC to comment. He eventually looked at Kelly. 'Four glasses please Kelly,' and he produced a half bottle of Scotch from one of his desk drawers.

They all had at least two fingers in lead crystal glasses. John knew it tasted so much better in a decent tumbler. The DAC confirmed that authority for the two maverick detectives to be attached to the Surrey and Sussex Major Crime Unit investigating the murder had been sought by Ashurst. He was happy to confirm her request. It amused him as to how John had engineered her into agreeing. His conclusion was that she wanted rid of them. The chief constable of Surrey was happy to welcome the unasked for assistance.

'I think Ashurst may soon be trying to work out who you two actually are. A new recruit should be able to do so in half an hour. She has a team of graduates with a combined IQ of astronomical proportions so one of them should be able to check police indices. When she finds out your histories, and she will soon, it will be intriguing as to what she does,' and he burst out laughing. 'One thing I would say to you Clive, is watch and learn and don't do anything illegal. It will stand you in good stead for the future.'

In the outer office, Kelly told them, 'I've received the transcript from the lip reader of the female's side of the conversation. Not much to it I'm afraid. Obviously, nothing from your original target as he had his back to you both. I've put a copy for you onto a USB. You are welcome to use one of our office machines.'

John stated, 'We'll have a quick look.' All three settled around a computer as the file on the USB was opened. It was the video recording but now with the words typed across the screen in thick bold script just like subtitles.

Hello. It's been a long time.
Reply.
Please call me Chloe.
Reply.
It's good of you to come at such short notice.
Reply.
What happened to the police who were following you?
Reply. Laughter.
I've been here a while, and no one has followed you in.
Reply.
Down to business. I presume you know why I'm here?
Reply.
He was shot the other day.
Reply.
He's dead. I need to speak to the person with the cash and let them know some new details.'
Reply.
I'm sorry. I thought you knew.

Reply.

You were sent a bible some years ago. Am I correct?

Reply.

If I said you were known as Luke, what would you say?

Reply.

He was a disciple.

Reply.

Where is the bible now? It'll prove my credentials.

Reply.

Why won't you tell me? You haven't lost it?

Reply.

Thankyou. Does your wife know?

Reply.

Will you call me when you have got it?

Reply.

I use a burner. It's safer that way. I change it quite regularly.

They both took out their mobile phones from pockets and each appeared to be typing into them.

Thankyou. Please don't let me keep you.

Reply.

Scrolling across the screen was the statement, *The female is holding a hand over her mouth and is drinking preventing full transcription. Not deliberate.*

Kelly said, 'Why on earth are those subtitles so thick? They block out a lot of the video.'

John asked, 'Can you tell me the name of the lip reader and where I might find him or her?'

Kelly jotted down the lip reader's details on a slip of blank paper and handed it to John, 'Keep it confidential.'

As the two left the Yard, Clive enquired, 'What did the

DAC mean when he said, "Don't do anything illegal"?'

'No idea whatsoever. Something is worrying me though. Perhaps you noticed it when we saw Ashurst?'

'Other than she seemed overtly upset at our presence in London instead of Carlisle and she'd had a large tipple. Nothing.'

'Think again. Come on Clive, you are nearly there.'

'Give me time.'

'I know what may help. Meet me at 4am at the entrance to the Yard and we will have a mooch about.'

'You're kidding! Why then?'

'It's quiet then and we shouldn't be disturbed,' replied John.

'Is this what the DAC meant when he said, "Don't do anything illegal?"'

'Oh. Make sure you wear something dark and shoes that don't make a sound. Ditch the leather.'

14

11TH DECEMBER 2011
4AM

'My girlfriend was not amused with me eating a whole pizza all by myself and then a couple of hours later coming out to meet you. I hope it's worth it?'

'You need to get used to odd hours. You won't solve crimes while you're at home lying about in bed.' John looked Clive up and down. Dark blue jeans, black shirt and a black anorak. Then red trainers with a white flash drew his attention, 'You're good as there, Clive. The trainers are a bit over the top.'

'I don't have any other soft shoes.'

'Get yourself a good pair of brothel creepers,' John retorted.

'OK then. Where are we going?'

'Clive, I would have thought you might have worked that out?'

'Cobalt Square by any chance?'

'Now you're thinking straight.'

'How do we get in?' asked Clive.

'The front door is always open. We stroll in. No one will ask where we are going or what we are doing.'

'You know exactly what I mean. Ashurst's office. There is a security keypad. I'm sure she didn't tell you the code and she definitely didn't tell me.'

'There you are. Think logically. Consider everything. Think fire alarms,' replied John.

Clive pondered the question out loud, 'Who would need to enter the office? The security officers who are always in the building and possibly the Fire Brigade? How would they get in? They would need to know the code. Perhaps there is a list of codes kept by the security officers somewhere. But then they would know Ashurst and tell her someone had accessed it. The people who fitted it may have a 'back door' in. That would be the maintenance department probably based in Brixton. That's where I would go. They wouldn't know Ashurst from Adam.'

'Spot on. That's where I went. All the digital code locks they have fitted have the same 'back door' in. I didn't even tell them which office I was interested in. Always think logically and you will find an answer.'

'Thinking logically then. Are we breaking and entering?' asked Clive.

'There you are not thinking straight. It is police building and an office within that building. We are police officers who are entering that office. No problem.'

'Erm. Is this what the DAC said about you sailing close to the wind?'

'I don't know what you are alluding to. We'll park round the corner just for security reasons.'

They walked up the steps and into the foyer of Cobalt Square police building. Both displayed their warrant cards to the semiconscious security officer who nodded them in. Up two floors to the deserted corridor. The whole of the outside of the building was covered by CCTV cameras but none inside the building above the ground floor.

Tapping the code into the pad by the door caused the office door to click open. Both entered and went to Ashurst's inner office. Clive whispered, 'What are we looking for?'

'I don't know, and by the way you don't need to whisper.'

'That's helpful,'

'Just make sure that what you look at is put back in exactly the same place. If you check her desk, I'll do the cupboards.'

Both began their search. John searched the two cupboards and shelves as Clive sat in Ashurst's seat as he went through the unlocked drawers. A Met issued address book and desk diary held pride of place in the top drawer. He flipped through the address book but saw nothing of note before checking the diary more thoroughly. Just general meetings and phone calls and people spoken to or to be spoken to. Something seemed to be missing. Clive went through the diary twice. He couldn't find it. Then he thought, I won't if it's missing.

On the desk were two pictures in silver frames. Clive assumed them to be of her children. Her daughter was smiling proudly in the familiar pose of a newly qualified lawyer in gown and wig. Her son was pictured smartly dressed standing outside an imposing doorway pointing at a brass plaque. Between them was a Kodak digital picture frame which changed the image displayed every thirty seconds. Clive sat looking at it as John finished up searching a shelf.

One caught his eye. It was a grainy black and white photograph of the Ashurst's wedding. She was in her prime wearing a flowing veil and a white dress. They appeared to Clive to be at the wedding breakfast. Both her and her husband sat in the middle of the top table with the best man, the maid of honour and two sets of parents around them. Clive could see it was obviously an expensive gathering looking at the table settings and bottles of champagne scattered about. He watched the images change until John said, 'Anything?'

'Nothing.'

'There is something wrong and I can't put my finger on it,' John remarked.

'Strange. I had that feeling. It's as though we are missing the obvious.'

'Well we can't do anymore here. Let's get over to Reigate Police Station for the morning briefing.'

Clive sank lower in the passenger seat with his eyes closed as John passed Lower Kingswood in Surrey. Less than three miles from Reigate. Something was bugging him, and it was starting to irritate. It was the diary. He was sure of it. Or was it one of the photographs. Perhaps the photo frame? John knew he was awake and could tell he didn't want to be disturbed.

As John drove into a cul-de-sac close to the police station and parked, Clive said, 'I want to go back.'

15

11TH DECEMBER 2011
6AM

The briefing room gradually filled up with the detectives from Surrey and Sussex MIT who were to investigate the murder. Forensic experts, fingerprint officers, analysts and explosives officers were among civilians who were also present. John and Clive being two of the first to arrive had snaffled a couple of comfy chairs.

At 6.15am, DCI Groves and DS Murray walked into the room and the general hubbub abated. John knew both having worked with them earlier in the year on the serial killers' enquiry and had developed a mutual respect for them. He noticed Murray walked with a slight limp as he was still recovering from injuries he had sustained during that enquiry.

'Good morning ladies and gentlemen. I am DCI Groves and will be the SIO for this enquiry and the office manager will be DS Murray. We are both from Sussex Constabulary. The majority of you are from Surrey as this murder occurred on your manor. At the conclusion of this first full briefing I would like you all to ensure you get to know each other and be willing to work as one team.

For our sins, we have the pleasure of two Metropolitan police detectives attached to us. Later in this briefing their reason for being here will become obvious.

One thing I want to mention straightaway is that if anyone wants to raise a point, please do not hesitate to come forward. You never know, you may have thought of something that could advance the enquiry no end. Just because I am a DCI does not automatically mean I know everything and am infallible. If, however, you would rather speak in confidence, myself or Murray will always be available.

The exhibits officer will be DC William Shaw from Surrey and he will always be available to accept exhibits in the evenings. At the moment, we do not have an office typist. I shall arrange that asap. As most of us can't hold a pen correctly it is a post that must be filled. Now the preliminaries have been complied with, I think we should start with why we are here.

Although this is a murder investigation, we already have a good idea of the culprit. It may be best described as a hunt. We believe it to be a female and have a lot of images of her taken from a video recording. Her method of dispatching the victim was unusual to say the least. It was a form of explosive that has already been established as dynamite. I want you all to see the official photographs so you know what sort of person we may be dealing with. It will also, I hope, make you more cautious.

Now before we go any further, I would ask our colleagues from the Met to explain why they are here. Please come up to the podium where we can all see you.'

John looked enquiringly at Clive, 'No way John. This is down to you.'

'Coward,' and John got up and walked to the front of the room.

He stood as straight as he could with his hands grasping either side of the lectern and surveyed the people in front of him. Flying through his head was how much should he divulge. The original surveillance operation? No. Not just yet. The meeting in the café was the most important. Not the message about a dangerous female. Again, not just yet. The murder itself and the item tossed into the vehicle. Then the murderer's escape. Definitely not the lip reader's account. Ample.

He began. From driving into the car park at Morrisons to seeing the suspect leaving in the Mercedes. Everything he said was correct. It was just that a lot was left out.

Groves and Murray watched him carefully. They had worked with him before in the protracted investigation earlier in the year. Both had come to realise he had exceptional investigatory powers. They both suspected he utilised unauthorised equipment but didn't know for sure and would not dream of asking him for clarification. Two serial murderers had been brought to book and another murder solved and as far as they were concerned, it had been a good result.

Instinctively, the two Sussex officers knew John had provided an edited version of events. They both decided independently of the other that they would have to ask him privately. Whether they would get the full story was doubtful, but they had to ask.

Some of the more inquisitive detectives also quickly concluded there was a lot more to John's narrative. One, an old sweat who, in a way, looked similar in stature to John, stuck his hand up. His casual jacket was patched at the elbows. His hair had streaks of grey and was unkempt and he had sideburns that were cut at an angle below his chin and had fallen from fashion decades previously. His face was weather-beaten and was pock-marked from an illness long forgotten. 'DC Shackleton. Why did you follow the victim into the car park?'

John realised that he was cornered, 'He had been a target of a surveillance operation. We happened to be behind him when he came into Reigate.'

Shackleton wouldn't let it go. 'Where were the rest of the surveillance team?'

Groves could see that John was struggling. He found it amusing. 'They were following another target in Carlisle,' John replied.

Shackleton continued to probe, 'So only the two of you out of your team were following the victim?'

'And a helicopter with some new equipment on board which negated the need for any other officers.'

Groves decided to rescue John. 'The gismo on the helicopter was new and experimental. That's why it wasn't mentioned in DC Whiles' primary account. It's good to see you are considering other aspects to this case. Tonight's briefing will be at 5 o'clock and then I hope we may be able to say a bit more. Thank you for your account so far DC Whiles.'

John was grateful to be able to return to his seat. He was expecting Groves to want to know more. Clive couldn't resist a little jibe, 'That went well.'

The meeting continued with Murray deputing officers to obtain statements from all the people in the car park. He confirmed interviewing specialists to interrogate the chauffeur who was recovering in hospital. Shackleton and a young officer were tasked with ascertaining everything that they could establish about the victim.

Collection of CCTV was Murray's priority for the uniformed officers as they were the people who knew the area best. It had to be collected from the route the Mercedes had taken as it left Reigate. There would be a lot. John and Clive were left as free agents to conduct enquiries that they thought fit. Murray knew that John would go his own way anyhow so why hinder him?

The meeting continued for another twenty minutes with Groves scribbling notes into his murder book as he was listening to questions from the floor and answering them as best he could. Murray was also writing in a notebook as to additional actions for officers to conduct.

As the officers drifted away at the conclusion of the meeting, Groves called out to John, 'Before you run away, Oscar, can we have a quick chat? My office in ten minutes?'

'Good to see you again, guv'nor. I didn't realise you'd made DCI. This is DC Clive Lavington. We started working together yesterday.'

Murray and Groves greeted him, and Groves said, 'You'll learn a lot from Oscar. Probably not what you want to know but it'll be entertaining.' Turning back to John, 'What can you tell me and what can I put to the meeting tonight?'

John told him everything. Then Groves asked, 'What did you make of Ashurst's attitude?'

'It seemed strange. A target who is suspected of being a major drugs importer gets killed. Why would that upset her?'

Clive chipped in, 'It definitely wasn't seeing us that upset her!'

Murray couldn't resist a comment, 'Be honest John. You upset a lot of people without much effort.' All bar John smiled.

'Clive wants to go back and have another look around her office tonight. We'll let you know if we come up with anything before tomorrow morning's briefing. I'll run you off a copy of the video with the lip reader's note but I'd rather that stayed confidential for the time being. I need to ask him what agency he was working for when he first saw her. The more I think about yesterday the more it worries me. That woman was totally ruthless in the way she killed someone she knew. I think this is going to mushroom and others may die.'

16

11TH DECEMBER 2011
11AM

John drove into the rear of Kenley Police Station ignoring his own edict of taking a surveillance vehicle into a police yard. He'd never been there before. It was only a small police station but had a huge car park and secure vehicle compound. It was the sort of station that John knew the locals cherished. A PC in overalls was busy cleaning a marked police car and looked up as John and Clive got out.

'Excuse me but do you know where I can find an officer called PC Horace Brown?'

'You're looking at him.'

Clive said, 'We're from CO. I am DC Clive Lavington and this is DC Whiles. I think you did some lip reading yesterday for DCI Sylvester. It was video we took. Can we speak somewhere?'

'Come with me,' and Brown dropped his sponge into a bucket. John and Clive followed him through a door into a wooden hut which was just large enough to house a billiard table. He added, 'No one comes in here till late afternoon. How can I help you?'

Clive asked Brown, 'We had been following a target who went to Reigate where he met the female we recorded on the video. We are intrigued why you sent a warning. Can you tell us why?'

Brown responded in a relaxed manner, 'The police allow me to work for different agencies as and when they want me. Twelve days ago I was approached to watch a recording of a female passing through Heathrow Terminal 5. The same one that you videoed. She had flown in from Miami. Unfortunately, the film was a day old. The Americans had informed the British that she was suspected of murdering a lawyer in Long Island, New York.'

Clive asked, 'Why wasn't she arrested when she landed?'

Brown responded as though the answer was obvious, 'The usual. She used a false passport, different hair style and strolled straight through. Border Force were looking for her coming from New York. The name they were given by the Americans was different to the one on the passport she used. They had her photo but were watching the wrong planes. I was viewing the videotape to see what was said by her or her contact. I got nothing.'

John pushed the point, 'So when you saw her on our video, you recognised her and sent the warning. I don't know if you're aware but she killed the man she met with some dynamite. In the confusion, she got away.'

Brown's laissez-faire attitude slipped slightly, 'I had heard. From what I was told when I viewed Heathrow's cameras, I could only warn you to be careful.'

Clive said, 'Do you know what her true name is?'

'No. The Americans don't know and nor do the British.'

Clive asked what he thought was the obvious next question, 'What name did she have on her false passport?'

Brown was quick to answer, 'I wasn't privy to that.'

John changed the subject, 'Can you tell us the agency you

were working for?'

'Special Branch at Heathrow. The Yanks told them as soon as they realised she was heading for the UK.'

Clive persisted on the new tact, 'Why did SB want her lip read? Surely they would have arrested her as soon as they could?'

Brown seemed to suddenly recall an additional piece of information that would explain everything. 'Sorry. I should have said. You can't be aware that she may be responsible for a murder at Heathrow the day she landed.'

Clive and John looked at each other. Neither knew of any murder at the airport. They were both aware there were so many murders in the Met that it would be particularly hard to know about all of them. Clive shrugged. John said, 'I didn't know.'

Clive asked of Brown, 'Can you get us an image from your contact at SB?'

Brown's response was too fast for John's liking. 'You could probably get one quicker from the murder team at Heathrow. You'd also get a copy of the CCTV from them. You know how slow SB are at times.'

John was troubled, 'Good point. When you saw our video and lip read it, what did you think?'

Brown was hesitant, 'She kept putting her hand in front of her face and was drinking tea. It was not possible to get a true idea of her attitude or see everything she said. Now I know she killed the person she was talking to; it sends a shiver down my spine. I wish I could help you more, I really do.'

Clive concluded by asking, 'Well, thank you for your help. If we have any other questions, would it be all right to phone you?'

Brown's answer was short and uneasy, 'Any time you like.'

John and Clive left Kenley and drove south towards Godstone where John pulled the car into a layby. He turned the engine off and closed his eyes. Clive sat still. Nothing was said for five minutes until John opened his eyes again and smiled.

'What do you make of our *helpful* PC Brown?'

Clive wasn't sure how to answer, 'He seemed helpful enough. I'm not sure what you're getting at.'

'Did you believe him?'

'Yes. Why wouldn't I?'

'At one time he let slip that he was watching the Heathrow video to see what her contact said. He never clarified who the contact was.'

'We didn't actually ask him,' reasoned Clive.

'The Americans allegedly told SB that a murderer was travelling from the States to the UK from New York. They are not sluggish and nor are SB. Every plane from the States would have been monitored.'

'Before I accept that, I will check with SB.'

John pressed on, 'How come he was pressing home that images and photos would be more quickly available from the Heathrow murder team in preference to SB?'

'He was just trying to be helpful. Don't you remember him saying, "I wish I could help you more, I really do"?'

John said, 'Yes. It makes me think that he has some other information that he is deliberately withholding that would be of use to us. I have a feeling that he is frightened of something. Or someone.'

'I see. Are you implying he may have been economical with the truth? A bit like you at the briefing.'

'Touché.'

In the office they found Murray writing out actions for the detectives. The exhibits officer Shaw, an articulate and keen young officer was busy sorting out what needed to go to which scientist for analysis. A photographer was busy putting images onto a white board and an explosives officer was on a phone trying to locate the source of any missing dynamite.

Groves and Shaw had attended the PM conducted by a Home Office pathologist. He had deduced the obvious cause of death. Destruction of major internal organs due to an explosion. Now, both Groves and Shaw stank of formaldehyde and were seated at desks next to office windows which were wide open. Groves was busy writing up his murder book. Still no typist.

Murray greeted them, 'You don't look at all busy. How about making a cup of tea?'

Soon the office ground to a halt as Clive delivered cups to all those present. John could only marvel at the fact police officers lived on the stuff.

•

Back at Kenley, PC Brown was on the phone, 'They have been here this morning. Two of them. One a six-foot black man, bald as a coot, called Clive something. The other, an old, scruffy bugger without much idea. Turned up in a bloody great Volvo painted pale blue. Not even metallic. Never seen a car look more like an unmarked police car. Must be the only one like it in the Met.'

Tabitha wasn't interested in cars, 'And?'

Brown realised she wanted the points of the meeting and not the details of a vehicle, 'Sorry. I told them what you suggested. They will be hunting her for the Reigate murder.'

'I'll be surprised if they can find her. If she only kills drug dealers we don't really care.'

'They asked if I could get a photo of her from SB at Heathrow. I fed them the line to go to the murder team as you wanted.'

'Good. Do you think they bought it?' Tabitha asked.

'Yes. It was just a simple courtesy visit. Part of the murder enquiry. Nothing to worry about,' Brown tried to say convincingly.

'If they come back let us know.'

'Yes. I will.' and then they hung up.

Tabitha placed the phone gently back on its cradle. She didn't like Brown's comment, 'Nothing to worry about.' He was too blasé for her liking. A bit of pressure and he might crack. That could not be allowed to happen. Her extravagant lifestyle would be seriously undermined if she were locked in a prison cell.

She spoke to Derek who had been listening in on an extension, 'He seems confident enough. I don't think there is anything to worry about. They'll probably get a copy of our doctored video from the Heathrow murder squad. That'll get them nowhere.'

Derek thought there was a lot to worry about but was not about to argue with his boss, 'Do you think they'll actually find her?'

'No. I doubt it. There are now two police murder teams looking for her. What I like is she doesn't seem to care. She can disappear at the drop of a hat. Just text her and update her with what's happened. We can keep her apprised if the police start to get too close. Think what an asset she'd be if she'd work for us.'

Derek didn't like the prospect of a murderer working for them. He knew that Marchant had disreputable people she could call on and he didn't like that. He couldn't argue. She was his boss and what she said went. Then again the money that she bunged his way every month was useful and kept him silent.

When Derek left the office, Tabitha pulled a burner phone from her bag and made a call.

'Yes?'

'I need you to do a job,' and she explained what was needed.

•

John sat opposite Murray nursing his cup of tea. There was no coffee, which was his preferred tipple, so tea it was. 'What do you make of this enquiry, Murray?'

Murray thought for a while. 'I am surprised at the brazenness of the woman. To kill like that in a busy supermarket car park beggars belief. Why did she want him dead? She had her escape planned with her car outside the car park, leading to the conclusion the murder was premeditated.'

'I've been thinking about that. Svendsen thought he had ditched his tail and so made the meeting. There was a conversation. What if she was trying to ascertain some information from him? Then, when she got it, he was no longer of use to her? There are a lot of other questions but that intrigues me the most.'

Clive said, 'What if she had found out what she wanted to know. Then the target, or let's call him the victim, realised the importance of what was said. She'd anticipated ascertaining the information and was equipped to kill him and escape. If she hadn't got the information she wanted, she could have just walked away.'

Murray, John, Groves and Shackleton were all listening. Each was taking in what Clive had said. Shackleton cautiously hypothesized to himself. It was loud enough for the others to hear. It was the sort of thing John was prone to doing.

'Perhaps it involved money. Between them they worked it out. Like buried treasure. Each had part of the information. Put it together and bingo the location is revealed. Then like pirates, one of them decides she wants it all instead of fifty per cent and kills her partner. Greed always wins.'

John stared at the old sweat. 'I like that. Not a bad analogy. That is something that needs looking into.'

17

11TH DECEMBER 2011
3PM

John and Clive sauntered into the DAC's outer office. DCI Kelly Sylvester looked up, 'I have soon learnt that when I hear or see you two my day will become enlivened. I just know it's going to be stimulating.'

Clive said, 'I want to point out I am a passenger in his vehicle and am still learning. Any grief has nothing to do with me. It's all down to him.'

Kelly laughed, 'You're learning the wrong things then. What have you discovered now?'

John collapsed onto a chair, 'Come on then, Clive, what have we come here for?'

'Are you aware of a murder at Heathrow about a fortnight ago?'

Kelly replied, 'Yes. Some minor league druggy found in a disabled person's toilet with a hypodermic stuck in his arm. At first it was considered an overdose. It became a murder enquiry after the PM found strychnine was the cause of death. Nasty way to die and I'm told very painful.'

Clive kept up the questions, 'Did Brown tell you that the first time he saw the Reigate murderer was on Heathrow's CCTV?'

Kelly was shocked, 'No. He only told me to warn you that

she was dangerous. Are you telling me it's the same killer?'

Clive was positive, 'We believe it is the same person.'

Kelly looked at John who was sitting with his eyes closed. It was clear to her that he was leaving everything to Clive. Clive asked her, 'Can you see when the PM was conducted and what day the murder squad was formed?'

'No problem. Give me two minutes,' and she picked up a phone.

Clive confirmed with John, 'What did Brown say? Twelve days ago, he viewed the Heathrow CCTV and it was one day after she had killed the junkie. That would have had him view the video on the 29th of November and her entering the country on the 28th of November. There's no way that a PM would be done the following day on a suspected overdose and then establish strychnine poisoning.'

John's eyes flicked open. 'Just what I was thinking. How are you doing, Kelly?'

Kelly had the facts, 'Cleaners discovered the body on the 28th and uniform officers attended. They assumed it to be an overdose. The PM was done on the 29th and toxicology was completed on the 3rd of December which is when the murder squad was formed.'

John considered the information and started to talk to himself, 'Brown claimed he viewed the tape before the police knew it was a murder. Did he see two go into the toilet and one come out? If SB asked him to view it for lip reading, they would have been aware of two going into the toilet cubicle and one coming out. They would have seen the uniform officers going in and would have then instigated a murder investigation. Confirm that. Who did he really view the

CCTV for and why?'

Kelly and Clive listened. Both were thinking along the same lines.

John kept talking, 'Check with Heathrow murder team and find out if Special Branch are liaising with them. Ask SB if they know PC Brown. Get hold of a copy of the CCTV from the airport. Let's get another lip reader. See if she says anything on Heathrow's video or on ours that Brown may have *inadvertently* missed.'

Kelly cut in, 'Brown's credentials are second to none. From what you are saying? You don't appear to trust him.'

John replied curtly, 'No I don't. Clive, what about you?'

Clive replied cautiously, 'Something is not right. I agree. He seemed confident enough when he was talking to us. The more you think about what he said though just doesn't add up.'

Kelly was reluctantly considering her options, 'Where am I going to find another lip reader? He was the only one on the Met intranet?'

John said, 'Try the Nuffield school for the deaf in Redhill.'

Kelly and Clive looked at him in astonishment. Kelly said, 'How the hell do you know about that?'

'Not sure, but I think I have heard of someone there having done a bit for police in the past.'

'I'll look into it. How soon do you want to know?' Kelly said, looking enquiringly at both John and Clive. 'OK, I'll crack on straight away.'

The two detectives made their way back to Reigate for the evening's meeting.

Before they got into the office, Groves called to them,

'What have you got for me that I can put to the team?'

John told him about the meeting they'd had with Brown and how they both felt he'd been lying to them. To confirm his lip reading was accurate, he updated him about Kelly making further enquiries to authenticate it. Then he said he was going to go to Heathrow to see someone he knew there and probably talk to the murder team.

Groves was happy. His team were working flat out to obtain all the witness statements. All the Surrey CCTV had been collected and was being viewed to track the Mercedes. A shop's camera had recorded the vehicle's index plates and ANPR cameras were being checked to trace it. The owners of the Mercedes had been identified from the PNC as a rental company who were being interviewed the following day as to the hirer's documentation.

DC William Shaw had submitted exhibits to the relevant laboratories and the fingerprint officer had submitted marks he'd recovered from the café in the supermarket for checking. The explosives officer was waiting for confirmation from his phone enquiries as to any stolen or missing dynamite.

As they walked into the office they saw all the chairs bar one were occupied. John hated standing during any meeting. He decided to perch on the end of Murray's desk. Slightly better than propping up a wall. Groves took the vacant seat as the office came to order waiting for him to speak.

It was a short meeting. Groves ran through what had occurred during the day. Murray updated the team as to how the statements had revealed extraordinarily little of note and the specialists explained what they had done. The meeting was thrown open for any questions or suggestions. In the room the atmosphere was positive. All believed that the female would soon be identified and located.

John was worried. Thoughts swirled around in his head. Why was Ashurst upset? Why was Brown apparently lying? What had happened at Heathrow? Why had she killed Kristoffer Svendsen? What was her motive? Was anyone else going to die?

Murray was worried. Statements were all handwritten. Results of officers' actions were all handwritten. Copies of forms were all handwritten. Everything in the office was handwritten and still they didn't have a typist. Everything needed to be typed up onto the HOLMES computer as a matter of urgency.

To aggravate him even more, he'd been told by Groves that the chief constables of both Surrey and Sussex would be visiting the following day. Probably about midday. Fancy that! Just in time for a liquid lunch.

•

As the meeting was in progress, an S-Class Mercedes car with false index plates pulled up and parked opposite Kenley Police Station. The occupant surveyed the surroundings as he lit a cigarette. He saw the police station comprised of two buildings with the public's entrance to the front of the one on the right. There was an area between the two buildings where officers who had parked their vehicles in the yard walked through and entered via a side door.

He saw the building to the left also had a side door but no front entrance. The only person he saw go into that building was the garage man and when he exited he watched him slam the door behind him. It appeared to be offices and a storage unit of some kind. Most of the uniform officers he saw went into a prefabricated hut towards the rear of the main building and nearer the car park. Some carried snooker cues.

The garage man stood between the two buildings as he wound up a hose. The man in the Mercedes easily recognised him from the image on his mobile phone. When the hose was neatly coiled he stood up and stretched and looked out towards the road. The man sank lower in his seat but knew his Mercedes tinted windows would protect him. Brown only saw the red tip of a glowing cigarette.

He'd seen the car earlier. Hardly anyone ever parked there. That's why he noticed it. It had turned up about an hour after he'd made the phone call to Tabitha. He wasn't stupid. He was frightened. He knew who the people were on the other end of the phone and he didn't trust them an inch. He needed a drink. He had to think.

The driver's window dropped down a few inches and the man flicked the cigarette out of the window. This was going to be easier than he first thought.

18

12TH DECEMBER 2011
4AM

As John was picking up Clive outside Scotland Yard, Horace Brown was lying on the floor of his living room breathing his last. He was gurgling involuntarily as the blood seeped down his throat into his lungs as he slowly drowned in his own fluids. A large yellow handled screwdriver was embedded in his throat. It had passed through his windpipe and voice box and was touching his spine. He'd grabbed compulsorily for the handle. The strength of the man was too much for him and he'd used all of it to drive the screwdriver home.

He was still in Brown's house. The Yale lock on the front door had been a minor irritation for him. A piece of mica had opened it within seconds and without a sound. When he had walked into the living room, Brown had been sitting in an armchair with a large kitchen knife beside him. The drink that he had had earlier to help him think had caused him to slip into a deep alcoholic stupor.

The man had seized his ankles and pulled him violently from the chair and onto the floor where he banged his head. He woke up in pain and in time to see the screwdriver in the man's hand. Then he felt it go in. He knew it was the end.

His hands were swift as they searched Brown's pockets. No

phone. His eyes took in the room. No phone. He walked around the house. No phone. Where had Brown hidden it? His temper was rising. The thought entered his head, if I can't find it, with a bit of luck no one will.

A Yankees baseball cap was hanging on a coat peg in the hall. The man tried it on back to front and checked himself in the mirror. He heard a moaning sound coming from the lounge. It didn't concern him; he knew Brown was nearly dead. He wore it the correct way round. That suited him better.

As he lay dying, the man turned up the edge of the rug. He thought when Brown was found it would be assumed that he had tripped while carrying the screwdriver. A tragic accident. Now he'd put the knife back in the block in the kitchen and was washing his hands before he left. He didn't want any of Brown's blood on the Mercedes' nice white leather upholstery.

•

John and Clive walked into Cobalt Square, past the recumbent security officer who nodded them in, and went up to Ashurst's office. They went in and Clive sat in her chair once again. He opened the drawer and took out the desk diary. Opening it he started at the 1st of January and read every entry to the 10th of December. It took nearly forty minutes.

John settled on the windowsill behind Clive. He was too far away to read the diary over Clive's shoulder so contented himself watching her photo frame flip from one image to another. He could see that a lot of the photos were good quality images and probably professionally taken. Lots of holiday snaps and weddings. Then something caught his eye.

'Clive, stop the images!'

It was too late. It had moved on. Clive was trying to get the images to rewind without much success. Clive said to John, 'What did you see?'

'I could have sworn there was a picture of Svendsen in a group of people. It looked like a wedding photo.'

Clive said, 'That's it!' and started to flip the pages of the diary, 'Nothing,' Clive said disappointedly. Then he grabbed the address book and flipped it open and shouted, 'Got it!'

John said, 'What?'

'Check out the address book. Under K and C.' Then he passed it to John.

'Kristoffer Svendsen. Entered under his first name. Can't see anything of note under C. So what?' said John.

'Now check out the diary from the 1st of December,' Clive instructed.

John read every entry for the first ten days of December, 'What am I meant to see?'

Clive said, 'The surveillance briefing was on the 10th when Phillimore told everyone that information had been received from Crimestoppers. He said that Crimestoppers had told Ashurst and then the operation was set up accordingly. Throughout that diary,' and he pointed to it for additional emphasis, 'she lists all the previous surveillance operations and where the information had come from.'

John flipped it open and confirmed what Clive had said, 'Sorry Clive, I'm still not getting this.'

'There is no mention in that diary of any information having been passed to her from Crimestoppers about Svendsen. When you looked in the address book under K, you saw Kristoffer Svendsen. He was the third entry and there are nine more names beginning with K after his. The implication being that it was written in there a long time ago. When you checked under C, there is no mention of Crimestoppers. You think you saw a picture on her photo frame of Svendsen. Yesterday, I now realise I saw a black and white picture of him with Ashurst. Not being in colour confused me.'

'Clive, that's brilliant! It explains a lot. If we can check with Crimestoppers that they haven't been in contact with her it will confirm what you say. It looks like Svendsen could be a friend. That's why she was so upset with his death. Then we need to know why she lied to set up the operation.'

At that moment John's mobile phone pinged indicating an incoming email: *If you receive this message, it means something has happened to me. The people I viewed the Heathrow CCTV for are on the following number,*' and a phone number was displayed in bold type. The email continued: *I have not told you the truth about what was said. Check it all out again. These people are dangerous and can't be trusted. Be very careful. There are some emails and texts on my mobile you will find interesting. To find my phone, you will need a PoLSA team. Start with the living room door.* It was signed, Brown.

John spun his phone so Clive could see and said, 'How could he send an email after something has happened to him?'

Clive replied, 'John, you have to learn to embrace

technology. He writes his message and then sets it to be sent a few hours in the future. If nothing has happened to him he just resets the time. If the allotted time is reached then the message is sent. From that message, I think we should try and find him.'

'Let's get back to the Yard. Time is marching on.'

In the car, John said, 'We need to get rid of this vehicle today. It sticks out like a sore thumb. I have an old Vauxhall that is fully equipped with everything this has got and a lot more. It's in a lock up garage. We'll swap them over later.'

Clive was desperately hungry. As they walked up the stairs from the garage below Scotland Yard at 5.45am he said, 'I've got to have something to eat. Let's just stop off in the canteen on way.'

Checking the time, John said, 'Yeah all right. We're quite early. Thirty minutes won't hurt.'

They both got an early breakfast at the servery and walked through to the seating area. It was practically deserted. A few early patrons were seated about. They both saw Kelly sitting alone at a table reading a copy of The Job.

Clive, ever mindful of manners said, 'Mind if we join you?' She looked up.

'What on earth brings you two here at this time of day? Or shouldn't I ask?' They sat down opposite her.

Clive said, 'One thing I've learnt working with John, sleep becomes a luxury, and the chance of food and drink must be taken whenever possible. Otherwise I'd starve.'

John feigned hurt. He took out his phone, found Brown's message and spun it round so Kelly could read it.

She immediately realised the implication of the message.

'Shit, you've just managed to ruin my day before I'm even on duty.'

John put the phone away and said to Kelly, 'We were just having a look around Ashurst's office when this came in. When Clive has finished his breakfast I'm sure you'll be fascinated with what he has to say. As to Brown, I think we need to find him. I tried ringing him but no answer. I was hoping you would be able to get his HA and see if he's there.'

'I thought all senior officers had security keypads on their office doors to keep unauthorised people out. It's obviously no bar to you two. I'll see you upstairs in the office when you're ready and I should have Brown's HA by then.' Kelly got up, collected her bag from the floor and started to walk away, then she stopped and said, 'I was going to have a coffee before work. Please bring one up when you come,' and she left the canteen.

Clive put the polystyrene cup on the desk in front of Kelly who automatically said, 'Thanks,' and took a long sip. Then said, 'I phoned Brown's HA but didn't get a reply. I've sent the local police round and they should be there shortly. What else have you got to tell me?'

Clive told her what he'd discovered and showed her photographs on his phone that he had taken of Ashurst's address book. She listened with growing incredulity. When he had finished, she sat in silence. Nothing was said for several minutes. She sipped her coffee. Then she opened a desk drawer and took out her own address book. Flipping it to C, she picked up a phone and dialled a number.

'This is DCI Kelly Sylvester. I am the DAC's staff officer at New Scotland Yard. I would like to speak to the director of

Crimestoppers as a matter of extreme urgency. Can you please ask him to call me as soon as possible?' There was a short reply. 'Thank you,' Kelly said and she hung up. She looked at Clive, 'My God. I hope you are wrong.'

The phone rang. Kelly answered it. For about two minutes she listened before saying 'thank you,' and hung up. 'It's not even 7 o'clock and we have the first suspicious death of the day. That was the local duty officer at Kenley who went round to Brown's HA. He's dead.' She told both Clive and John what the officer had found.

John said, 'Nothing suspicious about it. He's been murdered.'

19

12TH DECEMBER 2011
8AM

The DAC walked into the office. Looking at Clive and John in turn he asked a general question of either. 'Hello. What brings you two here this bright and beautiful morning?' Kelly butted straight in and quickly told him what had happened. 'Jesus Christ Oscar. Brown's one of our own.' John showed him the email. He seemed to study it for ages. 'With me Oscar,' and he went into his inner office with John and shut the door.

Once behind his desk the DAC spoke, 'Who the fuck has done this, Oscar? I want to know. Is it that homicidal female or the people at the other end of that phone number?'

'I don't know. Brown obviously told us lies. I suspect he was asked to by the people at that phone number and to bat off any questions. If it was the female: why would she want him dead? Then again, why would the people at that number want him dead? Could they be working in unison?'

'I saw the commissioner coming into the building. Once Kelly has confirmed either way with Crimestoppers what was or was not said, we'll all go and ruin his day.' Both John and the DAC went back into the outer office. There was no sign of Clive.

'I've sent Clive to warn the commissioner's secretary that

we will be there at 10am. The director of Crimestoppers has confirmed that they have never spoken to Ashurst or passed any information to her. I gave him the victim's name, but he declined to say at first if his details were on their data base. Once he knew he was a murder victim, he confirmed that his organisation had never heard of him. I've requested the inspector in charge of the Telephone Unit to come to the office. He should be here in five minutes.'

As if on cue, there was a gentle tap on the office door. An elderly uniformed inspector walked in. He was nervous. He worked in a large office where no one troubled him. There were nearly fifty civilians and a dozen police officers answering to him. He was God. Now he was standing before a more powerful God.

The DAC was brusque as he said to the Inspector, 'I want to know everything about this telephone number,' and passed him a piece of paper with the number on. The DAC continued his instructions, 'I want your best detective on this and it's to be treated with the utmost security. If anything gets out you won't be picking up your pension. Do I make myself clear?'

Inspector Goodall had worked in the telephone section for eight years and had never once had an ounce of stress. Now he was trembling a little and starting to sweat. He knew this was serious, 'Yes sir. It will take a couple of days…'

'Let me stop you there, inspector. You have till 5pm today. May I suggest you go now and get started.'

Goodall was grateful to be able to leave. He practically ran back to his office and summoned a detective.

'Kelly, get Ashurst's personnel file from registry. Go there yourself and deal with the supervisor. No one is to let any of this get out. Oscar, how much have you told the DCI running the Reigate murder?' John explained what he had told Groves and how trustworthy he was.

'Right. Get him here on the hurry up. I'll brief him before we see the commissioner. Bloody hell. I've still got my coat on,' and he went into his inner office, slamming the door behind him.

John phoned Murray who he knew would be in the office in Reigate from 7am. In reply to his question, Groves came on the line, 'Morning Oscar. What can I do for you?'

'We need you to come to the Yard urgently. We are going to see the commissioner at about 10 o'clock and the DAC wants to brief you personally. There's been another murder,' and John heard Groves yell to Murray about a car. John emphasized the urgency by adding, 'don't hang about.' The line went dead. No closure or social graces.

Now alone in the outer office, John sat in Kelly's chair. He couldn't see the logic of anyone killing Brown. Why did he have to die? What was it that the murderer thought he might disclose?' He knew he had to get the Heathrow CCTV and the video taken by Clive at Reigate checked.

John's phone rang. As he answered, he heard the wail of a two-tone horn in the background, 'Are you going to get here in time?'

Groves replied, 'Bloody Murray has found a mad man to drive me. I'm assured we will be there by about 9.15 unless we crash. Which is looking highly likely. Who has been murdered now?'

'PC Brown. Stabbed through the throat with a screwdriver.'

'Did our girl do it?'

'It's likely.'

Groves was quizzical, 'Why?'

John could only surmise, 'I think to shut him up from disclosing something.'

'Right. I'll be dropped off outside the front of the Yard. Can someone meet me?'

'I'll arrange it.' Again, no pleasantries. The line went dead.

Kelly strode back into the office. A file in her hand. 'This is Ashurst's personnel file. It contains her CV, application to join as a superintendent and everything since. Including her promotion. There's not that much to it.' She offered it to John who took it.

He went through it. He found her vetting history which confirmed her security clearance. Her CV contained the usual loose documents. Copies of birth and marriage certificates, educational qualifications, and references from eminent people. The writing on the CV showed a confident hand with a fountain pen. Answers to questions posed were brief and to the point. Her work history was short and concise but displayed a rapid promotion to the higher ranks of banking. As John skimmed the papers, he could understand why the Met entertained the application.

Clive came back into the office, 'Sorry I've been so long. Got held up in the queue.'

John handed him Ashurst's file. He started to go through it and said, 'Interesting,'

Both Kelly and John said, 'What?'

Clive was dismissive, 'Her name.'

Kelly queried, 'What about it?'

As thought it was blatantly obvious he replied, 'Well, she is using her maiden name.'

John cut in, 'Clive, Stop talking in riddles. Tell us what you have seen.'

'Her birth certificate shows her maiden name. Glynnis Ashurst. Then her marriage certificate Glynnis Jansen. That's a bit of a coincidence. Both her husband and the Reigate victim appear to come from Scandinavia. Oh my God. Look at the witness's name.'

John and Kelly looked over his shoulder at the marriage certificate. Bold as brass written on the bottom of the certificate in the box marked 'witnesses' was Kristoffer Svendsen. Kelly sat down. John's brain was racing. The DAC stepped out of his office now coatless.

Kelly gave him the new information. 'What the hell is that woman playing at?'

John said, 'Svendsen was renowned as a suspected importer of large quantities of drugs. He was a witness at Ashurst's wedding to Henrik Jansen according to that certificate. We need to know everything about Henrik and how he died. Was he connected in any way to drugs? If he was, did Ashurst know? Did that help fund her great wealth? Why did she set operation Barnyard in motion? How did she know about Svendsen's meeting?'

Clive addressed the DAC, 'I'd like to look into Henrik if that's all right with you, sir?'

'Do it.'

Kelly said, 'Without actually asking her, we're unlikely to find out the answers to the last two questions.'

The DAC said, 'Let's get her here and I'll ask her.'

John said, 'Can I recommend we hold off speaking to her for a while? It will put her on her guard. We need to know a lot more. Plus of course, the murder of PC Brown appears linked in some way to Svendsen. One course of action would be to conduct a surveillance operation on Ashurst. And am I right in thinking, that part of the conditions of service signed by a police officer, is that office telephones can be monitored?'

The DAC considered it and said, 'I'll get the phone sorted out. As for surveillance…' he stroked his chin for a few seconds then said, 'It needs to be an outside force to ensure no one is recognised. Who are you thinking of John?'

'Sussex.'

The phone rang and Kelly snatched it up from its cradle and said, 'DCI Sylvester.' She put the phone back and said, 'The back hall inspector says DCI Groves is at the reception desk.'

Clive quickly said, 'I'll go,' and left the office.

It took less than half an hour for Groves to be briefed. He had a lot of questions, but there weren't many answers. Then all five trooped along to the commissioner's palatial office.

Sitting to one side of the office was a staff officer and the commissioner sat behind probably the biggest desk owned by the Metropolitan Police. He smiled at them all and declared, 'Well. This is an interesting delegation. How can I be of assistance to you all?' Then he assumed the modern version of Rodin's 'The Thinker'. Hands steepled touching his chin.

The DAC spoke for twenty-two minutes. He covered everything including the unauthorised entry to Ashurst's office. No one else uttered a sound. At the conclusion, the commissioner looked at the four others in turn. Then he said to his staff officer, 'If you wrote any of that down, destroy it now. Not a word of what has been said leaves this office. This is going to take a while so cancel all meetings this morning.' The staff officer handed his notebook to Kelly and then left the office.

The commissioner continued, 'This is going to be a two jugger.' He picked up the phone and dialled the canteen supervisor's extension from memory. 'Hello Anita. It's your favourite client. Could you please bring up two jugs and biscuits?' Then he laughed raucously at some reply before saying 'Thanks.'

Looking at each of those sitting in front of him, the commissioner sought inspiration. He asked slightly rhetorically, 'Now what are we going to do about all this?'

20

12TH DECEMBER 2011
12NOON

Back in the DAC's inner office, there were five chairs all occupied. Behind his own desk, the DAC felt more relaxed. 'I'd like to thank you for coming at such short notice, Mr Groves. Should there be any problems about surveillance I'm sure, as the commissioner stated, he could clarify it with the chief constable. Clive, you seem to have a talent for gathering information. Henrik is all yours. Oscar, CCTV and lip reading is down to you. Kelly. If you could please sort out Ashurst's phone on my behalf? I shall make it my personal responsibility to find out who is on the phone number in Brown's last message. Can we all meet again say tomorrow about 11ish?'

All agreed. Then as a rider, Larry added pointedly at John and Clive, 'Do not break into her office again. I think the commissioner wasn't best pleased with that.'

John could not help himself, 'I think he's worried we might do his.'

They all went their respective ways. Clive made his way deeper into the inner offices of the Yard as Groves headed back to Reigate. John set off for Heathrow. Kelly set up all calls to and from Ashurst's phone to be tape recorded and forwarded to her immediately. Then she spent some time talking to people before finding the name of the person who had assisted police before in Redhill with lip reading and made tentative arrangements with them.

John drove into Heathrow Police Station's secure car park attracting curious glances from uniform officers at his powder-blue Volvo. In the police station he located the uniform chief inspector's office and rapped sharply on the door. The response came from within, 'Enter.'

As John opened the door and started to walk in, the officer looked up. 'Oh dear. John Whiles. Am I going to regret coming to work today?'

'Hello Kenny. Is that the way to greet an old friend?' For several minutes they nattered about past encounters before John said why he was there. Kenny listened agog. John trusted him unreservedly and gave him the whole story. 'So, the reason I have washed up on your shore, Kenny, is I need to get an original copy of all the CCTV from Terminal 5 for the 28th of November.'

'The murder team looking into the dead junkie is upstairs. They will have a complete set of the CCTV. If you want, I'm sure they could run you off a copy.'

John said, 'I don't think so. I have a horrible feeling that they may have a doctored set. Could I get one from the Terminal 5 security control room where I can see it being downloaded?'

'Yes. I'll take you there. I need to stretch my legs. Since becoming a desk jockey I rarely get out anymore. I am putting on so much weight my wife wants me to join a gym.'

John looked him up and down, 'I see her point.'

They made their way across the airport to Terminal 5 and

the CCTV security control room. It was a darkened room with concealed, non-reflective soft lighting and no windows. One wall was covered with thirty monitors surrounding one large screen. Each displayed the images being relayed in real time from a CCTV camera.

Facing the screens, John saw six people sitting behind a long desk. Each had a keyboard and a smaller monitor in front of them. Behind them, on a slightly raised platform, sat the supervisor at a small desk. He controlled the largest screen. As he saw the chief inspector he stood up.

The supervisor was polite, 'Good afternoon, sir. I didn't expect to see you today. What can I do for you?'

Chief Inspector Kenny stated their business, 'I'd like to see a day's CCTV if I could please.'

The supervisor was courteous, 'Certainly. Please come through to the side office.' Kenny, John and the supervisor went into a small room which also had subdued lighting. There was one large monitor and two computers linked to DVD recorders. 'Now, what day are you interested in?'

Kenny said, '28th of November.'

'That's fortunate. I have a complete copy of all the CCTV recorded for that date. It's here somewhere.' The supervisor sifted through a rack. 'Here it is,' he said plucking out two DVDs.

Kenny took them and said, 'Could you put up the original CCTV from the Terminal?'

John watched the supervisor. He saw his eyes widen and switch quickly between Kenny and himself. He suddenly became extremely nervous. A tick started under one eye which he couldn't hide. The supervisor stammered and said,

'I don't know if it's still available. It has probably taped over itself by now.'

Kenny was having none of it, 'It's not taped over for twenty-eight days. There will not be a problem. Please bring it up and download it while we are here.'

The supervisor was starting to visibly sweat, 'It will take an hour to copy it all. It you'd like to go and get a coffee; I'll have it ready for you when you get back.'

Kenny was getting irritated and sharply said, 'No. We'll wait and watch you do it. My colleague here is interested to see how you do it. Can you tell him how many cameras there are?'

The supervisor lied, 'There are ninety-two cameras in the Terminal and many more in the outlets.'

Kenny knew the supervisor was lying, 'I always thought there were a hundred. Am I wrong?'

The supervisor was becoming flustered. 'Eight are temporarily out of order. I am waiting for them to be repaired.'

'So they are not shown on these two DVDs you have given me?'

The supervisor was struggling, 'No. They shouldn't be. If they are, they would have been repaired by someone and they haven't told me.'

Kenny was annoyed, 'Well. Let's see how many you can find on the 28th of November.'

The supervisor's fingers were hitting a lot of the wrong keys on his keyboard. Normally he'd have had no problem, but John could see he was worried. Eventually he found all one hundred CCTV cameras were operating.

Kenny said, 'That's interesting. The eight must have been repaired and they forgot to tell you. I presume you can still put all one hundred of them onto two DVDs?'

The supervisor became resigned as to what he had to do. 'Yes. I'll put fifty on each,' he complied. Then he set the recorders in motion.

John and Kenny stopped in a café in Terminal 5 on their way back to Heathrow Police Station.

Kenny was the first to speak. 'There is something definitely fishy about these tapes. I've known that supervisor for a couple of years and never seen him act like that before.'

John said, 'He didn't want to copy them and was trying to get us out of there. I reckon he would have just copied the ones he gave us at the start.'

'I think you are right. Take them and let me know what you find. Do you want me to tell the murder team what we have done?'

'Not yet. They have what they believe is a genuine copy of all the active CCTV from Terminal 5. I am willing to bet it is identical to the two DVDs he gave us first from the rack. I'll see if the ones he copied while we watched him marry up with them. If they don't, and I think that is likely I'll give them a copy.'

The two men chatted as they drank their coffee, oblivious to the CCTV camera focused on them.

21

12TH DECEMBER 2011
7PM

John decided he couldn't be bothered about the Volvo anymore and drove into Scotland Yard's underground car park. Walking up to the ground floor he met the back hall inspector who said, 'DC Whiles isn't it?'

'Yes, that's me.'

'Are you the guy who just drove that ludicrously huge blue Volvo down into the car park?'

'Yes. I know it's a surveillance vehicle. I'm sorry I am in a bit of a hurry.'

The inspector seemed rather worried and more concerned about another matter. 'No, it's not that. About an hour ago, Janine who is one of our receptionists, got a strange phone call. Someone claimed to be a police officer and needed to talk to you urgently. They couldn't remember your name, but knew you drove a large light blue Volvo. You are the only person we know of at the Yard who drives a light blue Volvo. They asked her who you were and what department you were in. When she asked the caller for their warrant number and name before she would divulge any details, they hung up.'

'How interesting. Was it a man or woman enquiring?' asked John.

'It was a man.'

'If anyone else makes enquiries about me, could you blank them?'

'If a genuine police officer makes any enquiries, we'll find out who they are, and I'll let you know.'

'Thanks a lot,' said John. 'Please thank Janine for me. Good to see the reception is still on the ball.'

John bounded up the five flights of stairs and was out of breath when he got to the DAC's office. Kelly was just putting her coat on when he walked in. Despairingly, she took it off and hung it up. John dropped into a chair breathing heavily. She sat back at her desk and waited.

John, breathing heavily, said, 'I'm going to have to start using the lift.'

'While you're getting your breath back, I'll fill you in. The guv'nor has got the details of that phone number and he isn't happy. It comes back to a private number inside the Foreign Office in Whitehall. He wants to discuss it tomorrow at the meeting. The tap on Ashurst's office phone is active. We would need a warrant to tap her home phone and mobile. I think that would never get past even the most generous magistrate. Mr Groves tells me that surveillance will start at 6am tomorrow. I haven't seen or heard from Clive since this morning. I think that about covers what I know. What have you got to add?'

John told her about obtaining the CCTV from Heathrow. Kelly turned two computers on and said, 'It won't take long to check the provenance of one against the other.' She placed one of the first DVDs that the supervisor had given Kenny from the rack into a disc drive. Then she placed the corresponding disc that John had watched the supervisor download into the other computer's DVD drive. Checking the times shown were identical, she set them both running at four times normal speed. They both sat back in their chairs and watched the swiftly changing pictures.

They soon noticed that the disc that the supervisor had tried to get Kenny to accept first, was in advance of the one John and he had watched him download. Kelly looked at John and said, 'That confirms the disc has been doctored by someone. Some of the tape must have been removed so it's shorter than the one you saw him download. The murder team looking into the dead junkie hasn't got the true version.'

John said, 'I don't suppose it's worth checking the second DVDs just yet. They are likely to be wrong as well. Can you run off a quick copy of the two true tapes? Then I'll get it to the Heathrow murder team. I think the supervisor has a few questions to answer.'

●

The supervisor left the control room at the end of his shift at 9pm. His earlier phone call, whilst watching John and Kenny in the café, had eased his mind a little. He stopped en route to the underground station at his usual haunt in Terminal 2 for a latte. He had not noticed that he had been followed in by a female, but when she sat down, every man noticed her.

He couldn't help himself. The skirt of her suit rose higher than was respectable. She was smiling at him. He smiled back. Then she stood up and walked to where he was seated. 'Can I join you?' she said.

'Please do.' This had never happened to him before.

'You look like you know your way around. Do you work here?'

He was nearly tongue tied, 'Yes. I've just finished and was on my way back to London.'

'Such a coincidence. I thought I would have a quick coffee before I made my way there. Which way is quickest?'

'I normally use the Tube.'

'Could you show me the way? I tend to get lost very easily in a new airport.'

He was elated that such a beautiful woman was happily talking to him. The earlier problem had completely slipped his mind. 'I would consider it a privilege. What is your name?'

'Please call me Chloe.'

As they left the café, she slipped her arm under his. She pulled him gently closer and her perfume wafted around him. It never crossed his mind that she hadn't asked what his name was. It didn't even occur to him that she had no luggage. She spoke of travelling from America, but he ignored the fact she would not have been at Terminal 2. He laughed freely at her pitiful jokes and disclosed what his job was. Her hand delicately removed his mobile phone from his jacket pocket.

They stood side by side on an escalator and she put her arm around his back to pull closer to him as faster passengers tried to pass them. On the platform, he moved to nearer where the front of the train would stop, explaining it was quicker to alight in London. It was not overtly crowded, and she guided him to within a foot of the platform's edge without him realising.

They knew a train was coming by the rush of cool air preceding it along the platform and the growing noise as it entered the station. She lent slightly forward and watched it approaching causing him to lean slightly forward as well throwing him a little off balance.

She knew it was a forgone conclusion. Although the train was slowing, he was as good as dead. A swift push in the middle of his back sent him spiralling off the platform in front of the train. He clutched at thin air trying to save himself. Somehow he started to turn towards the platform. Shock had spread across his face as he saw her already walking away with his mobile phone in her hand.

The train hit him dragging him between it and the edge of the platform. It cut him in two just below his waist, dropping his legs and hips onto the track. Then it stopped with his torso tightly wedged between the bottom of a carriage and the platform's edge. All his vital internal organs were intact held by the constriction of the small gap. Blood was dripping but not freely flowing.

He was conscious. He had no feeling below his waist but didn't realise he had nothing there. His thoughts were positive. I've got away with it. People rushed towards him. 'Can someone help me up please?' he said. The train driver knew when he saw him he was as good as dead. As soon as the train was moved his organs would succumb to gravity.

The supervisor watched in puzzlement as the driver and station staff moved the public away and cleared the station. Police in uniform were everywhere. Medics had rushed up to him and stuck a needle in him. No one tried to help him up. 'Can someone help me up please?'

A police officer asked, 'What is your name? Have you any family?'

'I am the CCTV control room supervisor for Terminal 5. I am single. Why do you ask? Why won't anyone help me up?'

The policeman told him, 'We are going to have to move the train. Do you want to send a message to anyone?'

The supervisor realised with foreboding the blatantly obvious outcome. 'I was pushed by a woman who I met in Terminal 2. She called herself Chloe. Tell Chief Inspector Kenny that it was me who altered the tapes. I did it for the country. He will know what I mean.' A medic stuck another needle into his arm. He was unconscious in seconds.

When the train was slowly reversed, the supervisor died.

22

12TH DECEMBER 2011
10PM

John's mobile played a nondescript piece of music and vibrated in his pocket. He drove to the side of the road and stopped. 'Hello.'

'Oscar, it's Kenny. Just been called by the duty officer at Heathrow. The supervisor is dead. Apparently been pushed under a tube train by a woman. She gave her name as Chloe. He claimed to have altered the tapes. The strange bit is he said, "he did it for the country". I've no idea what he means by that. They have checked the CCTV and sure enough he was pushed. It looks like she nicked his phone for good measure.'

'How did he say all this?'

'Long story: he lived long enough before he died.'

'Kenny, if it's the woman I think it is, she has done for your junkie at Heathrow, my victim in Reigate and a uniform PC in Kenley. Make sure you are careful. She doesn't seem to worry about who she kills.'

'How come every time I meet you, something bad happens?'

'Just lucky I suppose.'

Kenny said, 'From what the duty officer said, I think the murder team are going to take it on with their junkie as it's sort of related.'

John advised him, 'There's a copy of the true tapes on their way to Heathrow via a "Black Rat". I've got a meeting tomorrow morning. I should have some more information by then. I'll call you afterwards.'

Kenny chuckled as he said, 'If you would. The DCI running the murder team is at twenty thousand feet and still climbing.'

John slid the phone back into his pocket. He sat in the car for a while as he considered what Kenny had said. Then he thought about their visit to the supervisor. He had obviously known who Kenny was. At no time had he been introduced and only addressed by Kenny as Oscar when they spoke together. The CCTV in the airport did not cover the police station or it's car park. That was a separate system. Therefore, the supervisor did not know his name although he could have 'grabbed' a still of him from the CCTV as he was in Terminal 5.

When they had visited PC Brown, Clive had introduced himself first. He had identified John only as DC Whiles and said they were from CO. John pondered the hypothesis that most people would only remember the first person named who did the opening spiel. That had been Clive.

He cursed under his breath. Brown had seen them getting out of the Volvo. He knew he shouldn't have taken it into Kenley's yard. That, he thought, explained why the enquiry had been made to the Yard receptionist. He knew he had to get rid of the car and quickly.

Then he remembered the remark made by Kelly about not seeing Clive. He whipped his phone out and dialled his number, 'Come on Clive, answer.'

'Hello Oscar.'

'Clive, thank goodness you are all right. Where are you?'

'On a train coming back from Birmingham. Good to know you care about me.'

'It looks like she's done another murder at Heathrow. I'll fill you in tomorrow but be aware of those around you. What were you doing in Birmingham?'

'Chasing up a lead about Henrik. Got a lot to tell you. Can you pick me up in the morning from my HA?'

'Yes, will do. Seriously, Clive, be careful. See you about 7ish.'

'Wow, I might actually get some sleep tonight,' and Clive hung up. His eyes darted about the train's carriage. What the hell am I looking for? No one was paying him any attention. Before John's call he was nearly asleep, now he was wide awake. The thought of shutting his eyes horrified him. Bloody Oscar, putting the fear of God into him.

As the train pulled into Euston, Clive slung a door open. When it had slowed enough, he jumped from it and ran down the platform, slapping his ticket into the startled collector's hand. He didn't slow down as he ran across the concourse. The directional sign pointed the way to the taxi stand. When he arrived, several cabbies were standing about chatting.

He got into the first vehicle as the driver disgorged himself from the group. Clive was looking back for anyone following. No one. Then he realised he was puffing. The speed he had run was his fastest sprint, Bloody Oscar, he thought again. Telling the cabbie his address, he settled back in his seat to recover his composure.

The taxi dropped him at his front gate. He paid and strode up to his front door. As he put the key in the lock, the door flew open and his irate girlfriend Celeste stood in the way. 'I'm sorry I'm so late, I've just got back from Birmingham and I am dog-tired. I need to sleep.'

She glared menacingly at him, and then gave him a mouthful. Why hadn't he called? Didn't he know she was cooking an evening meal? Every night she cooked. It shouldn't have been a surprise. Then finally with gleeful satisfaction, she disclosed his food was in the bin.

Then he made the fatal error of many a man before him. He told her he had eaten a couple of sandwiches on the train.

She stomped off up the stairs shouting, 'You will be in the spare room tonight,' and the door to their bedroom was slammed shut.

Clive stuck a chair under the front door handle and then went round the ground floor of his house checking and securing all the windows. The last thought as he lay on the bed in the spare room before falling into a deep sleep was 'Bloody Oscar'.

•

The woman lay on her bed in the Holiday Inn at Heathrow and scrolled through the supervisor's phone. No messages to worry about. She checked the phone's log. There was a dialled call to the number she knew. Using a nail file, she prised off the back of the phone and removed the battery. Then she took out the sim card. She knew even if the phone was turned off its location could often be traced.

Snapping the sim card in two; she threw one piece into a waste bin next to the bed. Getting up, she dropped the smaller piece out of the window. She watched it land in an ornamental flower bed. The battery and phone would have to wait till the morning when she would dump them in different rubbish bins.

Using a burner phone, she sent a text.

I've got rid of the supervisor. He had your details on his phone. Keep me informed.

Derek was just leaving his club in Park Lane to go home when his phone alerted him to the message. Swearing to himself, he forwarded the text to his boss.

Tabitha was at home watching television with her husband. Her phone was on a side table and pinged to let her know she had a text. Checking her mantle clock for the lateness of the hour she looked at her phone. Her text reply to her underling was brusque.

We'll sort this out tomorrow. Then in reply to her husband's curious look, 'It's work. Nothing to worry about.'

•

John parked in a side road about a hundred yards from his registered address in Fulham. He walked round the corner and towards his flat but on the opposite side of the road. There were a lot of parked cars, but all were empty. Slowly he walked past the entrance and glanced in. Nothing of note. Still all the parked cars were empty. What the back hall inspector had said was playing on his mind.

John had a flat in Chichester that very few people knew

about and he liked it that way. It was in a luxury block of three with a secure entrance into a foyer and then a flight of stairs up to his front door. Next to the stairs was a private lift to take him up the single flight to his front door if the stairs were too much effort. His flat was the largest, sitting above the two on the ground floor. The security was exceptional with additional measures added by specialists and a protected garage. Over the few years he had owned it, he had furnished it in an opulent manner.

Now he thought how much he would have preferred to be there as opposed to Fulham. Turning quickly round he went into the shabby entrance to the block of ten flats. He was ready to defend himself. Up the stairs to his flat, opened his front door, entered and shut it behind him. A quick check revealed no one was in there waiting to do him harm. He slumped into his old armchair where he could think.

Kenny was at home. He lived in Windsor in a large house. Not the grandest residence in the area but he was happy there. His wife of eighteen years was a local teacher and his twelve-year-old son Ralph idolised him and wanted to follow in his father's police footsteps. John had worried him. The television was on, but he was miles away in thought.

His son was a car enthusiast who studied every vehicle magazine he could get hold off. His internet searches were mainly of vehicle specifications. When Kenny had arrived home from work his son greeted him at the front door.

'Dad, look at that black Range Rover. It's got one of those new dash cams,' and he pointed to a parked car. 'They haven't adjusted it right. It's pointing at the pavement.'

Kenny turned to look at it more to humour his son than

out of interest. He saw it was only a few yards from his garage drive and facing it, 'I've not seen that car before.'

His son was positive, 'It's not been in our road before. Maybe one of our neighbours has bought it.'

Now he picked up his phone, 'Hello Oscar.'

23

13TH DECEMBER 2011
7AM

Clive saw John arrive and was instantly out of his house. The morning had been fraught. Celeste was in a worse mood than the night before. Getting into the passenger seat of the Volvo he relaxed. Neither spoke a greeting. Each had a lot to say but were not in any hurry. John drove off.

As he drove, John passed Clive a folded piece of paper without comment. Clive just opened it without remark. He read, *Do not say anything controversial. We'll go to Morrisons for breakfast. Once we are in the café, please pass me your mobile. I'll explain after that.* Clive looked at John who was looking straight ahead at the road.

They were soon at Reigate and John drove into Morrisons' car park. Both strolled into the café. The car park and the café had been thoroughly cleaned and bore no sign of any untoward activity. Each bought a large breakfast. John's was cholesterol-inducing and Clive's was healthy. Clive put his mobile on the table within John's reach.

'Damn! I've left my wallet in the car. I'll be back in a second,' and with that he snatched up Clive's mobile and rushed back to the Volvo. Clive watched him through the windows. In the short time he had come to know John, he'd learnt that he invariably had a reason for everything. Clive watched as he opened the boot.

Four minutes later, he returned to the café and rejoined Clive. He passed the phone back to him. 'Sorry about that. I just wanted to check that your phone wasn't bugged. I checked mine this morning. Trouble is, I can't check the car. So be careful what you say when we are in it.'

'How can you check the phones?' asked Clive.

'I've got a bit of kit that can do it.'

'Where did you get it from?'

'Some people I know.'

Clive was interested. He loved technology. He was struggling with the fact that John didn't seem to understand how delayed emails were sent. Yet here he was saying he could check if a mobile phone was bugged in a matter of minutes with kit that Clive never knew existed. Then another thought flew into his head, 'Why did you think our phones might be bugged?'

'I'll tell you when I have finished my breakfast,' then with a flourish, John set about a sausage.

After they had eaten, Clive bought the coffees and they settled back to discuss the previous day's events. John started by telling Clive about his visit to Heathrow. How Kenny had been given firstly, the doctored discs and then the true CCTV discs. He stressed the importance of the first phone call from Kenny which informed him of the murder of the Terminal 5 supervisor. Then he mentioned, as if in passing that he wasn't identified by name to the supervisor who had known Kenny.

Clive was shocked by the circumstances of the supervisor's murder by a woman, shortly after speaking to Kenny and John. He immediately guessed who she probably was. That

John had not been identified did not pass him by unnoticed.

Then after a pause to finish his coffee, John disclosed that Kenny had contacted him a second time during the previous evening. 'He told me of a strange vehicle parked close to his house. It had a dash cam which was directed more towards the footway than the road. Being worried by a comment I had made; he conducted a PNC check of the vehicle. It was blocked!'

Clive looked puzzled, 'Why would a blocked vehicle be outside a chief inspector's HA?'

'That was exactly what Kenny was wondering. He phoned a contact at the Yard who was able to tell him it was not a police vehicle. That means it was from a different agency. He established it was not from Church. Then he found out the army were the people who had blocked it. He didn't pursue which branch as that would have let them know he was checking. It leads him to think it could be one of the security services. They tend to block some of their vehicles via the military.'

'So he could find out who has blocked it if he wanted. I presume you asked him to hold off for a while?'

'That's what we agreed.'

Both men sat in silence for a couple of minutes before Clive asked, 'Why would the security services be interested in Kenny?'

John replied, 'Think what Brown said to us. He said he viewed the tapes for SB.'

'Let me stop you there, John. I checked with SB at Heathrow and they knew nothing about Brown or any lip reading requests. The guy I spoke to said he would check all

SB offices and let me know later today if any other office made the request.'

'That then is looking very likely Brown lied to us. If it was the security services he was doing the lip reading for, they would have known the tapes had been doctored. Brown may have contacted them after we left Kenley to fill them in on what we asked him. Say the supervisor did the same. Now the two are dead. Why?'

'The British security services don't go around killing people,' said Clive.

'While Kenny was on the phone to me, he saw someone go to the vehicle and drive away. That made him think his phone is tapped. Is someone worried about what the supervisor may have disclosed? Is that why his phone was stolen? We need to find Brown's phone as a matter of urgency,' said John.

'Who is this woman doing these killings?'

'I wish I knew. Is she working for whatever agency it is or is she an independent? Maybe she is both. Has she a separate agenda? We are still in the dark.'

'Not entirely,' replied Clive.

John said, 'Wait. I need another coffee. I'll get you one.'

Clive thought he had discovered a serious flaw in John's hypothesis and wanted to press home an advantage. 'Why did you tell me all about your exploits yesterday before checking my phone?'

'Because everything I told you is common knowledge to someone. They knew we had seen Brown. He more than likely told them. Same with the supervisor. Then Kenny's phone if it was tapped, and we both believed it was. They would have known what enquiries he had made and what he said to me. Did I mention the phone call to the Yard receptionist?'

Clive gave in, 'What phone call?'

John told him chapter and verse about the enquiry to identify the driver of the light blue Volvo. 'As soon as we can, we get rid of this car and use mine. Do not tell anyone what we will be using. As far as the job is concerned, we will still be using the Volvo. People seem to want to find out who we are. You must be careful, Clive. They may have got your name from Brown. Be cautious if anyone you know contacts you who hasn't spoken to you for some time. And be aware if you bump into someone out of the blue.'

'You really know how to put a guy at ease.'

'The more careful you are, Clive, the safer you stay. Enough of my story, what's yours?'

24

13TH DECEMBER 2011
8AM

'I spent some time in CRO with a friend of mine. We soon found that Henrik Jansen had an old criminal record. I wasn't surprised to see it was two convictions for possession of drugs with intent to supply. I'm sure you can guess who his main associate was?'

'Kristoffer Svendsen. Hang on. We have both seen his previous convictions. Phillimore had put them on the briefing sheet which he gave us the morning of the original surveillance operation. 'Barnyard', wasn't it? I can't remember Henrik Jansen being shown as an associate of Svendsen.'

'He wasn't. My friend told me that originally both files were paper, and they were later upgraded to digital. He found it very unusual that the main associates had not been cross referenced. We checked and everything else was correct. It took a while, but we were able to trace the firm who did the digitalisation. At the time it was a private company owned by one man. If I told you his name was Olaf Larsen would it shock you?'

John was contemplative, 'The way things are going, not at all.'

Clive continued his account. 'I had a long chat to the Norwegian consulate who were extremely helpful. They were able to say that both Svendsen and Henrik were suspected drugs couriers in their youth, although neither had a recorded conviction. They emigrated to the UK together. The most interesting bit of news was all three had attended the same school.'

Sarcastically, John enquired, 'Were they in the same class?'

Clive responded caustically, 'Now you're taking the piss.'

'Sorry. I couldn't resist it. Please. Carry on.'

'I was able to trace Olaf Larsen to an address in Birmingham. So I went there to see him personally. A lot better, I find, to talk to someone face to face. One can soon see if they are lying. That is what he tried to do. Once I had explained the potential outcome he soon told me the truth. He had married a rich French woman who provided the funds for him to set up his company. The digitalisation of the CRO files made him a millionaire in his own right. It was common knowledge what his company were doing and various people approached him. They were willing to pay for alterations to files. He swore blue blind that he cannot remember how many he altered, nor whose files they were. It became easy money for him. Being rich attracted a lot of classy ladies and he soon started to play away from home which resulted in his divorce.'

John queried, 'Was he able to say who asked him to alter Svendsen's file?'

'No. I asked him why he hadn't altered Henrik's and he said he had probably not paid.' Clive opened his man bag and took out a statement made under caution by Olaf Larsen in his own handwriting and gave it to John.

John read it and could see it was all written down, 'How on

earth did you get him to write this?'

'I just asked and he said OK.'

John looked at Clive who seemed to have seen something that took his eye elsewhere, 'I'm impressed.'

They left the café and drove to Reigate Police Station. On arrival they were greeted by Murray. A coffee machine had miraculously appeared overnight and was being utilised by nearly everyone who entered the murder team's office. John and Clive gave it a go. Sitting with Murray they were joined by Groves and brought both up to speed with everything that had transpired the previous day.

Groves said, 'This is getting ridiculous. People are being killed all over the place. Who the hell is behind it all? Who has the authority to conduct surveillance on a Chief Inspector? Why? We need a serious powwow with the Heathrow murder team. We could all soon become targets if we're not careful. Murray. Can you sort something out with them please?'

Murray acceded and then brought them up to speed with the progress of the enquiry. It wasn't good news.

'We have all the witness statements from those in the car park. No one except you two saw anything of note, and in fact no one else can recall seeing the killer. The car rental company has been visited and their CCTV obtained. It was hired by a male. We have checked with the Heathrow murder team and it wasn't their victim.'

Clive queried, 'I suppose the driving licence and ID used were false?'

'Correct. We don't seem to be getting anywhere. All the CCTV of the vehicle has come to nothing. It passed through

Woodhatch village and then disappeared. There has been no trace of it since on any ANPR cameras. We have to draw the conclusion the number plates have been changed.'

John said, 'I know it would be labour intensive but have you thought of checking each ANPR camera covering every route out of Woodhatch for a Mercedes?'

Groves said, 'We have thought of that. We checked with traffic officers and it worked out there are a total of fourteen cameras that would have to be viewed to cover every exit. Some are up to five miles away. We estimate anything up to fifty S-Class Mercedes matching the suspect one within that area. It would take the whole team three to four days to do it properly and we still might miss it. Then we would have to check each one out which would add more days. I think it's our last choice at the moment. A bloody nightmare.'

John concurred. 'Just a thought.'

Murray said, 'The fingerprints have come back as no trace. And, as far as we know, there is no missing dynamite or strychnine. There is only one good bit of news.'

John could see Murray was waiting for a response. Clive obliged, 'What would that be?'

'We have a typist. She's busy trying to catch up. You may recognise her.'

John knew who it was straight away. When he had last worked with Groves and Murray, Doreen had been the typist. Some of her input had helped to solve the crime and detect the two serial killers. He knew both Groves and Murray would have fought tooth and nail to have her on the team. He looked forward to renewing her acquaintance.

'Does she still dress the same?' he asked.

From behind him a female voice replied, 'Yes I do. Have you any objections, Mr Whiles?'

John spun round to see Doreen. She was dressed exactly the same as she had been before. Black shoes, knee length dark skirt and white blouse. Her hair was tied back in a bun and her complexion was sallow. She still looked older than she was. John had never been able to ascertain her exact age but reckoned she was somewhere near forty.

'Great to see you again, Doreen. How are you? Still living with your mum? Reading every afternoon? How do you get here? You don't drive.'

John was aware that she lived with her ageing mother and used to have to be home for 5pm every evening for tea. She had to be at the bus stop at the right time or be late and incur her mother's wroth. It was common knowledge that she would finish her typing and then read a book until it was time for her to leave.

'Mr Groves was good enough to arrange transport for me. He is a gentleman, not like some!'

'It's still good to see you again,' said John.

'I'll reserve judgement as to whether it's good to see you again.' Then Doreen walked away to her desk next to Murray's. Making a big show of removing a book from her bag, she placed it in her top drawer. Smiling at those watching her, she started work.

Clive stated, 'She seems to know you well.'

Murray called to her, 'Your tea will be ready shortly,' and then to John, 'She still runs the place.'

Groves ran the early morning murder team meeting and passed on all the negative responses. He concluded with the words, 'It's a straight man hunt at the present time. Go to it and see what you can find. Just remember, be very careful. This woman is a nasty killer.'

25

13TH DECEMBER 2011
11AM

John drove down into Scotland Yard's underground car park. The Volvo attracted the usual quizzical stares. Groves was in the back seat behind Clive and said, 'What the hell are we doing in this car? It sticks out like a sore thumb. Everyone in the world will know it soon. Where's your old car?'

Clive said, 'Even I can see this has got to go.'

John ignored the comments. 'I'll swap them later. Let's get up to the office.'

Clive and Groves strode into the office greeting Kelly. John walked in a few seconds later out of breath and with a reddened face. He plonked himself down on a wooden chair. Kelly picked up a bottle of water and threw it to him which he easily caught and said, 'For everyone's sake, John, take the lift in future.'

The DAC stepped out of his office, 'That's good advice Oscar. You're getting on. What news folks?'

Clive explained all the information gleaned by both John and himself. When he produced the statement he had taken under caution, Kelly, Groves and the DAC looked at it in amazement. The DAC couldn't help himself, 'How on earth did you get Larsen to write that? I hope you didn't promise him anything?'

Clive was slightly indignant at the thought, 'No sir. I think he wanted to get it off his chest before he died. He has cancer and a poor prognosis.'

Kelly told the group about rubbish spoken by Ashurst to various people on her phone. Then she confirmed a PoLSA unit would be at Brown's HA at 2pm. Groves confirmed that the Sussex surveillance team had been on Ashurst since first light. The DAC stood nodding. He liked what he heard.

'That phone number courtesy of Brown is interesting. It comes back to a number allocated to a department in the Foreign Office in Whitehall. Our people could not get any further than that. We don't know who has it or why. If we pursue the enquiry, we will probably show our hand. Has anyone got a thought on that?'

John had recovered his breath, 'I have a contact who may be able to help. I will see if he is available.'

The DAC looked sternly at John, 'Just keep it legal.'

John, Clive, Kelly and Groves sat in the outer office discussing tactics while the DAC was in his inner office with the door closed. Occasionally they could hear him shouting, presumably on the phone.

Groves said to John, 'If you pick your motor up today, I'll give the Volvo to the officer who drove me up here yesterday. He can run it about. He's an advanced driver and should be able to spot a tail and lose it if necessary.' Then, as a rider, added, 'Or nick them.'

John expressed his thoughts, 'OK. Just remind him to be very careful. Any of us may become a possible target. That would include any driver of the Volvo.'

Groves replied, 'I don't think there is anything too urgent

at the moment. We can check in with the PoLSA team at Brown's on the way back to Reigate.'

Clive asked John, 'Where's this car of yours?'

'Tucked away.'

John, Clive and Groves left the office and walked down the stairs to the reception desk at the front door to the Yard. All three spent another five minutes chatting to Janine. Then they went into the basement car park. As they were starting to get into the Volvo, a shouted greeting from some way off attracted their attention.

'Clive, long time no see. How are you?' They all looked in the direction of the call and saw a tall, uniformed PC striding towards them.

John whispered to Clive, 'Remember what I said.'

Clive looked mystified at the approaching officer. He had no idea who he was. The PC reached them and said to Clive, 'Jack Scrivener. You remember me. We were at Hendon together. Well I was two classes in front of you. Didn't you get posted to St John's Wood?'

Clive still had no recollection of the officer and said, 'No, I went to Bow Street.'

Scrivener probed further, 'What are you doing nowadays? That is a snazzy car you are using. Who are your colleagues?'

Clive rallied and lied, 'I got transferred and we've all been lumbered sorting out all the old court papers that need to be digitised. At least I get to move around a lot. So we got given this monstrosity of a car. No one else wanted it. Anyway. What about you?' Clive ignored the part about colleagues.

Now the initiative was on the other foot. PC Scrivener looked a bit taken aback. He hadn't expected to have to answer any questions. He was there to find answers. He didn't know how to lie quickly when put on the spot. Truth was out.

'I went to Bromley. Anyway. Must go,' and Scrivener ran off.

Before he was out of sight, John got out of the car and moved a few yards away from it. Then he phoned Kelly. He knew she could get Scrivener's personnel file within minutes. Then she would be wanting to know why he was at the Yard in full uniform and whether he was on duty or not.

Both Clive and Groves joined John away from the car. All three knew that every vehicle in the basement car park should be left unlocked with the keys in them. It was in case something happened and they had to be moved quickly. Anyone could have left a listening device in the vehicle or stuck a tracker on it.

John made a mental note to get the day's CCTV of all the vehicles that went down into the basement car park before they were approached by Scrivener. He knew the CCTV of the parking area was mainly to monitor the vehicles moving around, but he'd request it anyhow from the back hall inspector. It was possible he'd see if anyone went near the Volvo or tampered with it.

'Nice one, Clive. Interesting that he claimed he left Hendon sometime before you. In my day we were posted to our first police station after we had completed our final exam. That would be in our last week. Therefore, how, if he left sometime before you would he know of you or be interested in where you were posted? I think he had been tasked to find out who we all are and where we are currently posted to. Then of course he might have wanted to confirm this vehicle's registration number.'

Clive said angrily, 'Or stick a bug on it or listening device in it.'

Groves said, 'At least we know he is a genuine PC. He'd never get down here without having to show his warrant card at least once.'

Clive was more thoughtful, 'He knew my name. How? Since I have been working with you, I have given my name and rank but not where I'd been posted. I have mentioned the murder investigation but only to Brown. Furthermore. If he'd been tucked away down here waiting for us to return to this car, he might have had a camera.'

John said, 'Hold on Clive. He only used your first name.'

Groves said, 'Well. I recorded him on my phone if it's of any use.'

They all laughed. Clive more out of nervousness.

John drove out of the Yard and to Brown's HA. He parked behind the PoLSA team's Ford Transit Van and they all ducked under the police tape strewn about the front of the house. A uniformed officer recorded their details as they entered the property.

DS Grant Brahms was in the hall reading the report from John. His searching partner was sitting in the kitchen drinking a freshly made cup of tea courtesy of Brown. A large toolbox was by Grant's feet. He looked questionably at John saying, 'What the hell is all this about, Oscar? Why am I to start at the lounge door? Why aren't we searching from the front door?'

John had known Grant for years. He knew his nickname was Liszt and that he hated being called it. John said, 'Hi

Grant. It's all written down there for you. That was the last thing PC Brown wrote.'

'All right. You're the boss. It'll still take a couple of hours. Nice to meet you two. I'm Grant. He'll never introduce us. You are?'

Groves and Clive introduced themselves.

Grant continued with a warning, 'If you want to wait you can sit in our transit. Just don't eat my sandwiches.'

As they stood chatting in the hall, Grant took an electric screwdriver from his toolbox and started to take the lounge door off its hinges. Three hinges, three screws in each one. 'Strange, John. I've never had a door where the screws haven't been painted over.' His partner had entered and was holding the door steady.

Then with gloved hands they started to lift the door away from the jamb. As they moved it, a mobile phone fell from the top of the door which was neatly caught by Grant's searching partner. Grant looked at the door and saw a small chamber had been chiselled into the top. When the door had been on its hinges and in place it was not visible. The cavity was just large enough to hold the mobile phone without it moving and making a sound.

Grant said, 'That explains the screws. To chisel that into the door, it had to be taken off its hinges.'

John, Clive and Groves were more interested in the phone. Clive put it in an evidence bag but didn't seal it. It didn't go unnoticed by Grant.

'Trained by Oscar, I see. Just don't leave your sticky mitts on it when you check it. Remember. It's got to go to fingerprint branch and technical support. As far as I'm concerned you put it in an evidence bag and that's what I'll be saying.'

John said, 'Thanks Liszt. If I were you, I'd knock this search on the head. We only wanted the phone.'

'Call me that again and I won't even make a statement,' Grant threatened.

The three left as Grant was taking photographs of the door and its chiselled hiding place. He would still continue a search. His attitude was, if there was one thing hidden, there may be something else. Grant was pedantic.

26

13TH DECEMBER 2011
4.30PM

John parked in the car park at the rear of Reigate Police Station and they all walked into the office as Doreen was making the tea and said, 'Just my luck. I thought I'd get a half hour's reading in with a nice cup of tea and the three amigos walk in.'

Groves said, 'Just two more teas and one coffee please Doreen. Then we'll have a chat with you and Murray, if that's all right with you, in my office.'

Doreen busied herself and soon they were all nursing cups in the DCI's office. John, Clive and Groves discussed the day's events as Murray and Doreen listened. Groves phoned Kelly who updated him about Scrivener.

'Kelly has gone through Scrivener's records. He has had a couple of unproven allegations made by fellow officers who thought he was taking bribes. She found out he wasn't at training school within two years of you, Clive. She spoke to the duty sergeant and his duty officer at Bromley who told her Scrivener was on night duty and had no business being at the Yard. Kelly wants to know how we should handle this. Any suggestions?'

Murray said, 'Arrest the bastard and stick him in a cell incommunicado. There are plenty of empty ones downstairs.'

John said, 'I agree. I will be curious to see what he says. It'll be interesting to see if anyone actually tries to find him. I'm sure that when Clive interviews him and explains all the people dying he will spill the beans.'

Clive whined, 'Why me?'

'Because he knows you, Clive. Remember, he was at training school with you. He said so.'

'Yeah right! I get all the rubbish jobs,' Clive said, secretly looking forward to it.

Groves said, 'That's agreed then. I'll tell Kelly and get Shackleton to arrest him asap,' and he left the office.

Doreen said, 'Have you looked at Brown's phone yet?'

John replied, 'No. We'll give it to the exhibits officer and let him sort it out.'

She pressed, 'There may be a lot of emails or texts that will need to be checked urgently as well as logged call numbers. We need to see them before it's sent off to the labs for them to play with.'

Murray said, 'All right, Doreen. Go through it with the exhibits officer. Before you do though, get the SOCO to check it for prints. Then it's all yours. You'll have to make a statement later.'

'Thanks.'

Murray said to John, 'If you want to pick your car up tonight you can travel down to Chichester with Doreen when she goes home. You should be safe enough.' Then turning to Clive, 'I'll fix a lift for you when you want it. With a bit of luck, you might get an interview in with Scrivener tonight.'

Shackleton wanted to know why he was being sent to arrest a police officer. Groves told him the story and what Kelly had told him. He looked aghast, 'Bloody hell. There's one PC been murdered and another doing dodgy deals. What the hell is happening in the Met nowadays?'

Groves ignored the question, 'Go three-handed. I don't want any trouble. If you can, nick him when no one sees you. The fewer people who know he's been lifted the better. If anyone asks where you're from or where you are taking him, lie.'

'My sort of arrest. We'll have him here soon,' and Shackleton walked off to find his partner and another officer.

•

Tabitha said to Derek in a partly rhetorical statement, 'This is serious. I doubt whether anyone cares much about the druggie at Heathrow. The police must have known Svendsen was a drugs importer. There's something strange about that,' and she cast him a quick sidelong glance to see if he was showing any tell-tale signs of understanding. 'Now there's Brown, the dead copper and that supervisor at Heathrow who doctored the tapes. She's starting to get out of control.' Tabitha focused on Derek's face. It was blank.

'I don't understand why she killed Svendsen.'

Tabitha replied wistfully, 'Something to do with drugs from Columbia.' She wasn't going to say any more to Derek. Any monies that might come her way weren't worth sharing with an idiot like him.

'Do you think Brown told us the truth about what was said between her and Svendsen?'

Tabitha looked at Derek. He had a point. Brown wouldn't have lied to her would he? He'd lied to the police. Were they convinced? Where the hell was his phone? The man hadn't found it. He'd searched his house and hadn't found it.

Thoughtfully she said, 'You know, Derek. You may have a point. She's told us she hasn't got Brown's mobile. If she hasn't got it, where is it?' Tabitha was racking her brains. She obviously knew the woman hadn't got it. Nor had the man she'd sent. So who the hell had it? If the police recover it what will they find. Not her mobile number because any texts or emails from Brown went to Derek's phone. Like all department landlines and mobiles, she knew his was a protected number so they would know straight away if anyone was trying to find out who it belonged to.

Then she remembered, she'd spoken to Brown from her office phone just the once. She thought hard. She doubted he'd remember any number. Would his phone have the number stored? If the police found the phone, they'd see her number in the phone's log. Simple problem to answer; Derek obviously used her landline.

She looked at Derek. If anyone does get too close he was expendable. She didn't like him that much anyway. Eton to Cambridge and straight into the civil service probably thanks to someone at his posh club. How he ever got a degree baffled her.

Now she thought about it, why would the police have got the supervisor to run off the original tapes at the airport? Why didn't they accept the doctored ones offered? Someone was starting to look too closely. Why and who?

●

John was dropped off at St Richard's Hospital in Chichester and wandered into the accident and emergency department. The waiting room was chaotic. People holding various parts of their anatomy. Some were crying softly and others were just looking into space hoping the next name called was theirs. Then there were those waiting to be reunited with loved ones already in the treatment area.

The receptionist behind the strong Perspex screen saw him as he entered the main door. She picked up the internal phone and spoke to someone within the department. As John got to her she was putting the phone down. 'She'll be with you in a minute,' the receptionist said to John.

'Thanks Grace. I see you're as busy as usual.'

'This is the quiet period. Come back in a couple of hours if you want to see us busy. You look like you've been dragged through a hedge backwards. I think we could borrow an old comb for you from one of our local vagrants, if you want?'

A doctor in a creased white coat walked into the waiting area. Lots of faces looked up in anticipation. Carol said to Grace, 'In all the time I've known him, he's never used a comb.'

'Hello, Carol. Won't stop long. When do you finish tonight?'

'1 o'clock tomorrow morning. I presume you're staying the night at your place.'

'Yes. I thought if you fancied a glass of wine you might join me when you finished?'

'I'll be there,' and Carol walked back into the treatment area, as John marched out of the unit with a spring in his step to the cab rank.

Clive asked, 'Did anyone see you nick him?'

Shackleton said, 'No. What really got me was when I told him he was being arrested for corruption and cautioned him he replied, "I suppose it was inevitable."'

'Do you think he'll put his hands up to it?'

'I think he is worth talking to straight away. In the car coming back here he was miles away, probably thinking about what he's going to do.'

'Right. Let's go and see what he has to say?'

27

13TH DECEMBER 2011
9.30PM

John was on the phone for just shy of eighty minutes. Rocky was at home in Kent. He'd listened to what was being asked and if it was possible. They discussed the potential pitfalls. How would he get into the building? How would he get his gear through the scanner without it alerting all the security officers? Could he get into the office if it was locked? It seemed impossible.

John had never spoken to him before. His reputation was well known in certain circles. Rocky Boulder was one of the best, if not the best. His nickname was given to him by his best friend at school and it had stuck. No one had called him Richard since then. He had been the youngest person to get an electronics degree, then a Master's in engineering and a PhD in computer science.

The government had somehow got to hear of his talents, and GCHQ had quickly come calling. The military taught him things that civilian authorities would baulk at. He learnt from the Americans, Germans and other friendly nations, techniques that most individuals would call illegal. He had climbed the slippery ladder of promotions to the very top and then he went on some spurious mission into Africa.

One badly aimed snipers bullet was all it took. He lost his

left leg below the knee and the government decided he was no longer of use to them. Rocky had never understood how that had stopped him from being useful. A pension wasn't what he wanted. He'd loved his work. He wasn't going to sit back and do nothing.

Then an acquaintance told him of a unit in Kent that supported talented, disabled service men and women. Rocky travelled to Kent to visit the site and was impressed with what he saw, who he met and what he was offered. Within a month, he was equipping his own workshop and discussing radical ideas with other disabled and retired personnel. Several months later, they were inventing equipment which was being sold to various governmental organisations. Rocky was in his element.

Now he was considering all the options. There was always a way. His original lecturers and tutors had always told him. There is always a way.

Rocky knew of John and how the unit had come about because of a police operation that he had been involved in. He wasn't privy to the financial details and wasn't concerned. Monies made from inventions or other work were poured back into the unit's financial coffers and wages were paid from them. Any additional equipment was also funded from them. Both men trusted the other implicitly although they'd never met.

Rocky was positive, 'Let me think about it. It's certainly a challenge. Obviously illegal, but a challenge. Can I speak to one of my colleagues in the unit?'

John confirmed his consent with a proviso, 'I have no problem with that as long as it's treated as strictly confidential. Nothing written down or recorded.'

'Obviously.'

'When do you think you'll have an answer for me?'

Rocky was enthusiastic, 'I'll start now. I should have a reply for you tomorrow morning. Is that soon enough?'

'That's great Rocky. Thanks,' and they hung up. John was thoughtful. If anyone could tap the phone in the Foreign Office it was Rocky. How he would do it was anyone's guess.

14TH DECEMBER 2011

Carol tapped the doorbell four times before entering the foyer with her key. She walked up the stairs and knocked four times on the front door before opening it, again with keys. John had agreed the system with her some time previously so he didn't think it was an intruder. He'd patiently explained that people normally knock on a door three or five times. Rarely four times. As she walked into the lounge she saw him fast asleep in his favourite reclining armchair. Contemplatively, she said, 'So much for security.'

Carol went into the kitchen and found a Chablis in his wine chiller. Opening it she filled two large glasses and went back into the lounge. She kicked John's feet and he woke with a start. Taking the glass proffered he said, 'Thanks.'

'So much for your security system. I could have been a murderer,' and she sat down in a Stressless recliner chair.

'No, I would have known.'

'Of course you would. I haven't seen you so relaxed for

years. You can't be busy.'

'I think this is the calm before the storm. I want to take advantage of it.'

They chatted for an hour and finished the wine before retiring for the night.

●

Rocky was wide awake in his workshop. He'd made a call after he'd spoken to John and had been joined by Zina. She had been in the signals corps but had suffered from depression. The military had looked after her as best they could but eventually they had to let her go on an ill health pension. Then the Kent unit had taken over her treatment and she had been free of any problems for three years. Now the two of them were collaborating and checking manuals and papers in their own reference library. A soldering iron was on a bench warming up for action.

At 5.30am as dawn was considering breaking, a strange looking drone lifted off from Kent. It had a long way to go. Zina was piloting it. She knew what building she was going to but did not know which room, or more importantly, what window she needed to be above. Her laptop displayed and recorded what the camera on the drone showed. It overlaid a scrolling map which enabled her to navigate easily from such a long distance.

Rocky was busy trying to hack into the Foreign Office email system. It took him six minutes. GCHQ had taught him a lot about hacking which he had put to good use when he worked for HM Government. Now it was being put to use again. He set a computer programme running which started to call email addresses within the Foreign Office, ostensibly from another internal account. So fooling and circumventing the internal security system. Each time, a window was illuminated on his 3D mapping system, letting him know in which room the email was being received.

Then the computer swiftly searched each email for the relevant phone number in the contacts' folders. Before the drone had passed the Thames barrier, an email account displayed the name Tabitha Marchant next to the phone number. Rocky took control of the computer and sent an innocuous email to the one within the room containing Marchant's phone number. A red light blinked in a window on his 3D map. He drew Zina's attention to it.

Rocky was in his element. He downloaded every email to and from Tabitha's account and set his computer to mirror hers. Then with another piece of home-made kit, he rang the actual phone number. No one was in the office at that time of night and the phone went straight to answerphone. Rocky pressed the only button on a box of electronic equipment and a pulsating signal was sent down the line. Nothing was recorded but the phone was intrinsically linked to a tape recorder on Rocky's bench.

Zina hovered the drone above the roof of the Foreign Office and lowered a hair thin wire from beneath it. She couldn't land as the roof had sensors to detect any untoward objects. She let the wire slowly down to a foot below the top of Tabitha's office window. Zina moved the drone slowly so the wire just touched the metal handrail surrounding the roof. Then she released it from the drone. It's magnetism caused it to grasp the rail in a vice-like grip. Now the handrail became an aerial.

The wire blew in the wind for a few seconds as Zina watched what looked like a small spider slide down it. As it was about six inches from the end of the wire it automatically stopped. It was perfectly positioned right at the top of the office window. The wire drifted about like spider's silk and then the minimal weight kept the wire reasonably taut, just long enough for it to stick itself to the glass.

She flew the drone to a high rise block of flats and landed strategically on the roof of the lift housing. No one would stumble across it. They'd programmed the drone to act as a relay from the little spider to the workshop. It would take up most of its remaining power so would have to be recovered in person. Neither considered it would be a problem. The camera was shut down to conserve as much power as possible. Rocky estimated a fortnight before it went flat.

28

14TH DECEMBER 2011
7.30AM

At 7.30am John strode into the office in Reigate Police Station. His old Vauxhall was tucked away out of sight in a side road. He was taking no chances. It had two separate alarm systems. There was a lot of sensitive equipment in the boot and some wired into the vehicle itself. To open the boot was not as simple as using a key. Even to start the vehicle required a sequence of switches to be pushed. He couldn't afford the vehicle to be stolen. The gun secreted under the driver's seat couldn't be allowed to fall into the wrong hands.

The sound of his mobile phone seemed to shock him. Doreen saw him jump.

'Bit twitchy this morning?'

'I think today is going to be a long day, Doreen,' and he answered his phone, 'Hi Rocky.'

John went to a chair and sat down heavily with the phone still clamped to his ear. He said nothing for eight minutes and then said, 'That's brilliant. Can you forward the emails to a computer without disclosing where you are sending them from? I don't want anyone knowing who got them or who sent them?'

Clive looked up and thought, what the hell is he up to now?

John continued his phone conversation, 'Let me fill up the printer. How many sheets do you think it will take?'

John said to Doreen, 'Can you fill up the printer with paper please Doreen. Five hundred sheets should do it.'

Doreen looked at Clive and cast her eyes upwards as she opened the huge, printer tray of the laser jet and stuffed it full of A4 sheets of paper.

John told Rocky the office email address and then said, 'Are you sure? That's amazing. I never knew you could do that!'

Both Doreen and Clive were studying John. When he hung up he sat at a computer terminal and said to the pair of them, 'I may need some help here please.' An email from Rocky started to download to the computer. It contained attached word documents, photographs and emails from within the Foreign Office. Four hundred and twenty in total.

Doreen looked taken aback. Clive looked at John and said, 'Are these from where I think they're from?'

'Yes. We have less than thirty minutes to print these off. Then they will disappear from this computer and we'll lose them all,' said John.

Doreen pushed John and he realised she wanted him out of the way. He stood up as she sat down in his vacated seat. Her fingers skipped across the keyboard and the printer burst into life. Clive collected the papers as they were spewed out. John watched them. Cheers Rocky, he thought. A lot more than I could ever have hoped for.

The printer eventually stopped. Two minutes later Doreen said, 'Look!'

John and Clive looked at the computer screen. A skull and crossbones was in the centre. A red flash burst from the eyes in the skull. As it subsided the image was on fire. It burnt fiercely for a few seconds and as the embers drifted away, the email with all its attachments broke up into pixels and fled from the screen. The actual printouts were all that remained.

Shackleton called to Clive, 'I've run off a couple of tapes for Doreen of last night's interview with Scrivener. Mr Groves is going to suspend him from all police duties on behalf of the Met commissioner and seize his warrant card.'

Doreen cut in, 'I'll type them up first thing after this morning's briefing.'

John asked Clive, 'What did he say? Did he want a brief?'

Clive replied, 'He must be the only copper ever arrested who hasn't asked for a brief. He didn't seem concerned. When I asked what he was doing in the Yard's underground car park, he made no bones about it. He told us he was taking our pictures and clocking the Volvo's details. When I asked "why?" and "who for?" he said because we were criminals and he was gathering evidence. I asked him what offences we had allegedly committed. He said we would be told in the future. Then I asked him who he was reporting to and he didn't answer. I pointed out he was off duty and he said he knew where we would be so that's where he waited for us. Again I asked how he knew and he clammed up. DC Shackleton asked him if he remembered when he joined the police that he took an oath to uphold the law without fear or favour. If he believed we were criminals why hadn't he reported us to senior officers who would take the relevant action. He told us that people way higher than the commissioner were aware of our crimes but wouldn't say who. I asked him if it was someone in the Foreign Office and he looked a little startled.

He stuttered a bit but didn't answer. I pointed out that four people had been murdered including a police officer who had probably been carrying out clandestine duties for that person. He started to shake and turned red so we had to abandon the interview so he could be seen by a doctor,'

John asked him, 'Do you think he will talk to you this morning without a brief?'

Clive was slightly agitated. 'I don't know. DC Shackleton probably went to the same interview techniques course as you. As we were leaving the custody suite he said to me, "I don't think he'll need a doctor if we release him on bail, the coroner will be dealing with him." It was obvious he had overheard, as DC Shackleton intended, because he fainted.'

DC Shackleton said, 'No. I was obviously talking a little too loudly. Never mind. I'm sure he'll be happy to chat to us. Anyone want a coffee?'

John was amused. It was the sort of thing he would have done. Clive, Doreen and Murray who had been listening didn't seem to appreciate the humour. Coffee and tea were served in proper mugs. Where they had come from was anyone's guess but John hated paper ones and was grateful. The office was running a lot more smoothly since Doreen's arrival.

Groves started the morning's meeting at 8.15am. Enquiries were drawing blanks at every turn. No one had gathered any useful information of note to pass on. Liaison officers at Heathrow were briefing Murray who was reciprocating with Reigate's information. Groves and Murray were putting on a brave face but were running out of ideas. The meeting was thrown open to all. Groves informed the team that all fourteen traffic cameras were going to have to be checked for the S-Class Mercedes. An officer pointed out the obvious that if the vehicle left the area with false plates there was nothing to say that they hadn't been changed since. All reluctantly agreed it was the only positive way forward.

Then Groves told the team about Scrivener. Rumours had already circulated and it had been agreed with John and Clive what should be disclosed for safety reasons. No one seemed to question what all three were doing at the Yard. Doreen and Murray had established Scrivener's mobile had been reset to factory settings just prior to his arrest so would have to go to the lab to be examined. The exhibits officer was tasked to prioritise it's delivery. Clive stated he planned a morning interview with Scrivener if a doctor declared him medically fit. Everyone present saw a potential new avenue in the investigation developing although they weren't sure how.

The officer who had inherited the Volvo was asked if he still wanted to use it. When he answered in the affirmative, Groves insisted that there should always be an armed passenger. He pointed out quite forcefully that whoever was in it must remain constantly vigilant as they could become inadvertent targets. John had already checked the vehicle and removed a small tracker which he had thrown onto the back of a European registered lorry heading for Poland.

Murray deputed the officers. He sent a couple to the Kenley area to check if they had missed any CCTV from around the police station and then to the area around Brown's home address. He was sorting out who did what when the office phone rang.

Doreen said, 'Incident room Reigate Police can I help you?'

Then she passed the phone to Groves and said, 'Vince.'

'Hi Vince. What's up?' said Groves. He listened without comment then said, 'Cheers mate. Stick with her and keep me up to speed. If I'm not here, let Murray know.'

He passed the phone back to Doreen who put it back on the cradle and said, 'Doreen, Murray, John, Clive. My office in ten.'

DC Shackleton enquired, 'Would this be something that concerns me if I'm to assist Clive with the interview?'

'Yeah. You as well. Sod it. We'll stay out here, there's more room. Let me know when everyone has left,' and Groves went into his office to think. It didn't take him long. He phoned Kelly and told her what Vince and the surveillance team had seen. She told the DAC. He went to the commissioner's secretary and was with the commissioner before Groves could brief any of those within feet of him.

Doreen knocked on his door and walked in. 'The office is clear,' she said.

The two went back into the main office where a cup of tea was waiting for Groves and he began to speak, 'Cheers, Doreen. Right people, you're going to like this. Vince and his surveillance team have had a lot of boring hours plotting up Ashurst. This morning they followed her to Cobalt Square and she came straight back out and went to Bromley. To Svendsen's home address.'

Shackleton was the only one in the group who had no idea who Ashurst was. He didn't even know that the premier Sussex surveillance team was conducting an operation in connection with the murder investigation. From his years in the military and his long service in the police he knew to keep quiet and listen. Then when the time was right, to ask the right person the right questions.

John was the first to respond, 'I suppose it's no surprise. It just confirms everything we knew. I think we need to speak to the DAC and see what he and the commissioner want to do about it.'

Groves said, 'I told Kelly just now so I presume the commissioner must have been told already. I personally think she should be arrested and questioned. What's your take on it?'

John declared, 'After Scrivener's interview, me and Clive will go to the Yard and see what they decide. I think it's got to be considered. It's something the commissioner would have to approve.'

Groves queried, 'Do you reckon she knows where our killer might be hiding?'

John thought for a few seconds before saying, 'No. I don't believe she expected Svendsen to be killed. I don't understand why she set the surveillance operation up. What was her ulterior motive, what did she know and how? What do you think, Clive?'

Clive detailed his thoughts, 'I think her information originally came from either Svendsen himself or his wife. If he had told her, why would he have deliberately lost the surveillance team she had put on him. I reckon more likely his wife. But why would she have spilt the beans on her husband if he was doing a dodgy deal? Surely his wife would not want him arrested. Was she worried for his safety and if so why?'

John said, 'Ashurst has a lot to answer for but unlike

Scrivener she would definitely ask for a brief. He or she would tell her to say nothing and Ashurst would likely follow the advice. She is probably only aware of Svendsen's murder and wouldn't be intimidated by the disclosure of all the other murders. A dilemma.'

Groves said, 'Not for us. Just the commissioner. That's why he's paid so well.'

Shackleton was catching up quickly and considered another option. 'Why don't we arrest Svendsen's wife and ask her what it's all about? From what I've heard, although I don't know the full facts yet, she might be a weak link in this chain.'

They all turned to look at Shackleton. No one spoke. Shackleton was apprehensive. Sod it he thought. Should have kept schtum.

Groves was the first to speak, 'That is a damn good idea.'

John said, 'I like that. We could bring her here and let Ashurst run and see what she does.'

Clive was quick to comment, 'We haven't got much, if any, evidence to justify arresting her. Why don't we invite her here for an informal interview to assist us in the investigation of her husband's murder? Then we can put questions to her without a brief?'

Groves agreed, 'Yes. If she doesn't like the questions we could consider arresting her. Complicity in her husband's murder would do. I'll come with you to the Yard and we could discuss it with the commissioner.'

John liked Shackleton. He had good ideas and thought laterally. He would bring him up to speed before the interview with everything that had happened so far.

Scrivener was asked if he was willing to be interviewed without a brief, and to Clive's amazement agreed. Shackleton smiled knowingly as they all entered an interview room. He set a video recorder in motion and conducted the compulsory introductions and official caution. Somehow, Scrivener had become aware of the brutal murder of PC Brown. Clive was surprised but Shackleton was sanguine. Now Clive was starting to appreciate Shackleton's methods.

Scrivener kept talking. A simple question elicited lengthy explanations. Prior to his joining the police, he had been a civil servant. When he had requested a reference from his line manager he was ordered to an office in Portcullis House where he was seen by a private secretary. He was informed that they would provide a glowing reference which would ensure a successful outcome. In addition, he was also told that in the unlikely event in the future that he was required for work of a secret nature, he would be contacted by officials in the civil service. He was given a code word 'Zanzibar' which would be proof of the official's accreditation. He stated he could not remember who the person was that told him this.

He said, 'I was phoned three days ago by a man who gave the code word and told me that two police officers using a big blue Volvo were engaged in treasonable activities. He said that a tracker had been left by my front door and that I was to put it in the car. When I asked how I was to find the car, he told me to hang around the Yard and wait for the car to turn up. He told me no one could miss it. It was a huge vehicle and a ridiculous colour and probably the only one like it in the Met. Then I saw you and that's when I photographed you and the car's number plate. I just tossed the tracker into the back of the car. I sent the pictures to the number I had been given. Within seconds I got a text back telling me to format my phone and if possible find out who you were and where you were working.'

DC Shackleton asked, 'What was the phone number?'

Scrivener replied, 'I don't know. It was sent to my phone via a text. Now I've formatted my phone, it's gone.'

'How were you going to be contacted to find out if you identified DC Lavington and where he worked?'

'I don't know. I'm sure they'll find me.'

Shackleton asked the most pertinent question, 'Do you know who they are?'

'No. I just responded because the person used the code word.'

Clive left the majority of the interview to Shackleton. He had a full grasp of what had occurred and Scrivener answered his questions quickly. Clive was sure Scrivener was petrified of what might happen to him if he didn't reply truthfully. When Clive asked a question, Scrivener didn't reply as quickly and treated him with slight disdain. He started to think his colour was anathema to Scrivener.

At the conclusion, Clive asked, 'Before we finally conclude, is there anything you want to ask?'

Scrivener said, 'What's going to happen to me now?'

Shackleton pressed home his advantage. Turning to Clive he said, 'If we release him on bail, do you think he'll be murdered like that unfortunate PC from Kenley?'

Clive understood what Shackleton was doing and said, 'Well he can't go anywhere near his family, home or station. He would likely become an instant victim. I don't think the commissioner would consider him a suitable case for the witness protection scheme. I can ask him.'

Scrivener was petrified. He had, like half the Met, heard about PC Brown and Shackleton had put the fear of death in him. 'Please ask him. I'll do whatever it takes to stay alive. I'll go wherever you want.'

Shackleton pursued his cause. As if rhetorically, 'You wouldn't be able to use a credit card or a phone. You know how easy they give you away. It's a hard question. I think we need to discuss it with the brass at the Yard.'

Clive said, 'We'll keep you downstairs while we see what the Yard's decision is.'

Scrivener went willingly into a cell to await his fate.

29

14TH DECEMBER 2011
1.30PM

John, Clive and Kelly were sifting through the pages of Tabitha Marchant's emails. Most were irrelevant. Some contained sensitive information relating to Foreign Office affairs. Then gradually a pattern started to emerge about foreigners of dubious character wanting visas to enter the UK and what they were willing to offer in exchange for one. Information being the predominant bargaining chip.

Large amounts of money were offered by the richest who had no information to offer. Their reluctance to disclose the source of their wealth should have prompted an immediate rejection. Tabitha gave some of these people hope along with a mobile telephone number she could be directly contacted on. Each number was unique to an individual. All three came to the conclusion they were burner phones and she was probably demanding bribes for visas.

There were emails about some diplomats who were attracting security services' scrutiny and Tabitha was able to express Foreign Office opinion. There was regular contact with someone in MI6 referred to only as 'B' about foreign operations against friends and enemies alike. Someone using the name Claudius in MI5 was briefed about UK based individuals and they reciprocated with information.

Not one email was passed up the ladder to a senior supervisor or the Secretary of State. John, Clive and Kelly all came to different conclusions as to what her job actually was and her seniority level in the Foreign Office.

The DAC and Groves entered the office noisily having been out for a sandwich in the Albert Pub on Victoria Street. It was like the tank: full of police officers discussing operations and court cases. Seeing all the different stacks of paper laid out over a couple of desks provoked a question from the DAC, 'What's that lot?' indicating the piles of papers.

John nonchalantly replied, 'They are all the emails to and from Tabitha Marchant that are still in her inbox on her computer.'

The DAC queried, 'Who is that?'

Kelly said, 'She is the woman responsible for the phone number in the Foreign Office.'

'How the hell did you get those?' Then as an afterthought, 'No. Don't tell me. Best I don't know,' and he went into his inner office with Groves.

Clive started to riffle through a small pile of papers and then moved to another pile. His eye for detail had picked something up. He flicked the papers as though about to shuffle a deck of cards. Both Kelly and John had stopped their searches and watched him. He looked at a couple of other piles and picked out a couple of sheets of paper.

Kelly wanted to know, 'What have you seen?'

Clive was checking pages and wasn't to be rushed, 'I'm not sure. Give me a few minutes.'

John said, 'I'll go and get the tea,' and left the room.

Clive knew, but wanted confirmation so asked Kelly, 'Remind me. What date did the woman kill the junkie in Heathrow?'

'28th of November.'

Clive volunteered a little of what he was thinking, 'These emails seem to be in groups. For instance, there are several from Russian Embassies around the world seeking visas for oligarchs who are obviously loaded. Their wealth resulting from fortunate: nay, lucky investments. Then there are Russian diplomats who don't need visas, yet they still let her know of their intended arrival. Interesting. They all arrived in her email account within two weeks of each other and less than a month before the murder at Heathrow. Strange?'

Kelly was not so bemused, 'I can't see a problem with that.'

Clive continued, 'A couple of these Russians arrived at Heathrow on the 28th of November and had emailed Tabitha to let her know of their arrival. Presumably in order that she could facilitate their progress through the airport.'

Kelly was getting irritable, 'If that is part of her job description, I still don't see a problem.'

Clive seemed to ignore her and asked imperturbably, 'Who would render the assistance at Heathrow on Tabitha's behalf?'

Kelly had no idea and said, 'Now that is an interesting question.'

Clive knew what he wanted and said to Kelly, 'I think we need to find out from the Heathrow murder team what the details were of our killer's false passport. And whether or not it was one recorded in these emails.'

Kelly picked up a phone and started dialling a number from memory.

Clive took a moment to think. Then he said to Kelly, 'Who arranged for the junkie to meet the woman. Can you ask them if they have traced the person's movements around the airport from the new tapes John sent them?'

It didn't take her long. She scribbled the passport's details on a piece of paper. Then she listened to a short account and said to the person on the line, 'Please email me a copy of the contact's photo.'

John returned balancing three cardboard cups. In his view, slightly more acceptable than polystyrene.

Kelly put the phone down. 'Right. The name on her passport was Chloe Mila. I've got the number and it was allegedly issued in Bogotá, Columbia by the Russian Embassy.' She looked quizzically at Clive and said, 'Interesting how you picked Russians as your example just now. What a strange coincidence.'

Clive looked nonplussed, 'Yes. Interesting coincidence.'

John handed the cups around and said, 'I've obviously missed something while I've been out. I don't believe much in coincidences. Would one of you care to fill me in with the coincidence you are referring to?'

Kelly swiftly brought John up to speed with Clive's examples of Russians seeking visas as Clive started scanning the emails again. He was shuffling the papers from different piles as previously and pulled seven sheets out and started to create a new mound. John looked at Kelly and raised his bushy eyebrows in an effort to imply, 'ignore him'.

Kelly continued her narration mainly for John's benefit although she had a few surreptitious glances in Clive's direction, 'The border force officer told the Heathrow murder team the passport went straight through the machine and looked genuine. He said if it was forged, it was the best he'd ever seen.' She sipped her tea and checked what Clive was doing before continuing, 'The office manager at Heathrow's murder team has personally viewed the new tapes you sent and found a man in a suit handing a bag to the junkie. He is going to email an image in a minute. What was interesting was that he tracked the suited man to the taxi rank and they are tracing the cabbie as we speak.'

Clive piped up, 'Five pounds says it took him to the front door of the Foreign Office.'

John said, 'That's a strong bet.'

Kelly said, 'Not for me. I only bet on certs.' She fired up her computer and didn't have long to wait. An email arrived with numerous images attached. Once opened they showed several photographs of a man smartly dressed in a blue suit. He was about thirty years old, five feet ten inches tall, mousey-coloured short hair, clean shaven and otherwise unremarkable. All three committed his image to memory.

Clive mused out loud, 'She wouldn't have risked bringing the poison in the syringe through customs. He supplied the bag to the junkie which was passed to the woman. It's likely the poison that killed him had been in the bag. Did he know?' Kelly gave an involuntary shiver.

John sat back in his chair thinking. He slurped his tea noisily. Kelly was getting irritable. Clive seemed to be ignoring her but was proving he could multitask. She hated being blatantly ignored. The DAC opened his door and was about to ask her for something but seeing her look decided against it and retreated back into his office shutting the door quietly. She rarely sulked but was approaching one rapidly.

Clive unwittingly provoked her, 'You haven't got any spare sugar have you? This tea is a bit strong.' Kelly opened a drawer and took out a handful of sugar sachets and threw them at him. He seemed oblivious. 'Thanks,' and he kept scanning the pages of emails.

John was no help. He had his eyes closed and to the unobservant could have been asleep. Then his eyes flicked open, 'Kelly. What's your opinion about Ashurst?'

She glared at him, 'What the hell has that got to do with these emails?'

He ignored her question and asked, 'Do you think she's bent? For instance. Maybe she found out about Svendsen's meeting by chance and saw a way of making some cash?'

Kelly was becoming disconsolate, 'What, and use an inept surveillance team to help her do it? I think she was primarily trying to protect an old friend of her husband who she believed was about to do a major drugs deal. How she was going to deal with the person he was due to meet is still open for debate. Was she going to arrest them or tap them for some cash? I don't know.'

John persisted, 'What if she was having an affair with Svendsen? Perhaps she actually found out about the meet by chance from him. He realised and took what he thought were appropriate measures.'

Kelly had considered that herself but discounted it. Now she was reconsidering. 'Possible. But then, why would she have gone to see his widow?'

John flippantly suggested, 'To pass on her condolences?'

Now Kelly was back to her inquisitive self, 'As you're

throwing thoughts about. What if the widow and Ashurst had come to some sort of agreement? That's why she has risked going to see her. Maybe to tell her what actually happened.'

John pronounced, 'We are going to have to bring one of them in.'

Clive pointed at the new sheets he'd put aside and said, 'Have a look at that little set of emails and see what you think?'

Kelly picked them up and looked at each one carefully before passing it onto John. He read them all judiciously and when they had both finished Clive said, 'Well?'

John said, 'From what some of these emails tell us, Chloe Mila applied for a visa on the 19th of November this year and Marchant granted it. There is a photocopy of her passport attached. The picture on it is a fair likeness of the woman who met and killed Svendsen. At last we might have the name our killer is using. Well spotted Clive.'

Kelly said, 'I see that, but what are all these other emails telling us? Is it something to do with the dates?'

Clive continued, 'To an extent, yes. What I found interesting is Mila applied for her visa on a brand new passport which had only been issued by the Russian Embassy in Bogotá allegedly on the 17th of November this year. She applied directly to Marchant, not via the British Embassy in Columbia. That in itself is unusual. The email she used was from within the Russian's Columbian Embassy. Marchant instructed Mila to send the original passport to her at the Foreign Office where she would have it endorsed and then returned directly to the Russian Embassy in Columbia.'

John asked, 'How did she know to contact Marchant in the first place and how did she get the passport from Columbia to Marchant and then returned in such short a time that she could use it to enter the UK on the 28th?'

Clive replied tersely, 'Now that I don't know.'

Kelly snatched up the papers again. As she perused each one, she handed it to John. When they knew what they were looking for it was a lot easier to see. She asked Clive, 'OK. And these other emails?'

'I noticed another person, Gleb Kuznetsov requesting a visa from Marchant on the 18th of November this year. The day after Mila. He had a Russian passport issued in Moscow but was also applying from the same email address in the Russian Embassy in Bogotá. His passport is several years old. The strange thing is that Mila's passport has an identical number to his.'

Kelly and John checked the other emails. Neither doubted Clive, but they checked his facts. They saw an attached photocopy of Gleb's passport and committed his image to memory. Both saw the same passport number as on Mila's passport.

Groves came out of the inner office. 'Some bad news. I've just been told by Murray that PC Waiters, who has been doing some house-to-house enquiries around Brown's HA, has been given some footage from a security camera at an address opposite. Murray has told me Waiters has viewed it on the owner's system. Apparently it clearly shows the person breaking into Brown's house. It is a man.'

30

14TH DECEMBER 2011
4.30PM

The evening's office meeting was scheduled for 5pm and Groves was not looking forward to it. He hadn't been able to view the security camera footage that PC Waiters had discovered. Murray told him the camera had been positioned under a first floor window aimed at the road outside the house seemingly to protect the occupant's vehicle. The view had extended across the road to the front door of Brown's address.

It was an expensive, specialist camera which produced clear, sharp images onto a mini DVD player. The two main shortcomings were it only filmed for one week before recording over itself, and it needed professional equipment and an unusual codec to view it. The force photographer had a copy of the codec and was in his lab duplicating it onto a normal DVD so everyone could view it on a computer.

He'd forwarded some pictures that he thought might help via an email to Murray. The first was of a male by the front door. His back was to the camera but his gender was obvious. Another individual frame showed the man with both hands by the Yale lock holding something. Everyone who viewed it swore they could see mica in the man's hand. They couldn't. A third image showed the male entering through the open front door. A later frame showed the same male leaving, wearing a baseball cap with the words 'Yankees' written on it pulled down over his face. Then the last isolated frame showed a side view of the male walking away.

Clive said to John, 'We need to view the full tape. It shows the road. Any car driving by will pass through the camera's field of view. If the person is careless, we might get a vehicle for the killer. It has been recording since the 7th of December.'

John suggested to Clive, 'We can forget anything before we spoke to Brown at Kenley on the 11th because he was alive then.'

Clive was adamant, 'No. That's wrong. He told us he viewed the CCTV from Heathrow on the 29th of November. So whoever he viewed it for is fully aware it must have been doctored: especially if the Terminal 5 supervisor did it for them. If Brown knew that, he may have been watched as a potential weak link.'

John asked, 'OK. Do you want to do it?'

'Yeah. It'll take me a day. Then we'll have to check all the passing vehicles that I can get index numbers for. It's a comparatively quiet side road with not much through traffic, so I'm hoping it shouldn't be too much of a problem.'

John told Clive, 'Tomorrow, I'm going to be in Redhill getting the CCTV from Heathrow and the video from Morrisons lip read again. I'll keep in touch. Just be careful Clive.'

Groves conducted the meeting and could see a lot of the officers were growing despondent. He tried to boost spirits with the images of Brown's killer. They had all assumed up to that point it had been the same woman who had murdered Svendsen. Murray thought to himself: We should never have assumed that. Big mistake. Groves instructed the team to have an early night off and a fresh start in the morning.

That applied to everyone except Shackleton. The local CPS had been consulted and had made their decision. Scrivener was to be charged with Malfeasance in a Public Office. The Chief Constable of Surrey had visited the head of Surrey CPS and after a convivial lunch had come to an agreement with him. There was to be no publicity and he would deal with it himself. Shackleton was to complete the paper work.

●

Isabella was relaxing on a large couch in the day room of an exclusive town house in Clabon Mews: the heart of London's Chelsea. There was a garage but her S-Class Mercedes was too big to go in it, so she'd left it in Cadogan Square. Within five minutes' walk, and just far enough away to spot anyone paying it too much attention.

She was aware that the house had originally been purchased with money from Jesús although the title deeds were in the name of a lawyer. She knew Pat had been charged by Jesús with the maintenance and day to day running of the property. At the time of purchase, Pat had been a newly qualified barrister and was looking for clients when Jesús had crossed her path.

He had easily induced Patricia to take on the ownership of the property. Large amounts of cash had changed hands and Pat's bank balance had grown substantially. Pat was fully aware that what she was doing was illegal, but the money seduced her. She agreed with Jesús to visit the premises once a week to maintain it and pay all the bills. A healthy retainer appearing in her bank account every three months ensured she complied.

Now Isabella was waiting for Pat to turn up at the house. She didn't know her full name, telephone number or where she worked. She had to sit and wait. Normally when she had visited the property she left a car outside and if Pat or the cleaner arrived and saw it, they didn't enter. Today was different. Isabella had a few questions.

She climbed to the top bedroom. The sheets were fresh. They always were. Isabella got into bed after hanging her clothes in the wardrobe and cast a casual glance at the large floor safe. She'd often wondered how much was in there. She'd soon know.

•

John drove down to Chichester. He got there in about the same amount of time that it would have taken him to get to Fulham. He'd phoned Carol and then booked a table at Brasserie Blanc. Leaving his car in his secure garage at the top end of West Street, he walked as quickly as he could to the bottom end of East Street and into the restaurant.

Carol was waiting with a glass in her hand and a bottle of one of the restaurant's best white wines in a wine bucket. 'I thought I'd start without you.'

John sat opposite her and was pounced on by a waiter. 'Good evening, Mr Whiles. Such a pleasure to see you again.

Your beautiful companion has studied the menu at length and I am sure she knows what she is going to order. Would you like your usual?'

John said, 'Maurice. You are such a sniveller. You know me too well. Yes please. My usual.'

'Madam. As a person of refinement and good taste, unlike your companion, what can I get for you?'

Carol laughed. 'It's always a pleasure to see you Maurice,' and she dictated her choices. Maurice did not need to write anything down. He was a professional of many years' standing and could remember any order.

●

Clive was dropped off outside his front gate after the Volvo had done a slow lap of his block. The two officers in the front scanned every parked car. Clive was not worried, just slightly apprehensive. He was probably more frightened of Celeste than any murderer. The car stayed by his gate until he had closed his front door.

She'd mellowed. The table had been laid and she'd got a steak on the grill. The wine was a cheap red bought from the local shop. Clive didn't want a row, so supped a mouthful and complimented her on her choice. The food was his favourite and she knew it. She'd even excelled with the oven-ready chips.

Clive knew she was a poor cook with little knowledge of wine. He didn't mind because he loved her. Celeste had been brought up by a mother who believed in ready meals and takeaways. Her father had rarely drunk alcohol and never wine. Because of this, Clive often cooked in the evenings because he was better at it than her.

After the meal, they snuggled down together on their sofa and chatted. Clive had decided to tell Celeste just a little about what the investigation was about. 'I know I don't normally tell you what I am doing but I think I must warn you. I am investigating a couple of murders where the culprits don't seem to worry who they kill. One of the victims was a policeman.'

Celeste was instantly worried for Clive. 'Are you in any danger?'

'There is a slight possibility, but I want you to be careful though. If you think anything is out of the ordinary, find a policeman and call me. Promise to do that.'

'Of course I will. If you think it's necessary.'

'Until we solve this case, I shall be wedging the front door and securing the windows every night before we go to bed.'

'Well hurry up and do it. I'll see you upstairs.'

•

Kenny was a worrier. Although he was looking at the television, he didn't register what was on. He couldn't get the Range Rover with the badly adjusted dash cam out of his mind. Who does the vehicle belong to? Why was it outside my house? It has to be connected to our visit to the Terminal 5 supervisor. But why?

The local police in Windsor had agreed to drive past his house at random times throughout the night. He felt safe. His wife noticed his agitation. 'Something on your mind?'

He told her about the visit to the supervisor, his murder and the vehicle. 'Jesus Kenny. Are you in trouble?'

'No. I just don't like being in the dark. I'll be stirring the shit tomorrow. Whoever owns that vehicle will wish they had kept away. I'll set up an ANPR alert so it will flash up whenever it moves. Then I'll know what this is all about.'

'Are you in danger?'

'No.'

'What about us?' and she nodded to indicate their son Ralph upstairs in bed.

'Well, you take him to school so he'll be safe there. I know you can protect yourself.'

She smiled. Twice she had represented the UK at Karate and won both times. She wasn't worried.

31

15TH DECEMBER 2011
7AM

Pat parked her BMW convertible sports car outside the house. She was conducting a quick visit before work to check the house was spic and span. Tonight she was going to be entertaining a girlfriend. The door seemed a little stiff and she realised the mortice lock was on. Cursing the cleaner, she opened up and went inside.

When she walked into the first floor day room, she was surprised to see that the room looked dishevelled. She'd spoken to the cleaner the previous morning who'd assured her the house would be pristine. Pat plumped up the cushions and arranged them on the sofa. She made a mental note to speak to her yet again. Then she noticed a wine glass on the coffee table.

'What's wrong with the woman? I pay her enough.'

Isabella heard Pat downstairs chuntering to herself. She rose quietly from the bed and put on her underwear. As Pat began climbing the stairs, Isabella stood to the side of the bedroom door. It opened and Pat saw the untidy bed.

'That's it. She's fired.' As she walked into the room, Isabella stepped behind her and shoved her hard pushing her forward onto the bed. Then she jumped on top of her pushing her face into a pillow.

In a muffled voice, Pat shrieked, 'Don't hurt me. Please don't hurt me.'

Although she knew who it was likely to be, Isabella asked, 'Who are you?' and allowed her head to lift slightly from the pillow.

'Patricia Ashurst. I'm a lawyer.'

Isabella remained straddling her with one hand on the back of her head still holding her face down on the bed. Pat's expensive perfume wafted up to Isabella. 'Who owns this house?'

'I do.'

'No, the true owner?'

'It's me'

'The person who put up the money?'

Pat tried to twist round to see her inquisitor. Her face was pushed hard into the pillow and she started to cry.

'Who?'

'A friend of mine.'

'Jesús Posda by any chance?'

Pat stopped crying and hesitated. She swiftly considered her options. The woman on her back knew his name. If she was police, Inland Revenue or any other government department, the method of questioning would never stand up in a British court of law. Was she a burglar? No. Burglars steal and leave. A rapist? No. It was a woman on top of her. She muttered something inaudible into the pillow as she fought for time.

'What did you say?'

She really had no choice. 'Yes.'

Isabella got off her and she turned around. She was

surprised to see a woman wearing only small black lacy underwear. An evenly tanned body, short blonde hair, pretty and mildly aggressive was an instant turn on for Pat. For a few seconds, she thought she saw the woman looking at her in an appreciative way. Her thoughts turned to sex for a few seconds more.

'I am Isabella Posda. I arrived last night. I don't know if you are aware that my father, Jesús, is dead. I am trying to sort out some of his affairs.' The blood drained from Pat's face. She sat up on the bed. 'I need to know some things from you,' and Isabella tapped her on the thigh to move her so she could sit on the bed next to her.

'What happened? When did he die?'

'A few weeks ago. He was shot.'

Pat was shocked and her hand flew to her mouth. 'My God.'

'It was just one of those things that happen to drug dealers in Columbia. You knew he was a drug lord in his own right?'

Pat whispered, 'Yes. The money to buy this house was obviously from drugs. He didn't need to tell me. At the time, I was just starting out and needed some collateral. Jesús was good enough to help me. The agreement has stood ever since.' Pat paused while she thought. 'What do you want to do now with this place?'

'It's in your name. Perhaps we could make a new agreement that would be suitable to you,' and her hand casually dropped onto Pat's hand as she smiled at her.

'I'd like that.' She didn't move her hand away.

'I need to know what's in the safe in the wardrobe?'

'There's about twelve thousand pounds left in there. It's

normally topped up every three months.'

Isabella was confused. There should be at least twenty million or more in the safe. Up until the time she'd made her hasty departure from Columbia, she knew no monies had been paid to the Posda family for drugs. Every three months, at least twenty million of laundered cash would arrive. She considered it an interesting coincidence that Pat claimed her account was credited every three months.

Isabella thought for a minute, and absently played with Pat's fingers. She recalled conversations of Jesús, overheard years ago, that mentioned Pat as the person sending the money from the UK. Then she remembered a brusque conversation between Thérèse and Pablo across a dinner table about Ashurst not sending the correct money. Now she remembered the name. It had to be Pat Ashurst. She was sitting next to her.

'How do you get the money?'

'It's put into my account by someone. I don't know who. I keep ten thousand and put the rest in the safe. It's used to run the house. Repairs, bills, that sort of thing.'

Isabella could spot a liar a mile off. She wasn't sure with Pat. If she was lying she was good. Someone had access to a large amount of cash and Isabella was determined to get her hands on it. She had something that would help loosen Pat's tongue: and her clothes.

'I'm sorry, I must have a coffee. Do you want one?' and she jumped off the bed and headed for the bedroom door.

Pat watched her go and decided the morning might prove enjoyable. She didn't need to be in the office until the afternoon. Plenty of time. 'Yes please. Milk. No sugar.'

Isabella went quickly down the stairs to the kitchen and grabbed her handbag. A small clear plastic bag containing an off-white coloured powder was in a side pocket. She palmed it as Pat walked in.

'I really should phone my secretary and tell her I'll be late in.'

'Use the phone in the day room. Please don't mention me.'

Pat went into the day room, which she considered a lounge, as Isabella made two coffees and emptied the powder into one of them. She was still on the phone when Isabella walked in and handed her a mug. By the time she'd finished talking to her secretary, she'd drunk half the mug of coffee. She'd found the taste unusual but thought nothing of it. She admired Isabella who was still in her underwear. She drained the mug and soon started to feel a little dizzy.

'Are you all right?'

'I think so. I feel a little dizzy.'

'Come upstairs. You can lie down for a while.' Isabella didn't want to have to carry her and knew she would need help within minutes. Pat was desperate to lie down. By the time she was upstairs, the drug was starting to take effect.

'Wouldn't you be more comfortable without your suit on? You don't want to ruin it do you?'

Pat was slowly becoming drowsy but wanted Isabella desperately. She started to struggle to take off her suit. Isabella helped her undo the buttons and zip. Pat was unable to remember what happened next. Isabella sat patiently for fifteen minutes contemplating Pat's body and waiting for the drug to take it's full effect.

'I want you to answer truthfully. Who sends you the

money for the upkeep of this house?'

Pat was practically unconscious. Isabella slapped her awake. 'Who?'

'I don't know.'

Isabella was annoyed. The drug had always worked before. She slapped Pat hard several times. It didn't help. It made her feel better, but it didn't help. Then she sat back to think. Pat Ashurst was definitely the name she remembered. Yet here she was and she was telling her it wasn't her. Isabella came to the conclusion she had assumed Pat would be the person holding the money because she was known to the Posda family. Then a stupid idea entered her head.

'Do you know... Wake up damn you!' and she slapped her twice. 'Do you know anyone else called Pat Ashurst?'

'My brother, Pat.'

Isabella was ecstatic. 'Where does he live?'

'I don't know.'

'Where?'

'I don't know. We don't talk,'

'How can I find him?' Isabella asked.

'Mum knows.'

Pat was feeling so tired. She wanted to sleep. Isabella slapped her awake.

'Where's your mum?'

Pat reeled off a phone number. 'My address book. My handbag.'

Isabella ran back downstairs to find Pat's bag. She opened it and emptied the contents onto a coffee table. A mobile phone fell out as well as a diary and an address book.

She checked the address book and found Glynnis Ashurst

and her office in Cobalt Square and the phone number was the same as Pat had said. Nothing for her brother. Isabella tried the mobile phone contacts and again found listings for Glynnis but not Pat's brother. Swearing loudly, she went back upstairs and found Pat fast asleep.

Isabella pinched Pat's ear lobe and she woke up in pain. 'What's your mum do at this place. Cobalt Square?'

'She's a policewoman,' and Pat started to fall asleep again.

Isabella was taken aback. She kept pinching Pat's ear lobe.

'Does she know about this place?'

'No.'

Isabella let Pat fall asleep. She had to think. How was she going to get Glynnis Ashurst to tell her where her son was living?

32

15TH DECEMBER 2011
7.30AM

Clive was watching for the Volvo to cruise past. He had agreed the previous day with the new driver that he would circle the block before stopping to collect him. Celeste kissed him goodbye as he left the house. Everything was rosy again and he was looking forward to the new day.

John arrived early in Morrisons' car park. He walked into the store and bought a paper and then joined a queue at the café's servery. A team of builders were in front of him and they weren't stinting on their breakfasts. John could appreciate that manual workers needed more than office workers to set themselves up for the day. For five minutes he chatted to them and found out they were going to be setting up a crane close by.

'Don't come anywhere near the High Street after we leave. We'll probably have it all blocked off for the day,' and the man laughed. 'It'll be absolute chaos.'

John found himself laughing with him, 'Cheers. I'll keep well clear.' He made a mental note to let Groves and the team know about the pending pandemonium.

As he was finishing his breakfast, one of the builders said to him, 'We're off now. You've got about fifteen minutes.' John wolfed down the last few mouthfuls of food and then went back to his car. He drove swiftly to the police station and parked in a different side road from before.

Everyone in the office seemed cheerful. Doreen was already typing up a few new reports and Murray was directing some of the officers with new actions. The exhibits officer was busy making tea and coffee for those who wanted it. No one was concerned that open milk was kept in the exhibits fridge, together with various unsavoury and unhygienic items.

John and Clive had a short discussion with Groves as to what they were going to be doing during the day and some of the specialists were telling him about their work. Vince, the leader of the surveillance team, had attended the office and was going to stay for the morning's briefing and was monitoring his team through a covert ear piece. He heard them following Ashurst from her Docklands penthouse apartment towards Cobalt Square.

Shackleton was suited and booted and ready for a court appearance where he was going to request that Scrivener be remanded in custody, pending a trial on a future date. He confidently told Groves that Scrivener would not be requesting bail and Groves deemed it inappropriate to ask him how he knew.

The photographer gave Murray four DVDs which he said would play in any computer. He told him they were true copies of the tape which PC Waiters had obtained.

Clive stated, 'I certainly hope so. Can I take one?'

The photographer didn't understand Clive's comment, nor did he understand the look that passed between him, John and Groves. Murray handed him one of the DVDs and told him which computer was going to be free throughout the day.

The phone rang in Groves's office. He heard it over the hubbub and darted back in to answer it, slamming the door to shut out the din. Kelly was calling to let him know there was nothing of use on Ashurst's answerphone overnight. He gave her a quick briefing as to the progress made by the murder team. Both agreed that things seemed to be becoming bogged down.

John felt his mobile vibrating in his pocket. He couldn't hear it ringing over the growing clamour of many voices in the office. Stepping out he walked downstairs and into the station car park answering it on the way. There was no identifying number in the display to say who was calling.

'Hello?'

'Hi Oscar,' and John recognised Rocky's voice. 'Just a quick update for you. Yesterday the lady in the office was working normally during the day for most of the time. Twice she used different burner mobile phones. The first to speak to a man in Hungary about him getting a visa valid for a year. She blatantly asked for ten thousand pounds in cash and he agreed. I'll email you his details and the arrangements they made for payment which will stay in your inbox for ten minutes.'

'That's terrific.'

'The next was really fascinating. When she speaks to her husband, she uses the office phone. Her second call on a burner phone was to a man who definitely wasn't her husband. They are, without a doubt, in the middle of an affair. She is meeting him tomorrow at 6pm in Victoria railway station and then going to the Grosvenor hotel. I'll forward his details as previous, and I'll email a picture of her to you. She is wide open to blackmail if you get my meaning?'

'Oh yes, I certainly understand. Thanks for that.'

'No problem,' and the phone disconnected.

At 8.30am Groves walked back into the office which instantly came to order. It was a comparatively short meeting as there was little to say. He was glad to see that people were looking a lot more optimistic than before. All the specialists seemed upbeat and constructive although they had nothing new to add. At the conclusion of the meeting, everyone set about their respective tasks with gusto.

John told Clive what he had learnt. Then he showed him the printouts of both emails. Neither meant anything to Clive. When John took out a folded piece of paper and opened it, Clive saw an A4 picture of the woman known as Tabitha Marchant. She was facing the camera but oblivious to it.

'How the hell did he get that? It looks like she could be posing for it.'

'I've no idea and I won't be asking him. I've saved an unfolded copy in case we need it later. I'm off to get the lip reading done now and I hope we'll learn something new from it. Think about how we should proceed with this. Should we tell the Yard or take it on ourselves?'

'Bloody hell, Oscar, we've overstepped the mark already. What I think you're suggesting is way over the top.'

'Just think about it?' and John left with true copies of the Heathrow tapes and a copy of the video from Clive's mobile phone taken in Morrisons.

Clive sat at the designated computer terminal and put in the DVD copied by the photographer from the original tape from the premises across the road to Brown's address. It began on the 7th of December at 4pm and was of exceptional quality. Each passing vehicle was easily identifiable as were all the index plates. Diligently, Clive filled in a spreadsheet he had created leaving columns for PNC checks and dates when owners were to be contacted and eliminated from further enquiries.

Doreen kept putting mugs of tea in front of him as the DVD played on. Clive's gaze never faltered. He sped the tape on whenever he could see clearly and rarely played it at normal speed. He stopped the tape only to record vehicles and then set it going again. Even during the hours of darkness, the camera clearly recorded everything. By 4.20pm on the 11th of December Clive had recorded the details of a hundred and ninety-three vehicles. Then something caught his eye on the very edge of the video.

A figure of a man moved into view. He was smoking as he slowly walked along the pavement and hesitated when he was level with Brown's front door. He looked around but not up at the camera that captured his every movement. Clive instantly recognised him from one of the images on the passports from Tabitha's emails. Gleb Kuznetsov. Then Gleb turned around and went back the way from which he had come.

Clive started whispering to himself. 'Come on. Drive past. I dare you.' For twenty more minutes nothing moved. Then he saw a large silver S-Class Mercedes move slowly into view. 'Gotcha, you bastard.' He watched as the vehicle actually stopped level with Brown's front door for a few seconds before continuing on.

Clive froze the tape when the index plate of the vehicle was clearly visible on the screen. He called to Murray who walked over to him. 'Can you do a PNC on this vehicle. I think it's Brown's murderer.' Murray jotted the number down and went back to his desk.

'I think you're right. It's not even a cloned number plate, it looks like a number plucked out of the blue. It comes back to a black Vauxhall Nova registered in Leeds. I'll set a warning on ANPR and with a bit of luck we'll find it. Then we can nick him. Great work.'

Murray called Groves from his office and he rushed out to see the image frozen on the screen. He'd been desperate for some good news and now he had some. All the others in the office crowded round to have a look. The photographer offered to download an image and Clive made room for him. Soon the vehicle and the image of Gleb Kuznetsov were being stuck on to one of the white boards.

Clive said, 'I still need to view the rest of the tape,' and people moved away to give him room. The tape continued and then on the 12th of December at 3.22am, Gleb Kuznetsov strode into view. There was no hesitation. He walked straight up to Brown's front door and was soon in the house.

Murray said, 'Clive. When you have a minute.'

'Problem?'

'Not at all. There have been quite a few hits on ANPRs and it looks like the vehicle is mainly in the Richmond area of London at night. It last set off an ANPR forty minutes back in Paddington on the Westway. I think we are going to need some help though. I'll suggest we do a street search as soon as it triggers an ANPR tonight. What do you think?'

'I agree. Strike while we're on a roll.'

'Good. Let's go and see the boss.'

33

15TH DECEMBER 2011
2PM

The Mercedes cruised around the block. There were CCTV cameras high up on every wall covering the pavements and entrances to Cobalt Square police building. There was no way past them that Isabella could see. Driving into a side road she parked and lit a cigarette. She didn't even know what Glynnis Ashurst looked like.

She'd seen the entrance to the secure car park. A large blue metal gate that slid back and forth to permit authorised vehicles in and out. There were two cameras covering it and the layby she'd have to park in to watch it. That's if the bloke in the crappy old plumber's Transit van, who was having a nap, would clear off.

It was out of the question. She'd have to think of something else. The driver's window lowered without a sound and she threw her cigarette butt out. Isabella quickly closed it again to keep the warmth in the vehicle. It was her own fault she knew. Had she questioned Pat more thoroughly she'd probably have come to a better decision. She set off back to Clabon Mews.

A man on a motorbike roared past her and glared at her through the un-tinted windscreen. Isabella cursed him as he swerved in front of her. A battered old Peugeot nearly rammed her as it pulled out in front of her from a private block of flats and then seemed to dawdle along Nine Elms Lane towards Chelsea Bridge. Isabella suddenly thought of the plumber's Transit.

She knew something wasn't right. She swung a complete U-turn in front of a local authority dust cart and floored the Mercedes back towards Vauxhall. Checking her mirror, she saw the motorcyclist catching her up. Her speed was soon up to 60 mph and the motorcyclist was gaining. She started to dodge round a few slower moving cars but the motorcyclist had the edge.

Gently she eased off the accelerator as the motorcyclist was about thirty yards behind her. She stamped hard on the brake and did an emergency stop. With her eyes glued to her rear view mirror she saw the motorcyclist was unable to stop and was going to pass her on her offside. As he reached the rear of the Mercedes, she accelerated and veered to the offside.

He couldn't swerve out of the way and just hit the Mercedes a glancing blow. It sent him flying across the road in front of oncoming traffic. He fell off his machine and rolled in front of an old Saab. Isabella smiled to herself as she continued on back to Vauxhall and over the bridge towards Victoria and on to Chelsea via the longer route. She didn't care about a few scratches on the Mercedes: it wasn't her car.

Vince had instructed the occupants of the Transit van and a Ford Mondeo to remain at Cobalt Square to watch for Ashurst. The rest of the surveillance team were either going the wrong way or were trying unsuccessfully to catch up with the Mercedes. Vince went to the assistance of his motorcyclist. It was his worst day ever.

•

John was at the School for the Deaf in Redhill with a man affectionately known as 'Lips' who was looking at the CCTV from Heathrow. He'd been stone deaf from birth and over the years had become an expert in lip reading and sign language. His speech was occasionally stilted and sometimes he didn't enunciate his words correctly. He'd understood what John wanted without a problem.

John started the first DVD as the unknown suited man stepped out of a taxi as he arrived at the airport on the 28th of November.

Lips read the cabbies speech to the unknown passenger, 'Call it 45 quid.'

John saw the man take two twenty pound notes from a wallet and a ten pound note. Handing the cash to the cabbie he told him, Keep it,' and he walked into the terminal carrying a zipped up tote bag about a foot square. John changed the cameras accordingly as he followed the man through the terminal into a convenience store. At the sandwich display he picked up a packaged sandwich which had a split wrapper.

A very thin white male about twenty-six years old with straggly hair and wearing a green Parka stood next to him. 'I wouldn't eat that. You don't know what germs are in it.'

The suited man handed the bag to the male. 'You know who to give this to?'

'Yeah,' and he walked off.

John tracked the unknown suited man back to the taxi rank and he watched him get into a cab. He knew the

Heathrow murder team were conducting enquiries as to where the taxi took him.

There was a few minutes' delay while John found the white male wearing the Parka arriving at the airport from the underground. He tracked him to the convenience store and the collection of the bag. Then he followed the male to the seating area just outside the arrivals gate. The male sat down and held the bag on his lap looking towards the gate.

John recognised the woman straight away as she stepped into the arrivals terminal. It was Svendsen's killer: the person in the email to Tabitha Marchant who called herself Chloe Mila. She looked about and stopped when she was looking straight towards the male. He didn't move as she walked towards him and sat down next to him.

Lips read her, 'I've come a long way. Is it always cold here?'

'This is what you want. There's something in it to keep you warm,' and he handed her the bag. She partially unzipped it and looked inside.

'Needles! They're not my thing. Do you want to try it?'

'You're kidding me. 'Course I do. There is a disabled toilet over there. That'll do,' and he stood up and walked to the toilet as she followed. He opened the door and they both went inside as the door closed behind her.

Within ten minutes she exited the toilet alone, carrying the small bag and closing the door behind her. John tracked her to the taxi rank. She spoke to no one else. He couldn't see or make out the number of the cab and again he knew Heathrow murder team were conducting enquires to trace it.

Lips said, 'When she offered him the chance to try the

needles, did you get the feeling that was his payment for delivering the bag?'

John was thinking along the same lines. 'Yes. I did.'

'If that's the case, she probably knew or suspected what was in the syringe and that it would kill him. Or, of course, the person who provided the bag had put the poison in it to try and kill her thinking she would take it.'

John looked at Lips, 'You should be a detective. All you have to do now is tell me which one it is?'

'Sorry. Not for me. I am happy teaching lip reading and sign language. What's your next tape?'

John gave him a USB stick and said, 'It's on here.' Then he said, 'This is the same woman who killed the man in Morrisons' car park the other day. Perhaps you read about it in the papers? She was waiting for him in the café when he walked in. This tape only shows her side of the conversation.'

'Yes. I saw a report about it in the local press. Not at all pleasant.' Lips plugged it into his computer. It didn't load as quickly as the DVDs and wasn't the same quality. 'I know I can't hear it, but can't you enhance the sound so you can hear what both parties have said? I saw it once on a television programme.'

'We've tried that already and it can't be done.'

'OK. Let's crack on,' and he set the tape running. It was a copy of the original without Brown's subtitles. John put a small Dictaphone onto the table next to the computer and turned it on. Lips spoke as he read the woman's words.

'Hello. Good to see you again. It's been a long time.'

'Please call me Chloe. I don't use Isabella here.'

'It's good of you to come at such short notice.'

'What happened to the police who were following you?'

'I've been here a while and no one has followed you in. The last person who came in met the black guy sitting a couple of tables behind you.'

'Down to business. I presume you know why I'm here?'

'Jesús was shot the other day.'

'He's dead. We're ensuring the supply routes aren't disrupted. I need to speak to the person laundering the cash and let them know some new details.'

'I'm sorry. I thought you knew. Who do you give the cash to then?'

'You were sent a bible some years ago by Jesús. Am I Correct?'

'If I said you were known as "Luke", what would you say?'

'He was a disciple. Jesús called all his distributers by the names of disciples.'

'Where is the bible now? Check the heading for the Gospel of Luke. It'll prove my credentials.'

'Why won't you tell me? You haven't lost it?'

'Thank you. Does your wife know what you do?'

'Will you call me when you have got Pat's number?'

'I use a burner. It's safer that way.'

'Thank you. Please don't let me keep you.'

Svendsen left the café and within a minute the woman stood up and followed in the same direction. The video stopped abruptly.

Lips said, 'I couldn't see everything she said because she occasionally had her hand in front of her mouth, but I got at least ninety-five per cent.'

'Thank you for doing this for us. I appreciate you haven't charged us for this work. So your charity will receive a donation from the Metropolitan Police within the week.'

They parted company and John returned to the police station.

34

15TH DECEMBER 2011
5PM

John strode purposefully into the office and was slightly bemused at the amount of activity. Clive briefed him as to what they had heard from Vince.

'The surveillance team were plotted up around Cobalt Square and the eyeball saw a Mercedes cruising slowly around the block a couple of times. It looked extremely odd to him and he updated Vince who wanted it checked out. They lost sight of it for a couple of minutes then their 4 2 spotted it going along Nine Elms Lane towards Chelsea Bridge. He saw the driver was a female and with another vehicle they tried to slow it down so the rest of the team could catch up. At that time they obviously weren't sure if it was our lady's Mercedes. When they did a PNC on the index number it came back to an entirely different make of car. Vince wanted uniform to do a hard stop on it and arrest the driver. Then it gets a little blurry. It looked like she spotted the tail, did a hairy U-turn and took the 4 2 out. She scarpered and they couldn't find her again.'

'What was she doing around Cobalt Square?'

'You should've asked how the 4 2 is. He's OK.'

'That's good. What was she doing around Cobalt Square though? The only person of note there is Ashurst. We need to think about this, Clive.'

Clive said, 'At least we have the index plate that is currently on the car. We are assuming of course that it is Chloe. An S-Class Mercedes with 'Mickey Mouse' plates in that area acting suspiciously: it has to be. Murray has checked ANPR and found a few random hits. Its plates are from some obscure vehicle down in Plymouth.'

John said, 'One thing of importance that I have learnt today is that her real first name may be Isabella.'

John looked towards Doreen's desk and he saw she was getting ready to go home. He put his little Dictaphone on her desk and said, 'Could you please type this up before you go. It'll only take you five minutes?'

She made a little show of looking at her watch. 'You know I used to have to get home for tea with my mum by 5.30. She reluctantly agreed to alter it to 6.30 while I'm working here. One day, I'm going to introduce you to her. I'll explain that you alone are responsible for every time I am late. She'll wipe the floor with you!' Her computer burst into life.

'You know I love you Doreen?' teased John.

'Huh!' and she started typing. It took seven minutes and then the printer spewed out five sheets of paper which John picked up. He read the typed pages before giving them to Clive.

Clive said to John, 'A long way to go for such a short meeting. Shame we can't hear what Svendsen said. Some of her words would probably make a lot more sense. I see she says her real first name is Isabella. I presume that was on our tape?'

'Yes. Can you look into it Clive? I don't know how it'll help.'

Clive replied, 'OK. I'll work on it.'

John added, 'Another name mentioned was Pat. It means nothing to me. What about you?'

Clive racked his brain, 'It rings a bell. Can't say why at the moment. I'll think about it.'

Doreen was already wearing her coat. 'If you need more, you know how to copy them. Goodnight.' She left the office and ran down the stairs to the station car park and got into a car. Her driver, who had been studying the latest football reports, left the car park at speed and headed for Chichester.

Clive was still busy and showed John the images stuck on the white board of Gleb and the S-Class Mercedes. John easily identified the person whose passport they had seen bearing the name Gleb Kuznetsov. Clive explained the false index plates on the Mercedes and the hits on the vehicle by ANPR cameras around Richmond.

'I presume we're going to do a street search?'

Murray said, 'Even without your participation, we'd thought of that. Heathrow murder squad are giving us a leg up. I've got a street map of Richmond and when the Merc hits an ANPR tonight, we'll move in. Does that meet with your approval?'

'I knew I could rely on you Murray. Let's hope it's not the genuine vehicle from Leeds doing some overnight work in the borough.'

'Catered for Mr Whiles. The local constabulary are making sure it's at the registered owner's address tonight. Anything else we may not have considered?'

'What if the car is in a lock up garage?'

'Then we plot up every road out of Richmond and wait for

the car to pass by tomorrow morning. We will have additional uniform officers available from 7am. Anything else?'

'Not that I can think of at the moment but I'll definitely let you know if anything springs to mind.'

'Well, in that case, while you're trying to think up something useful, how about you making everyone a nice cup of tea or coffee?' said Murray.

John was caught. And he knew it. There were seventeen people in the office and they were all calling their orders to him. He tried to claim there wasn't enough milk but got shouted down. Groves, who heard the racket, came out of his office.

Murray said, 'Just in time sir, Mr Whiles is making the tea and coffee, and I'm sure he'd like to make one for you.'

'Looks like you've been caught Oscar. This must be the first time ever? Do you know where the kettle is?' said Groves.

'All right. You win. Once a year is acceptable I suppose.' John spent the next twenty-nine minutes making the teas and coffees and taking them to everyone in the office.

Murray couldn't resist one more dig. 'Don't forget to make one for yourself.'

Clive, Murray, Shackleton and John sat together with their drinks. John said, 'Something is worrying me about our two killers. We know about their application for visas coming from the same place. Now they both appear to be here in the UK but not together. Chloe, possibly Isabella, has killed the junkie, the supervisor and Svendsen. Gleb has killed Brown. Have they got separate agendas or are they working together or even for Marchant?'

Shackleton said, 'At least Scrivener is tucked away and is unlikely to speak to anyone. If he does; we'll know straight away.'

Clive said, 'They could still get to him in prison if they locate him.'

'He's been put in solitary confinement in a medical block. They seem to think he has a rampantly contagious case of TB. The only one allowed near him is the prison doctor.'

Clive stared at Shackleton, 'Are you sure you're not Oscar's brother?'

Murray cut the exchange short and said, 'If all goes to plan tonight, we should have Gleb in custody soon but I doubt that he'll be as cooperative as Scrivener. Vince and his team have got the hump about this afternoon's debacle and are sorting themselves out and will be with us tonight. That'll speed the search up a bit.'

All the officers spent time updating their loved ones as to the fact they would not be home until tomorrow and arranging evening meals from various local eateries. Soon the office reeked of curries, pizzas and burgers. Not one person seemed to object.

At 10.46pm Murray got a phone call. An ANPR on the outskirts of Richmond recorded a hit on the Mercedes.

'Let's go folks. Meet at Richmond nick in the canteen at midnight.'

35

15TH DECEMBER 2011
11.50PM

Pat was drowsy. She was naked and in a bed. Her mobile which was on the coffee table downstairs was playing a digital ring tone. She couldn't muster the strength to go and get it. Then it stopped and she heard a muffled voice. Someone was downstairs. They'd tell her if there was a message. She drifted off back to sleep.

On the bedside table was a syringe. It had been used twice and was ready again. The next dose would keep her asleep all night. Isabella would administer it before she went to bed in another bedroom. She wanted a clear head in the morning and didn't want to be disturbed by Pat waking her up.

•

The canteen, which was so big everyone had a seat, was alive with noise. There were fifteen officers from Heathrow, Vince and nine other surveillance officers and twenty detectives from Reigate. They were going to be doing the main street by street search. There were six specialist officers from a Trojan CO19 team who were going to make any arrests. Murray busily handed out Airwave radios to any officer without their own personal issue.

Kenny was chatting to John, 'I put an information request on ANPR about the Range Rover outside my house. Got a lot of hits all over London and the home counties. I'm deciding what to do. If all goes to plan tonight and this guy is nicked, I'll arrange a hard stop on it and arrest the occupants. What do you think?'

John said, 'It'll stir up a hornet's nest and probably drag whichever agency it belongs to out into the open. I think it's a good idea. Leave it till we can have another chat tomorrow.'

Groves called above the noise. 'Settle down folks, we've a lot to get through,' but didn't have time to say anything else.

The canteen door opened and the chief constable of Surrey and the DAC walked in. The chief constable apologised to all those present, 'Sorry we're late.' Chairs slid over the floor as officers started to stand. He added, 'Sit down. We're here to observe tonight. The bastard you are looking for has killed a police officer. When you nick him, we want it done by the book. I don't want any fancy lawyers getting him off on a technicality. I want him locked up for the rest of his life. Please carry on.'

Groves continued. The briefing was lengthy. Coloured photocopies of Gleb and the Mercedes were handed out. His name was not mentioned nor written down on Murray's briefing sheet. Officers were making notes. At the conclusion of the briefing, Groves asked the DAC if there was anything he wanted to add.

'Please remember, this man is dangerous. I don't want any more funerals. Do not take any chances. The members of CO19 are not here for the overtime. They are going to be making the arrest.' Then he looked directly at the sergeant in charge of the unit, 'If you have to shoot him I will back you up all the way. There are enough witnesses here who will verify what I have said. Good luck people.'

Groves added, 'All communication to be addressed through me. Get going.'

Officers began to troop out of the canteen, each with the list of roads they were to search. John thought Richmond was the safest place to live that night as he and Clive headed for their designated area. Parking up, they left John's Vauxhall and each walked down one side of the street. Officers were doing the same all over Richmond and into parts of Twickenham.

For three hours the searching continued. Every car park at the rear of buildings or unlocked garages in blocks or under flats were checked. Secure car parks where a bit of climbing gained entrance were checked. All vehicles in drives to private houses and parked on the street were checked.

Groves was ticking off the roads as officers radioed in. He was getting despondent as negative results kept being reported. Then he got the message he craved. Two of the surveillance officers had broken into the secure car park under the Premier Inn and found the Mercedes parked in a bay.

Groves was elated and told the officers via the radio, 'Maintain observation on it if you can. Don't take any chances.'

There simple reply was, 'Will do.'

Groves summoned everyone else back to Richmond Police Station. The armed unit readied themselves. By 3.30am the canteen was buzzing again.

'Right people, the time has come. Vince, I want you to go into the Premier Inn and find out which room he is in. Call me as soon as you know.' Vince left the canteen. 'Murray will give everyone else a point to hold just in case he breaks out.' Then looking straight at the firearms officers, 'Sergeant: I want you to take charge of entry to which ever room he's in and I want him nicked.'

'Understood.' The firearms officers moved to the back of the room to discuss tactics.

Groves continued, 'I want everyone out on the plot by 4.15am ready to hit the room at 4.30. Grab a cup of tea. The local boys have found enough milk for all of us and have provided their kettle. Don't break it!'

There was a friendly clamour to get a cup of liquid. It mattered not to them what it was providing it was wet and warm. The chief constable of Surrey and the DAC moved about chatting to officers. No one disturbed the firearms officers except to pass them cardboard cups of tea.

Vince got to the entrance of the Premier Inn and found it was open. He pushed the door and went to the reception desk which appeared unmanned. As he stepped behind the desk he nearly stood on a man asleep on a camp bed and out of sight to anyone entering the building.

Gently, he shook the man by his shoulders. Slowly he woke up and was immediately frightened when he saw Vince towering above him. 'It's all right, I'm a police officer. I need some urgent information from you.' He produced a picture of Gleb. 'This man? What room is he in?'

The receptionist recognised Gleb immediately. 'He's in room twenty-two on the first floor. Obnoxious bastard. No manners. What's he done?'

'I'll tell you in a minute. Have you a floor plan of his room?'

'No. Sorry.'

Vince asked, 'Can you please draw a rough plan on the back of this photo?'

The receptionist stood up and put the photo paper on the desk. Then he quickly drew the layout of the room. 'It's right at the end of the corridor. Furthest from the lift and stairs. He insisted on it. The window overlooks the gardens. He didn't look like someone who was into gardening if you ask me.'

'Does the window open wide or has it a limit as to how far it will open?'

'It should only open six inches and is held by a chain which sets off an alarm if it opens any further. I suppose if he wanted and didn't care about the alarm he could force it wide open.'

Vince noticed a fire evacuation plan fixed to the wall showing the layout of the corridor. Right in the furthest corner he saw room twenty-two marked.

'Have you got a master key for that room?'

'Yes of course. Before I let you have it, I'll have to clear it with head office.'

'No need. Where do you keep this camp bed?'

'In the store cupboard just here behind the desk.'

'I suggest you put it away now.'

The receptionist looked quizzically at Vince. 'Why?'

'You'll have to come with me to a safe place. You don't want to be hit in any crossfire.'

The receptionist turned pale and put the bed into the store cupboard. 'Let's go.'

Once the pair had got out of sight of the hotel, Vince called Groves, 'I'm with the receptionist,' and he gave his location. 'I need to talk with the firearms team. Can you ask them to meet me?'

'Will do. They will be with you in less than five minutes,' Grove said.

In three minutes they pulled up in a black carrier with some police markings. When they all got out the receptionist was petrified. He had visions of South American paramilitary hit squads. All were wearing heavy duty helmets with visors and cameras fixed on the top. Black combat fatigues overlaid with body armour and high boots completed the image. Hand guns, an Asp and a gas cannister hung from their waists and they were carrying what looked like machine guns. A bright yellow taser was slung across each of their chests next to looped Plasticuffs. One was carrying a metal battering ram know to all police as a 'door bosher' and another a Kevlar bullet proof shield.

The receptionist sat on a fence with his head in his hands saying the same expletive over and over again. Vince gave the Sergeant the drawing and told him where the evacuation plan of the floor was. The armed officers were all deputed to their respective tasks and were raring to go. At 4.25am they all walked as quietly as they could to the entrance of the Premier Inn. Four went to the stairs and two crept into the gardens.

At 4.30am the 'door bosher' was swung and struck the door by the lock to room twenty-two. It flew open.

Two retorts echoed around the corridor as Gleb fired from the bed at the oncoming police. The Kevlar shield stopped one of the bullets and the second struck an officer in the chest. He was knocked backwards by the impact but saved from serious injury by the reinforced metal plate in the front of his body armour. But he was winded and out of the fray with a couple of cracked ribs. At least he was still alive.

Gleb rolled off the bed away from the door and towards the window. He was into a firing crouch in seconds. His training was exemplary and his reactions were perfect. The Sergeant and another moved into the room behind the shield and split up. Two more rounds were fired at the Sergeant. One glanced off his helmet destroying his camera but he barely felt it.

The officer who had stayed by the door fired his taser at Gleb and the barbs stuck in the bare flesh of his chest. Thousands of electrical volts shot along the wire and should have knocked him to the floor. Gleb felt them but didn't go down. He yanked the wires free. A jet of tear gas from a canister flew across the room and hit him in the face but had no discernible effect. All three officers realised they were now going to have to use their firearms.

Gleb could see he was probably going to die if he stayed in the room. He fired several rounds at each officer and as they recoiled slightly from his onslaught, he threw himself at the window. His weight forced the chain to snap and the alarm to activate at the reception desk downstairs. The window flew open as Gleb dropped through the opening to the flower bed a floor below.

There was a cold wind blowing, but Gleb didn't notice although he was only wearing underpants. He'd landed a little heavily but was getting to his feet when he heard an officer shout, 'Armed Police. Drop it or I'll shoot.'

Gleb was a believer in doing something unexpected. Most

people may have laid their weapon down. Some may even hold on to them and try to chat. He fired three quick rounds at the officer. Now he knew his gun had only one round left. All his spare ammunition was one floor above him in his room. The officer was hit in the chest and went down winded but alive. Gleb thought, either shoot or get shot don't talk.

The second officer in the garden was also a believer. He didn't talk. He fired three pairs of shots quickly as he'd been taught. The first two pairs were instinctive and aimed at Gleb's body mass. The last pair were fired slightly higher towards his head. Every bullet he fired sent Gleb reeling further backwards.

Gleb's gun spun away from his grip. He lay on the ground. He wasn't going to move again.

36

16TH DECEMBER 2011
7AM

The DAC and Chief Constable were as tired as their officers and looked slightly dishevelled in their uniforms. They'd sent most of their officers home for a few hours' sleep and a change of clothes ready for a full debrief at the Yard at 5pm. The only ones left were those from CO19, Groves, Murray, Shackleton, Vince, John and Clive.

The DAC spent some time talking to the IPCC explaining what had happened. He'd engaged in an argument with them about keeping officers on duty until they could arrive.

'My officers have been on duty for nearly twenty-four hours. If you think I'm keeping them on duty any longer so you can get out of your beds, have breakfast and turn up here at 11am you've another think coming. We have police work to do and can't wait for you to sort yourselves out. When you tell me a time that you are going to arrive, I'll arrange for the first ten to be available for two hours tomorrow. You have my number, call me,' and he cut the connection.

The canteen staff walked in to open up. They were greeted by tables and chairs scattered about with cardboard cups rolling about on the floor and coffee and tea stains on the tables. Firearms officers kit bags were strewn over a few of the cleaner tables. The CO19 sergeant was busy bagging the fired weapons as exhibits for the obvious enquiry to follow. John was sitting at a table with his eyes firmly closed. He could keep going another day. Shackleton seemed to emulate him.

Clive had spent half an hour talking to Celeste on the phone explaining that the news channels were not aware of all the facts. He wanted to close his eyes and watched the two older officers who appeared to be fast asleep whilst sitting upright in metal chairs. Murray was desperate for tea in a china cup as opposed to a cardboard one. He greeted the canteen staff with anticipation.

Groves was busy and didn't realise how tired he was. He'd made the shot officers go to hospital for check-ups. They'd both recovered and were busy downloading their camera footage for the inevitable enquiry. The one with the cracked ribs was told by his Sergeant that he'd be on light duties for at least a fortnight which didn't please him. A couple of photographers from Forensics were explaining how quickly they could create albums and video for the ensuing investigation.

Groves had arranged for the FME to attend in order to pronounce life extinct as required. He had completed his work and had already written his proforma statement and gone back home to bed. A tent had been requested from the Yard which had already been erected over Gleb.

The DAC arranged for uniform officers to secure the scene and a full PoLSA team which were to search the Premier Inn at 9am for any bullets, casings or other relevant material. Everything seemed to be going like clockwork. The DAC had just one more phone call to make.

'Good morning commissioner. I am calling because of an

incident that occurred last night in Richmond.'

'I heard the initial radio report on the 6am news. Are all the officers safe?' said the commissioner.

'Yes. Some have a few bruises and cracked ribs. Nothing serious. The deceased man is the person who we can prove murdered PC Brown. I fear we are likely to be criticised by some who will claim we assassinated him in revenge. We do have clear video from the helmet cameras of the firearms officers that show our team acted with great restraint. Obviously, we cannot put it in the public domain prior to an inquest or the IPCC investigation. I'd like to speak to you in person before we make any press statement. Richmond is waking up to reporters from all over the world.'

'I'll arrange for our press relations people to put out a noncommittal statement. When are you having the debrief?'

'I've arranged 5pm tonight in the Yard's conference room.'

The commissioner said, 'I'll keep it secure. I don't want anything leaking to the press. I'll speak to the IPCC and find out what they intend doing. They will not be at the debrief but I will be.'

'Thank you sir.' The commissioner hung up.

Both the DAC and chief constable left the building. They needed sleep. Each had summoned a car and driver from their respective force. They'd both sleep as they were driven home.

John's phone rang jolting him awake, 'Hi Oscar.'

'Hi Rocky.'

'You've certainly stirred the shit today. The lady's at work already and is busy on the phone and internet. I presume you're involved in Richmond?' asked Rocky.

'Yeah. We found the guy who murdered the PC from Kenley. It ended up with a shootout.'

'She already knows who it is. She's been in touch with the Russian Embassy in Columbia and told them. They are deciding what to do about it. They are claiming they didn't know he was in the UK. It looks like they aren't going to admit anything about him. They don't think the British can find out his true identity.'

'Does our lady know his true identity?'

'Apparently not. She's sent an email to the Russian Embassy in the UK saying she's heard a Russian national has been shot by police. She received a thanks for the information and that was it. It looks like the Russians are going to disown him.'

'Thanks for that Rocky.'

'One other thing. She's sent a text to an encrypted phone that I can't trace just yet. She said, "The gentleman has been shot dead" and that was it.'

'Will you be able to identify it?' asked John.

'Undoubtedly. As soon as I have it, I'll let you know.'

'Cheers Rocky,' and they hung up.

●

Isabella woke up and turned the television on in her room. The rolling news channel was covering the story of a shooting in Richmond. She paid it scant attention. Getting dressed she went into the main bedroom to check on Pat. She was completely out of it. Isabella shook her awake. Slowly Pat responded.

'What a night. You look like you need the bathroom.' The drug was building up in Pat's system and she couldn't help but agree. She tried to get out of the bed but couldn't stand. Isabella helped her up and into the bathroom. 'I'll come back and get you when you are finished.'

She knew that Pat would do what she was told. The drug ensured it. Once she got her back into the bed she'd give her another dose. It would probably be the last. If everything went well she'd deal with her later. Isabella made herself a coffee and scanned the images on Pat's mobile.

When she'd parked her Mercedes and returned to the house after her encounter the previous day, she'd been furious. It was as if she'd walked into a trap. Pat couldn't have known. The drug wouldn't permit her to lie and she was asleep when she left. So someone else was watching Cobalt Square. Who and why?

She slapped Pat a few times. Pat remained obedient and when questioned, pointed out images on her phone that showed Glynnis Ashurst and her brother Patrick Ashurst. She even recited details of Glynnis' car and her home address which was also in her phone's directory. She didn't know as much about Patrick other than he was the manager of a safe deposit company and a phone number for it.

Isabella knew she should have established the information instead of driving off half-cocked to Cobalt Square. What the hell was she thinking? She'd rapidly come to the conclusion that Patrick was the controller of all the monies and probably kept it in a safety deposit box that he could govern. Her way to finding him, she knew, was via his mother.

There were several new texts on Pat's phone from her

secretary asking her to call. A text from an irate girlfriend who was complaining she'd been stood up and never to call her again. It brought a wry smile to Isabella's face. A few new emails sat in Pat's inbox from various contacts confirming agreements or requesting legal representation. Isabella noted none would attract attention other than her secretary if there was no reply.

Isabella texted the secretary as Pat claiming she'd had some kind of medical issue and her doctor had prescribed a drug that had disabled her. Then as an afterthought, she added that she wouldn't be able to get into the office for several days. The text pinged a receipt message seconds after Isabella sent it. Deciding to keep the phone for the images that were on it, Isabella dropped it back onto the coffee table and it spun round ending up balanced on the edge.

She went back into her bedroom to get her own phone. The television was still scrolling the news of the death of a man in Richmond. As she was about to turn it off, she heard the anchor mention the hotel receptionist had said the male had given the name Gleb Kuznetsov. Her finger was just about to push the off button on the remote control. She froze.

Sitting on the bed she watched the news feed from Richmond and the reporter giving a resumé of what was known. Gleb had been a good friend and her true love. He'd arranged her false passport and the visa to enter the UK. Once she had the money, they were going to want for nothing and live life to the full. She knew he was in the country but didn't know where or what he was doing. An actual tear dropped onto her cheek which she wiped away with the back of her hand.

She would not have been so upset if she'd known he intended to double-cross her.

She turned the television off and went to get Pat to put her back to bed. In the bathroom, Pat had shaken off a little of the drug's influence whilst in the shower but still complied with Isabella's instructions although she tried to fight them. Once she laid back down on the comfy bed she started to doze off. The needle slid gently into her arm and Isabella slowly pushed the plunger down. Pat could do nothing to stop it. She was unconscious in minutes.

●

Groves said to those left in the canteen, 'I'm going to have a big boy's breakfast and then go and get a few hours' kip. I suggest you all do the same. The debrief will be in the conference room at the Yard at 5pm but I'll be there for 4.30 for a quick scrum down beforehand.' He then went to the servery and put his order in. The others queued behind him.

John was thinking how he was going to get to Victoria Station by 6pm to cover Tabitha Marchant's clandestine meeting. He came to the logical conclusion he wouldn't be able to make it. There was only one other way, he needed help. John grabbed his phone and made a call.

'Hello Simon. Are you busy?'

37

16TH DECEMBER 2011
9AM

John was at his flat in Fulham and asleep fully clothed in his old armchair. He was waiting for Simon who was driving up from Chichester. When the doorbell rang, he awoke and gave no appearance of having been asleep as he checked his caller's identity through the spy hole set in the front door.

Opening up, they shook hands and John invited him in. The cafetière hadn't been brewing long enough to let the liquid get cold, and they both sat in the lounge clutching mugs. John explained what had occurred in relation to Marchant and her dealings. Simon had an advantage that he often visited the Kent unit and knew Rocky well.

John's dealings with Simon had been well established earlier in the year when John's temporary partner, a Sussex WPC was kidnapped. Simon had kept her safe and dealt with the kidnappers and a major criminal and his cohorts in Birmingham. Not everything he'd done was legal, in fact hardly any of it was but it achieved the relevant goals. He had been a member of Her Majesty's special forces like his father before him and John was a friend of them both.

It didn't take John long to show Simon the picture of Marchant and tell him what he wanted. 'I'm after good video of Marchant meeting her fella and as much as you can get of them in the Grosvenor Hotel. If you can get a copy of the names they use to book in, it would help.'

Simon said, 'I gather this won't be going before a court.'

'No chance. This is going to be used sometime later. I think the Foreign Secretary would like to see it.'

'How come she seems to have such authority that she can make decisions without consulting anyone higher?'

'No idea,' said John.

'How do these people know she can get them a visa. Surely there is a system devised that they should follow?'

'I'm told that they should apply through a visa application centre or via the British Embassy or consulate of the country they are in. To be honest, I don't know much about it. All I know is she is charging a lot of money for one and that's illegal. It is rather interesting that people seem to know about her all over the world.'

'OK. I'll give you an update once I've something of note to tell you.' They both stood up and Simon added, 'You look like a bag of shit, John. Can't you get Carol to tidy you up?'

'It's been a long night.'

'Yeah, right. I'll speak to you later,' and with that he left.

John went to bed.

●

Isabella rang the office land line, 'Hello. Can I speak to Glynnis Ashurst please?'

'Speaking. I notice on my phone's reader display that you are using my daughter's mobile phone. May I ask how you came by it?'

'She gave it to me. I work in her office. Unfortunately, she is in a rather long and protracted legal meeting and mobiles are not permitted for security reasons. She said you would understand. She asked that I call you because she needs to speak urgently with Patrick at the meeting's conclusion. She thought you might know where he is or have his mobile number handy?'

Glynnis had never received a call from anyone other than her daughter calling from her office before. She immediately accepted the explanation that Isabella gave. It didn't cross her mind that whenever Patricia had called, she'd always used a land line.

'I'll call him and get him to phone. Can you hold a second?'

Glynnis tried to ring Patrick from her mobile phone. His phone didn't even seem to ring.

'Strange. His phone seems to be turned off. He does occasionally change it. Perhaps he's done that and forgotten to pass on the new number.'

'Do you know where he might be?' Isabella asked.

'He told me he's going to the house in Arundel for the weekend. He often sneaks off early on a Friday morning so he's probably driving and that's why he's not answering his mobile. He normally has it turned on though. That's strange. He'll be back in London late on Monday morning.'

Isabella didn't want to make Glynnis suspicious. She would ask Pat where the house was. She was sure she'd know. If Pat didn't, she'd have to consider abducting Glynnis from under the noses of those who were around Cobalt Square.

'Thank you very much. I shall inform Pat later.'

'No problem. Please pass on my love.'

'I certainly will,' and the call was terminated.

Isabella went upstairs to the main bedroom and shook Pat gently at first and then quite violently. She slowly woke up.

'Where is the house in Arundel?'

'Tarrant Wharf.'

'What number?'

Pat was drowsy, 'I can't remember.'

Isabella was frustrated, 'Where is it in the street?'

'It's the middle townhouse of the first three overlooking the river.'

'Who lives there?'

'No one.' Pat was asleep in thirty seconds.

Isabella went into the day room and opened a map on her smartphone. She soon identified the house. She lit a cigarette and lounged back on a sofa. Closing her eyes she thought of Gleb. When they were on the plane from Miami he'd told her he had work to do in the UK. She casually crossed her legs and one lightly touched the coffee table. Pat's phone dropped quietly onto the luxuriously carpeted floor.

She'd doted on Gleb from the instant they met in Columbia. A couple of secret trysts led her to believe they were in love. She'd told him everything about the family's drug trade. Ingenious methods of transport caused them both to break into bouts of laughter. When she'd mentioned the amounts of cash and methods of laundering it, he was often aghast.

He'd arranged for her false passport and the unlimited visas for America and the UK. They were to be a couple. She missed him already. The occasional dalliances satisfied her needs but he was going to have been 'the one'. She cried.

•

Tabitha was furious. She liked Gleb. He was like her. Kept things simple. A business man. They'd made an agreement. He'd told her what Chloe was up to. They'd agreed how they were going to take the money from her. He was going to make Chloe's death look like an accident. They'd both be rich. Well: one would be. The double cross had already been planned.

•

Kelly answered the phone for the nineteenth time. It had been ringing constantly since she'd arrived in the office. People asking to speak to the DAC; journalists asking for comments without going through Press Bureau and assorted other calls regarding older ongoing investigations. She'd fobbed them all off. As he was being taken home, the DAC had updated her from his chauffeured car regarding the night-time's escapade.

This call was from a man in a secure building in Denmark Hill and she didn't like what she was hearing. The person played a copy of the call that Isabella had made from Pat's mobile to Glynnis Ashurst. Then they stated they'd download both the audio copy and typed transcription to Kelly's computer. She checked and it was there already.

Kelly searched Ashurst's personnel file. There was no

mention of premises in Arundel. Something Clive had said made her turn to Henrik Jansen's CRO file. Buried in his antecedents she found a list of the houses he'd owned in the UK. It wasn't there. She was about to close the file when she saw Ashurst's name on the copy of some deeds. She read on and noted that they had jointly purchased their marital address in Tarrant Wharf in Arundel. The phone's incessant ringing was putting her off. She took all the phones in the office off their cradles and the noise ceased. Peace at last.

Checking the digital wall clock she saw it showed 9.50am. The DAC had told her he'd be back in the office about 4pm. She knew those engaged during the night would all probably be at home and in bed. She rang the Reigate murder office number more in hope than expectation.

'Good morning. Reigate murder enquiry. Can I help you?'

'Hello. I'm Kelly Sylvester from the DAC's office at New Scotland Yard. Who am I talking to?'

'Hi Kelly. My name is Doreen. I've heard a lot of good things about you from some of our more eccentric team members.'

'When they have been here they have mentioned you with affection. As to eccentric. I'd say unconventional. Odd even. But you probably know them better than me. I have a problem and I hope you may be able to help.'

'Try me.'

Kelly detailed the phone call that had been made to Glynnis Ashurst.

'It just doesn't sound right, Doreen. Why would her daughter ask someone else to call her mother? Surely she would wait until after the meeting and call Glynnis herself and get the information immediately. It worries me on numerous counts. Has someone harmed her and taken her phone? Is Patricia being prevented from using her phone? If so, why and by who? It then begs the question, why does the person want to know where Patrick is, and is he in any danger?'

Doreen considered the problem. 'I understand your concern. Give me ten minutes. I'll call you back.'

'OK. You have my number,' and they hung up.

Doreen sat at her desk alone in the office. She considered the problem. All the murder team had been involved during the night and were more than likely to be fast asleep somewhere. She walked absentmindedly to the coffee machine and pressed the button. Taking the full mug back to her desk, she opened a drawer and took out a new packet of rich tea biscuits.

Within seven minutes she was a quarter of the way through the packet. She'd dunked everyone and not lost any into the mug. Tea was her tipple so she didn't bother with the coffee but threw it in the sink. Picking up a phone she rang Vince. Doreen knew they weren't covering Cobalt Square that morning as they'd been up all night.

'Got a problem Vince. Can you talk?'

'Go on Doreen. I'll wake up as you talk.'

Doreen related the story of the mobile phone call and then said, 'I know most of your team live around the Chichester area and are likely to all be at home now. You are all close to Arundel. What's the chances of you and your team covering the address?'

'You've got it Doreen. I won't need a full team to start with.

I'll check out the house myself and see how the land lies. Depending on what I see will govern what I do next. If I need to call the team together, I think it will take us about an hour to get plotted up. I'll keep you informed and if you get anything else just give me a call.'

'One other thing Vince. The person who called Ashurst was a woman.'

Vince thought for a second, 'If there is a hit on any ANPRs for the Mercedes heading this way, please call me straight away. We have unfinished business.'

'Will do. Thanks Vince. I'll update Mr Groves later.'

Doreen called Kelly back and told her what she'd arranged.

Kelly was apprehensive, 'I just hope he can stay awake.'

Doreen was a lot more buoyant, 'I wouldn't worry about him. He's got a tremendous track record in Sussex. Have you got Patricia's mobile number?'

'Yes. Clive found it in an address book when they were, shall we say, engaging in night-time extracurricular excursions.'

Doreen laughed. 'Can you get a trace on it to locate it? The Yard would be able to do that a lot quicker than me.'

'Good idea. I'll sort that.'

'If you get any more info, please call me.'

'OK. Speak to you later.'

Kelly looked at the clock. It was already creeping towards 10.30am. She summoned the elderly Inspector Goodall from the Telephone Unit using the DAC's authority. He tapped lightly on the office door. He wasn't sweating as much as the previous time she'd seen him. He'd attended promptly, knowing to keep the DAC waiting could be a serious mistake.

'The DAC has asked me to come and see him.'

'He's tucked up at the moment elsewhere. Take a seat and I'll explain what he wants.' Kelly was brief. 'I assume you are up to speed as to the events last night that the DAC was involved with?'

Goodall was, 'I'd heard. I didn't know he was involved. How can I assist?'

'A mobile number has come to our attention and we believe the owner, a woman is in imminent danger. She may be about to be murdered.' Kelly noticed the inspector's brow started to show beads of sweat. It was obvious to him what he was about to be asked. 'We need to know it's location. Can you do it or do we need to go to a government agency?'

'We can do it. It's best to be kept in house.'

'I obviously don't need to tell you that this is a highly sensitive matter. As soon as you can locate it, there will be a major operation to rescue the woman.'

The inspector rose from his chair. He knew his unit could do what was asked. 'I'll phone you as soon as we have it,' and with that he left at speed.

38

16TH DECEMBER 2011
11.45AM

Vince drove into Tarrant Wharf and passed the house before parking in a visitor's bay. He saw a Lexus parked on the drive. Noting the index plate, he called Doreen.

'It's parked face in, and there's no sign of movement by the vehicle or in the premises. I'm going to call my team out so we can cover it in case it moves. If you could do a PNC on it and let me know the RO.'

'I'll call you back as soon as I can.'

The surveillance team arrived and took up their designated positions. Vince moved away and left the eyeball to a female member of his team. He was hoping to get a little shut eye further away and out of sight. It was only a few minutes later that Doreen called.

'The RO comes back as a painting contractors in Edmonton in London. I've updated DCI Sylvester and she's sent someone to find out if they still own it or have sold it.'

Vince acknowledged the information. Then ten minutes later Doreen called again with an update. 'They sold the vehicle to a dealer so they don't know who owns it now. DCI Sylvester is trying to ascertain the information but has drawn a blank so far.' Vince was feeling confident.

He needed to know if it was Patrick's car and if he was in

the premises. He instructed one of his team to knock on the front door and claim to anyone opening the door that they were collecting for a Christmas charity. If the person was Patrick they could get him to a safe place. If it was Mila it would be down to CO19. Vince had high hopes. The officer rang the bell several times and knocked on the door. There was no reply. The surveillance team settled down to wait.

There was no sighting of Patrick or anyone else going to or moving about inside the house. Vince changed the eyeball occasionally so most of his team could snatch a few minutes dozing. It helped. Now Vince made a decision. He sent the officer back to knock on the door. When there was no reply, he was going in.

With another member of his team, he walked casually to the front door, and rang the bell. As his colleague kept watch, Vince slipped a piece of mica between the door and the jamb. He slid it above the Yale lock and gently moved it up and down until it forced the lock back from its housing. The door opened and they both moved quietly in closing it behind them. Each extended an Asp for protection. They checked the building. There were no surprises.

Moving back to the ground floor Vince quickly drew floor plans. First the entrance hall with a cloakroom and then the downstairs room that had patio doors leading to a small balcony. They kept well away from the glass. The room was a computer and reading room. It overlooked the river Arun. Stairs to the first floor turned and Vince realised they would pose a problem for CO19. The first floor had a living room and a large kitchen and then further turning stairs to the second floor which comprised of two bedrooms and two bathrooms. The drawings showed which way doors opened and where obstacles and furniture were placed.

It was time to leave. Checking the coast was clear with the eyeball, Vince and his colleague left the premises exactly as they had found them.

Vince called Doreen, 'We are going to need a firearms team in case of problems. Can you please arrange it with Mr Groves as soon as possible? Let them know I have floor plans.'

Doreen set about her work.

Kelly sat quietly at her desk. She worried about Patricia. Was she in danger or was she over-reacting? Too late now. She'd set a series of actions in motion. Should she have consulted the DAC? How would she explain her actions to an independent investigation if she was wrong? The hardest thing she would have to explain was how she'd come by Patricia's mobile phone number. That would end up with Clive and John having questions to answer.

Doreen was in a similar situation. A fresh cup of tea was untouched in front of her. She was considering whether or not she'd done the right thing getting a tired surveillance officer to check out premises which could be the location of a potentially deadly meeting. Should she have consulted Groves? She was going to have to call him anyway.

Isabella was in no hurry to go to Arundel. She was debating what to do with Pat. If she killed her in the house the cleaner would find the body and a murder enquiry would commence. They might work out who she really was and who the house actually belonged to. She considered taking Pat somewhere in her BMW and killing her, but then she would have to get back to the house and her Mercedes. A taxi driver couldn't be relied upon to forget her. Could she make it look like suicide? What would happen if she left Pat to eventually recover? So much to consider? There was one thing she had to do which was paramount.

Kelly only just heard the light tap on the office door and Goodall walked in. 'Got it.' He'd written the address on what looked like a piece of scrap paper which he handed to her. There was also a car number plate written on it. 'The team who found the address saw this vehicle outside. They thought it might help.'

Kelly was becoming more optimistic as the clock ticked on, 'Take a seat.' Goodall was happy and without a trace of sweat. His unit had succeeded in record time to trace the phone.

Kelly tapped her computer keyboard and completed a PNC search on the vehicle. She saw the registered owner, 'Patricia Ashurst' and the registered address of the vehicle in Docklands. The inspector saw it as well. He started to worry.

'Is she related to Chief Superintendent Ashurst?'

'She is. Hence the strict security.'

The inspector slumped down in his chair. He'd had dealings with Glynnis Ashurst and wasn't a fan of hers. Kelly noticed his change in demeanour.

'Don't worry. I'm not too enamoured with her either.' It made him feel a lot better.

Kelly checked her address book and then phoned the duty officer at the firearms unit in Old Street.

'Hello. This is DCI Kelly Sylvester. I'm the DAC's personal assistant. Who am I talking to?'

'Inspector William Whetson, Ma'am. Can I help you?'

'You can. I need a Trojan team for an urgent job that may

mean storming a house. The Trojan team we had last night are not available at the moment. Can you get to the DAC's office at the Yard in fifteen minutes?'

'We are aware of our team's work last night. Is this in any way connected?'

'It is.'

'We are on way. Please tell the back hall inspector. He will arrange our parking,' and the phone went dead.

Kelly called the back hall inspector who knew exactly what the firearms unit needed. They never took their vehicles into the underground car park and needed room in Broadway to park. As they left them in the road, a uniformed armed officer remained with them. It took the back hall inspector four minutes to arrange.

Kelly phoned the DAC's home telephone number which was answered by his wife. She woke her husband who didn't sound best pleased. He listened to what Kelly had to say. She was concise and accurate as to what she'd learnt, set in motion and was about to do. The DAC concurred.

'Get on with it Kelly. If it all goes pear-shaped call me. Otherwise, I'll be in the office at 4 ish,' and he hung up. Kelly felt better.

Six officers from CO19 in full kit, minus their helmets, walked into the office. The inspector from the Telephone Unit hadn't been an active officer for some years. Now he remembered what he was missing.

Kelly briefed the firearms officers. She expressed her fear that she couldn't be sure who was actually inside the building. The only known fact she presented was that there was a mobile phone somewhere within the premises. She couldn't help when asked by Inspector Whetson about the layout of the rooms inside the house. The firearms team had worked with as little information many times before and they all seemed sanguine at the thought of entering a building that might hold a hostage and/or a murderous armed kidnapper. Inspector Whetson asked when the assault was to take place.

'As soon as you're ready and I can get a uniform backup team.'

Inspector Goodall from the Telephone Unit said, 'I have half a dozen uniform officers who have recently been on District. They could back you up if you wished?'

Whetson said, 'With due respect, aren't you a little out of touch with operational duties?'

Goodall was positive, 'I may be, but they aren't.'

Kelly said to Whetson, 'It would save time which I believe is of the essence. I'll arrange for a paramedic to be on standby. One of his team can cover the arrest. If it all goes pear shaped, I'll set everything in motion from here.'

Whetson asked Goodall, 'OK. Have you transport?'

The Telephone unit was not considered a priority for vehicle's and only had a few. Goodall knew which ones would be appropriate and said, 'A couple of nondescript vans.'

Whetson knew what he wanted, 'Right. Put one either end of Clabon Mews and don't move about in them. People spot rocking vans. Watch us go in. We'll signal to you to come to the house once we've cleared it. If there's any problems we'll deal with them as they occur. Can you be in situ at 1pm?'

'We'll be there,' and the inspector from the Telephone Unit left the office.

Whetson said to Kelly, 'I hope he's alright, Ma'am. He'll

have to arrange a new front door at the very least.'

Kelly was assertive, 'Think positive. Good luck. I hope we don't have another shoot out like last night's.'

Whetson was thinking the same, 'That goes for us as well.'

The firearms officers returned to their vehicles as two old Ford Transit vans drove out of the underground car park and passed them.

Kelly sat at her desk with an Airwave radio tuned to the firearms officers' channel. All the phones were off their cradles bar one. Depending on what would happen in the next thirty minutes would probably determine which way her career would go.

William Whetson spoke to his team. 'You all know what your responsibilities are. I don't want anyone getting shot because someone didn't do their job right. We don't know what the situation is within the building. We may find there is no problem, or we may be confronted by armed people. This is connected with last night's operation. So be prepared for anything. Any questions?'

There weren't any.

Whetson issued the last instruction prior to the assault on the premises, 'Helmets on. Let's go.'

At 1pm the firearms officers parked in front of Pat's BMW and decamped in a set order. The first man out swung the door bosher and the second man held the broken door wide open and yelled at the top of his lungs, 'Armed police. Show yourselves'. The next man in ran to the bottom of the stairs and kept his weapon covering the first floor. The next two moved around the ground floor searching each room before yelling, 'Clear'. The last stayed by the front door covering the two searchers' backs. The man who had used the door bosher left it on the floor and moved to back up the man by the stairs.

They had had training in storming houses for years and knew exactly what they had to do. When the last downstairs room was cleared, all formed up at the bottom of the stairs. Going up stairs was dangerous. A further call of 'police' elicited no reply. Then in a formed unit they walked slowly up the stairs. The first floor was searched in a similar manner. Two officers were at the bottom of the stairs to the top floor as two entered each room as the other two covered their backs. It was going like clockwork.

Outside in one of the Transit vans, a young officer was playing with his new camera taking pictures and doing a bit of filming. He recorded the arrival of the firearms unit and then snapped local neighbours stepping out of their houses to see what the commotion was all about. A silver S-Class Mercedes cruised down the usually vehicle-free road. As it drew level with Pat's BMW, Isabella could see the smashed door swinging about aimlessly. He snapped several photographs of the driver's look of surprise as the Mercedes approached and then flicked over to video and filmed the car's progress.

Isabella had been to her contact in Notting Hill and had the car's number plates changed. Curly had suggested a number and she'd agreed. He soon changed one set of false plates for another. Had either of them known they were originally on a mobility scooter in Cumbria they would probably have chosen something different.

The encounter with the motorcyclist and Peugeot had

bothered her. She couldn't make up her mind if they were police or someone else. The two big police carriers outside the Clabon Mews address left little doubt. She needed more time to think. Parking in Cadogan Square, she lit up a cigarette.

Inside the house, they'd found Pat. Still in bed asleep but alive. They couldn't rouse her and yelled down the radio to Kelly for an ambulance. The one on standby was quickly there. The uniform officers from the Telephone Unit moved into the street clearing onlookers from around the vehicles and the building. The youngsters knew what they were doing. They'd soon arranged the removal of Pat's BMW and had a contractor ready to install a new front door.

Pat was put into the ambulance and whisked off to hospital with a uniform officer. Kelly soon changed her for two trained armed officers from the TSG. She wasn't taking any chances. Two other armed officers were sent to maintain security at Clabon Mews. Kelly breathed a sigh of relief. The only fly in the ointment was the kidnapper was nowhere to be found.

The wall clock was showing 2.57pm. Kelly needed a quick debrief with the CO19 officers and the Telephone Unit's officers. She summoned them all to the DAC's office and they all crammed in together. She started by congratulating them all on a successful job. Then she requested the CO19 officers download their helmet camera's footage and forward it to her as a matter of urgency.

She asked Whetson, 'When you went through the house did you notice anything out of the ordinary?'

The inspector answered checking his notebook as he did so. 'The bed in the spare room had been slept in and was unmade. There were some clothes in the room belonging to a woman. We found the relevant mobile on the floor in the lounge and the contents of a handbag scattered about on a coffee table. There was a zip-up bag in the lounge which had a set of handcuffs in as well as nine small clear plastic bags containing white powder. Two syringes and two small vials of clear liquid. There was a flick knife and a wrist strap in it. More seriously, there were three small round items with what we believe were fuses attached. We'll submit them for analysis. There was a syringe by the unconscious woman's bed and three clear plastic bags that were empty. We didn't do a full search. You can arrange that later.'

'Thanks. Please get your camera feeds to me asap.' Kelly turned to the Telephone Unit Inspector. 'Has any of your team anything to add?'

Goodall said, 'No. As soon as CO19 called us, we secured the roadway around the premises. We have removed the BMW that was parked outside and belongs to Patricia Ashurst to a secure compound. The front door has been replaced,' and he handed Kelly some keys. 'One of my officers acted as an exhibits officer and will submit all the other items to the correct scientists for analysis. There is a premises guard in situ until you call them off and a guard on the lady in hospital. I think that's it.'

Kelly wanted some clarification, 'Did you notice anyone acting strangely outside the house?'

Goodall was surprised by the question, 'No, just the usual onlookers.'

Kelly persisted, 'Did you check all the other parked vehicles in the street?'

Goodall didn't understand what Kelly was getting at, 'There were only three others and all registered to neighbours.'

Kelly was desperate, 'Any Mercedes?'

Goodall was adamant, 'No.'

The young officer piped up. 'I saw an S-Class Mercedes drive down the street before we all got out of the vans.'

Kelly swore. 'By any chance, can you remember the index number?'

The young DC said, 'Afraid not ma'am,' and Kelly swore again.

Gingerly, the young officer continued, saying, 'Mind you. I think I may have photographed it on my own camera. I know I shouldn't have used it but it's new and I was trying it out.'

The DAC had arrived as the debrief started and was standing at the office door listening to everything that was said. He couldn't get in due to the crowd of officers.

He said in his loudest voice, 'Well go and get it quickly. We need that information. As the official photographer of the event outside the premises I see no problem.' The youngster squeezed out of the office.

Kelly said, 'Good afternoon, sir. Didn't see you there.'

'No problem Kelly. Congratulations ladies and gentlemen on what was a successful operation. It looks like the lady in question has a lot to thank you all for.'

There was a general movement as the DAC found a way through the throng and into his own separate office. Shutting the door he picked up the phone.

'Good afternoon commissioner. I thought I should give

you a quick update as to another incident that has occurred this afternoon.'

The young officer entered the office and a corridor in the crowd opened up allowing him to get to Kelly.

'Show me what you've got.'

The camera's small digital display started with the firearms officers and neighbours and then came the car. Kelly looked at the still images of Isabella that he'd taken through the only unsmoked window: the front windscreen. She recognised the woman as the person she knew as Chloe Mila. The camera started playing the film of the Mercedes and Kelly jotted down the number plate that was clearly visible.

She said to the youngster, 'Don't go anywhere.' Then she dismissed the remaining officers saying, 'You will be hearing from us soon, but in the meantime grab a drink and then please be in the conference room for 5pm this afternoon.' It was a surprise how quickly the office cleared.

Kelly did a PNC check on the Mercedes which came back to a mobility scooter. She knew they had the latest details of the Mercedes. Snatching up a phone she called Doreen with an update. Doreen phoned Vince. Before he knew, Kelly was alerting and searching ANPR cameras. There had been no hits. The Mercedes was still parked in Cadogan Square. Isabella hadn't even left London. She was in Harrods replacing her clothes.

When John and Clive strolled into the office, Kelly updated them. John sat passively at a desk with his eyes closed as the young officer with Clive's help downloaded his camera's digital footage to a computer. The small SD card was preserved as evidence.

John considered everything he knew. He was beginning to think the police had started to get the upper hand. Chloe Mila was now behind the curve instead of controlling it.

39

16TH DECEMBER 2011
4.10PM

Groves joined the small group in the office having been given a lift from Reigate in the blue Volvo. Doreen had waited till he'd arrived before fully updating him as to what had occurred in London and what she'd arranged with Vince. He thanked her and stated it was what he would have done but she should have consulted him.

When she told him he needed his beauty sleep, he laughed and said, 'There's a good reason you are so popular as an office typist. You know instinctively what should be done and you do it. All the other SIOs ask for you first. Just because you invariably ignore what they say and do your own thing doesn't seem to inhibit them requesting you.'

'Let's be honest Mr Groves, you and the other SIOs often don't know what day it is. Would you like a coffee before you head up town?'

Groves laughed again. 'You just twist us round your little finger. Yes please,' and he walked into his office. He made a swift phone call to Vince who quickly roused his team from their slumbers and updated them. They were soon back to dozing in their vehicles. Then Groves left for the Yard.

The young officer returned to the Telephone Unit as Groves, John, Clive, Kelly and the DAC had a conversation as to Glynnis Ashurst. They all agreed that as Pat was in hospital she had to be told before she heard from another source. A decision was made. The DAC made the call. It wasn't lengthy and he suggested she should visit her daughter without delay. Then at 7.30pm she should present herself at the DAC's office with her official diary and address book. He didn't add that it would allow them time for a meeting with the commissioner and the debriefing of the night-time's operation.

At 4.35pm Groves went to set up the conference room and the remaining small group of officers traipsed into the commissioner's office. There were sufficient seats for all of them. Although the commissioner was going to attend the debrief, he wanted to know the abridged facts beforehand about the night-time shooting. Then the DAC informed him about the afternoon's rescue of Patricia Ashurst.

The commissioner steepled his fingers. No one spoke for a minute before he said, 'Larry. When I asked you to look into Glynnis Ashurst, I didn't expect murder and mayhem. It appears that your little team have uncovered something that is extremely worrying. Tomorrow, I'd like you all to come here at 10.30am and meet a gentleman who may be able to help you. In the meantime let's go and see how this debrief unfolds.'

All went through the waiting area, which had pictures of previous commissioners around the walls, then into the conference room past three uniformed security officers. The huge room was half full and everyone rose to their feet as the commissioner entered and took his seat next to the chief constables of Surrey and Sussex. Mr Groves stood behind the lectern. He was in no hurry to start and looked around the room as they all resumed their seats. John, Clive, Kelly and the DAC took seats close by. At 5.30pm he began.

'What you are all about to hear and see must remain confidential. Before entering this room, you were all instructed that mobile phones had to be left with the security officers outside. The commissioner has informed me that noncompliance will be a serious misdemeanour and result in a disciplinary hearing and punishment and the chief constables of Surrey and Sussex have confirmed they will take the same measures. If any of you inadvertently forgot to hand over your phones, please do so now. You have one minute,' and he made a show of looking at his watch. Two detectives from the Heathrow murder team stood and walked out.

A muttered 'Sorry. I forgot,' from one of them caused the commissioner to glare at them. When they returned, they took their seats to angry stares from their other team members. Their careers had been put back and they both knew it. Groves continued.

'For those of you that don't know me, my name is DCI Groves and I am from Sussex. I am the SIO at Reigate. Although this gathering is ostensibly a debriefing, I am going to give you a resumé of incidents that led to last night's operation culminating in the death of a man. Should anyone here wish to correct me or add something they think is pertinent, please raise your hand. Now that's all clear, I'll continue.'

Groves gave a brief outline of the arrival in the country of Chloe Mila and the murder of the junkie at Heathrow. He didn't elaborate about the details. Signalling to Murray a still frame appeared on a drop down screen. It showed two people entering a disabled toilet then another frame of Mila emerging alone.

'Ladies and gentlemen. Remember this face. It may save your life.'

Then he gave a similarly short resumé of the murder of Kristoffer Svendsen in Reigate. An image appeared on the screen of Mila facing the camera and Svendsen's back to it. Groves explained what was happening. The next frame drew gasps as an official photographer's picture of Svendsen, with a large gaping hole in his abdomen, filled the screen.

'She has callously murdered him by throwing a small amount of dynamite into the car which exploded on his lap. As I said ladies and gentlemen. Remember her face.'

An image was displayed of the CCTV supervisor on the escalator with Mila close to him with her arm around him. Groves waited as the image changed to the pair of them standing on the platform. Then a short film played which showed her coldheartedly pushing the supervisor off the platform and in front of a train.

'Ladies and gentlemen, please take heed. This unfortunate man was cut in half and lived for several minutes before he died. The fact is recorded but I have deemed it too extreme to show you. Those that have had to watch it in the course of their investigation will confirm it's gruesome details should you want it confirmed.'

No one did.

Groves went on to give another brief resumé about PC Brown being a lip reader for the Met who read the lips of Mila during the meeting with Svendsen. He didn't delve into his other nefarious activities. Then a frame appeared of Gleb Kuznetsov outside a house which Groves stated was Brown's home address.

A hand shot up. 'I'm sorry to interrupt sir, but how did Gleb Kuznetsov know where he lived?'

Groves answered, 'We believe that someone who knew where PC Brown was stationed probably informed him. Then Brown may have been followed to his HA. At the moment, that's all I can tell you.'

Another hand was raised, 'Sorry to push the point, sir. I presume there are ongoing enquiries to apprehend that person?'

Groves replied, 'There most certainly are. One thing I will add. We believed before we saw these images that PC Brown's murderer was Mila. She entered the country on the same plane as Gleb Kuznetsov so the chances they knew each other are high.'

A film started to play and the audience watched Gleb Kuznetsov strolling about outside Brown's house. It then changed to show him walking up to Brown's front door and after no more than ten seconds opening it and entering. The last piece of film showed him leaving, wearing Brown's baseball cap. A single frame then filled the screen showing an S-Class Mercedes.

Groves continued and informed the officers that was how they came into possession of the number plate. He stated the obvious to his audience that the vehicle was tracked on ANPRs to the Richmond area and the ensuing street search.

He stepped to one side and said, 'The following film is what was taken from the CO19 officers' head cameras at the

Premier Inn. Please take note of the speed of actions of Gleb Kuznetsov and what he does.'

The room's lights dimmed slightly and the films played in chronological order. A lot of the viewers were shocked at how fast he reacted from sleep and the fact he was willing to take on heavily armed officers. His accuracy with a handgun within seconds of being woken up stunned all the authorised firearms officers. When they saw he was not affected by a Taser and his athleticism in going through a first floor window, they realised they would have been no match for him. As each officer was shot an audible gasp erupted. Then when he finally met his end, there was a palpable silence.

The commissioner rose, 'I have watched that film twice now, and I can only marvel at the bravery of our fellow officers. The reluctance to use firearms from the get-go is astounding. I would like the officers from CO19 to stand so they can accept our thanks.'

The six officers stood and took a rousing round of applause and shouts of appreciation. Then as the noise abated the commissioner said, 'What you have all just seen cannot be put in the public domain at the present time. We have to await the coroner's inquest and the investigation by the IPCC. We have all seen that what happened was totally justified. However, as you are all aware, we are going to be vilified by some sections of the press. I will instruct our Press Bureau to do what they can but without the video, they will struggle.'

Groves stood back behind the lectern as the commissioner sat down. 'Before we go any further, does any person present have any information to add?'

Nearly everyone in the room was still thinking of what they'd just seen. No one said a word.

Groves was brevity personified when he explained that through good detective work, a house was located earlier in the day where it was understood a female was probably being held captive. He glossed over most of the facts but explained that the house was stormed by CO19 officers who rescued an unconscious female. He apologised for only having two images which had just been added to the system.

The first flashed up onto the screen of Mila looking slightly bemused as she drove past the house. Everyone recognised her. Groves said, 'We all know who she is now. What more can I say?' The last image was of the S-Class Mercedes bearing the false number plate. Groves couldn't resist a glib jibe.

'That ladies and gentleman, according to the PNC, is what is known in Cumbria as a mobility scooter.' A light chuckle drifted around the room as the mood lightened.

Groves continued, 'I can only reiterate. This woman is as dangerous as Gleb Kuznetsov. At the present time there is an ongoing surveillance operation and tracking of the vehicle via ANPRs. As soon as we can house her, our colleagues from CO19 will be called upon once again. Ladies and gentlemen. There is still a large ongoing operation with different strands to it. Many of you here may be called upon at short notice to assist and I know we can rely on you. Just remember, please treat what you have heard and seen today in the strictest confidence. Thank you for your attention. If there are any questions, please ask.'

There were several questions put, and answered, before Groves said, 'That is all.'

The conference room gradually emptied as officers chatted to one another. Outside in the waiting area, all the mobile phones had been lined up on low chairs and coffee tables by the security officers. It took a while for the correct phones to be reunited with their respective owners. No one seemed too bothered about it.

The commissioner and the chief constables adjourned to the restaurant for a few snacks. They were all aware of the ongoing surveillance operation in Arundel. Within minutes they were engrossed in a quiet huddle discussing possible outcomes.

Groves, Murray and the conference room supervisor spent a few minutes packing up all the equipment as John sat chatting to Kenny.

'I think the time is right, Kenny, for you to go after that Range Rover. The only problem I see is if anyone should come after you. Could your family spend a few days away somewhere?'

'That won't be a problem. I'll change the ANPRs from alerting me to stop and arrest in connection with the murders of the junkie and supervisor. Then we might find out who's behind all this.'

'I have a friend who's in London at the moment who could stay with you for a couple of days. He was the person who helped us earlier this year. He prefers to stay out of view but is a formidable ex-member of the SAS. Having seen what Mila is likely to be capable of, I think it may be prudent.'

'What! A bodyguard?'

'Looked at logically, yes.'

Kenny thought for a while. 'I'll pack my family off by

midday tomorrow. Can he come to my HA?'

'I'll fill him in. He has a mobile but doesn't like using it. His name is Simon.'

'All right Oscar. I'll change the warnings at midday tomorrow. Just keep in touch.'

Kelly unlocked the office and with the DAC and Clive went in and sat down, picking up and then checking their phones. They'd left them in the office rather than with the security officers. They were joined ten minutes later by John, Groves and Murray. John collected his phone and saw an image on it of a man who looked vaguely familiar. He scowled at him. Clive put his phone away as John swivelled his mobile for him to see.

Clive asked, 'What have you got his picture for?'

John was surprised, 'Do you know him?'

Clive said, 'Yes. Of course. He is an MP and something or other in the Foreign Office. Why?'

John looked at the image again and said, 'I think this is the person Marchant is having an affair with.'

The others all looked at the picture. All six recognised the person but couldn't actually put a name to him. Kelly set about logging her computer on and Googling all MPs connected with the Foreign Office. She soon found a picture of him with the foreign secretary. He was shown as the PPS. An MP in his own right and number two in the Foreign Office.

Clive said, 'That explains why she has so much authority.'

John was more sanguine. 'Does he know what she is up to selling visas? Is he taking a cut?'

Kelly was on a different tack. 'The dirty sod's married. He's cheating on his wife and she's cheating on her husband. What a tangled life they lead.'

The DAC was cautious. 'Clive, could you do some research on this guy. We need to know a lot more about him.'

40

16TH DECEMBER 2011
7.30PM

Chief Superintendent Glynnis Ashurst didn't bother knocking but burst in. 'What the fuck have you been doing? My daughter is unconscious in a hospital bed and there are two armed police officers outside her room. They had the audacity to stop me and examine my warrant card before letting me in.'

Kelly, who was alone in the outer office was having none of it. 'I'd be obliged if you didn't come in here swearing. Please hand me your official diary and address book.'

Ashurst was indignant saying, 'I certainly will not.'

The DAC had opened his door, 'Please do as she asks and then come into my office.'

Ashurst threw both onto Kelly's desk and walked into the DAC's office. She stopped dead as she saw John sitting in the DAC's chair behind his desk. Kelly followed her in and pushed past her to sit next to Clive on one side of the desk. The DAC pointed to a seat which she took facing the desk and John and then he sat in an armchair to the other side after shutting the door.

Ashurst scowled at John, 'Who are you?'

'You know who I am. DC John Whiles. I am going to tell you exactly what has happened to your daughter, but first there are other more serious matters to discuss.'

Ashurst turned to the DAC. 'What is this fiasco?'

The DAC was calm, 'I deemed it more sensible if DC Whiles sat there where you could face each other. He will be leading this conversation and for the moment that is what it will remain. A conversation. To put your mind at ease, you are not under investigation or caution at the present time.' Ashurst glared menacingly at John who stared back at her.

There was a knock on the door and the DAC jumped up and opened it. The commissioner walked in. 'Sorry. Got held up. Please carry on,' and he sat next to the DAC in the only other armchair. Ashurst didn't know who to look at. She was thoroughly confused. Kelly handed the diary and address book to Clive who started to examine them.

John continued. 'Can you please tell us your married name?'

Ashurst was belligerent. 'It's in my file. Jansen.'

John was unruffled. 'Your husband was Henrik Jansen. A friend of Kristoffer Svendsen since their schooldays. They were both involved whilst in Norway in the sale of drugs. But then you know that. Svendsen was a witness at your wedding and was a godparent to your children. You are friendly with his wife. In fact you've visited her since the murder of Kristoffer Svendsen.'

Ashurst's face was going puce. She was furious. 'How the hell did you know that? Have you been following me?'

John remained calm 'Obviously, but to continue. Your husband, whilst he was alive, and his friend Svendsen were both actively engaged in the importation and distribution of drugs in the UK. Both were making large amounts of money.

A lot of which ended up in your bank account. Should you deny this, it can be proved.'

Ashurst said nothing. She knew it could probably be proved by financial experts probing her old bank accounts. She wasn't willing to take a chance that it hadn't already been done.

John was relaxed. 'You lied to set up operation Barnyard. You claimed it was as a result of information from Crimestoppers. A blatant lie. You wanted to know who Kristoffer Svendsen was meeting. Are you willing to tell us why?'

Ashurst realised she had been found out and could only just manage to speak audibly. 'No.'

The commissioner muttered, 'Oh dear.'

John pressed home his advantage. 'That is a shame. Perhaps you were missing the drugs money that your husband earned and you wanted to take his place in the supply and distribution chain. Before he left his house that day Svendsen knew he was going to be followed and took what he believed were anti-surveillance measures. It leads one to believe that your information was from Svendsen's wife. She is being spoken to as we speak. I'm sure she'll confirm it.'

Ashurst had recovered her voice, 'You bastard.'

Clive said, 'I've checked your address book and there is an entry for Svendsen. It appears to have been in the book for some time as there are a lot of entries after it. Nothing for Crimestoppers though. Your diary shows a lot of entries detailing other operations conducted by the surveillance team but nothing for operation Barnyard.'

John continued. 'Unfortunately, it looks like you were

preparing to engage in criminal activities and use your position as a senior police officer to further those aims. Svendsen's murder put the brakes on it. Before I go any further, would you care to comment?'

Ashurst sat with her arms tightly folded and was furious. She didn't know how to respond. Should she admit anything she could end up in court. Should she deny it and it could be proved she could still end up in court. With great effort she remained silent. How she hated all of them in that room. Her political acquaintances would not be able to defend her.

John was becoming annoyed with Ashurst's refusal to comment. He told her what everyone else in the room knew. 'You are not aware but there are a lot of other people, with differing agendas at play, who are extremely dangerous. You are out of your league. So far four people, including a police officer have been murdered. Your daughter was probably going to be the fifth and your son the sixth.'

Ashurst put her hand to her mouth. She was shocked. 'What are you saying?'

John was brutal. 'You took a phone call from Patricia's mobile earlier this morning. You told the caller where your son Patrick is. In Arundel.'

Ashurst was outraged, 'You've bugged my phone as well!'

John's reply was stinging, 'It was fortunate for your daughter that we did. As a result, we were able to locate the house her mobile phone was in. CO19 entered and rescued her. Luckily, she is still alive and will make a full recovery in the future. They got to her just in time. You likely told the kidnapper-cum-murderer where Patrick is in Arundel.'

Ashurst tried to rally. 'How dare you listen to my phone

calls,' but her voice faltered.

The DAC spoke, 'For goodness sake. If we hadn't had a surveillance team watching you, and someone listening to your phone, you and your daughter would probably be dead by now.'

Ashurst looked at him quizzically, 'What do you mean?'

The DAC was as harsh as John. 'The surveillance team spotted the murderer at Cobalt Square and chased them. That team saved your life but you didn't even know it.'

John continued, 'I am surprised that Patricia is the owner of an extremely expensive house in Clabon Mews in Chelsea, as well as a large penthouse in Docklands, close to your own penthouse.'

Ashurst whined, 'I didn't know Patricia owned a house in Chelsea.'

John mellowed as he sought the information they all needed. 'She is safe, but we are now concerned for Patrick. If he's in Arundel he's not at the house. Where could he be?'

Ashurst panicked. 'Oh God. I don't know where he goes when he's there. You have to find him.'

Clive said, 'We need a set of keys to the house. Have you got some with you?'

Ashurst scrabbled about in her handbag in a panic. She pulled out a bunch of keys on a silver key ring and held two separately. Clive took the bunch from her trembling hands and removed the keys from the ring and gave the rest back to her.

Ashurst looked around the room at all the faces and didn't know who to ask. She picked on John. 'Can you phone him? You've got to protect him. Will the local police help?'

John needed answers from her. He tried to remain relaxed. 'At the moment he is not answering the phone number we have for him. It appears to have been disabled. We have obviously tried it. The Telephone Unit are unable to locate it. There is a surveillance team. A truly professional team, totally unlike yours, available to watch the premises. As soon as either Patrick or the killer turn up they will take the appropriate action. Do you have the details of Patrick's car?'

'He's forever changing them. I don't know what he drives. He's not a strong character. Don't frighten him. He might do something rash.' Ashurst was close to tears as she thought of her sensitive son.

Clive was impatient. 'There's a Lexus parked on the drive to the house in Arundel. Could that be his car?'

'I just don't know. Please find him,' and Ashurst burst out crying.

The commissioner intervened. 'Mr Whiles, DCI Sylvester, DC Lavington. Would you please allow us some time? I suggest a long cup of coffee in the restaurant.'

The three left the office and went down to the restaurant. The commissioner moved to the DAC's chair and waited for Ashurst to compose herself.

'Chief Superintendent Ashurst, you have a lot to thank those three officers for. They have, with others, protected you. Last night they traced one of the murderers and there was a major operation culminating in the death of one of the assassins.'

Ashurst looked at the commissioner with reddening eyes. 'That was part of this?'

'Yes. They managed today, with others, to save your

daughter and now they are trying to save your son. You have acted dishonourably and potentially criminally. I am going to give you a choice. You can resign. If you resign and consult lawyers as to your method of removal, with intent to obtain a financial gain, I shall institute a criminal investigation. From what I have heard you would likely be charged and face a court. As a police officer in prison, you know the possible outcome. Should you decide to stay on, I will suspend you while the criminal investigation is completed - with the obvious outcome. Of course, Patricia's finances as to the purchase of a property valued in excess of a million pounds will also come under scrutiny. However, my main concern at the moment is the safety of your son. Officers from the Met, Surrey and Sussex are working to find and then protect him. I believe that you are no longer in need of protection and therefore I suggest you spend a day considering your options. I shall look for your papers of resignation at midday tomorrow.'

Ashurst put her face in her hands and cried. 'My son. Please save my son.'

The commissioner left the office. The DAC sat still and waited. He knew she had no choice.

41

16TH DECEMBER 2011
8.30PM

Isabella had a new trolley suitcase and a selection of clothes all purchased in Harrods with a credit card in a false name. She'd taken the time to have a full meal in one of the local restaurants before going back to Curly to pick up a small canvas zip-up bag with some items she considered essential. Handcuffs, flick knife, cherry bombs, syringes and drugs. Curly reminded her that the drugs in clear plastic bags with a minute single red self-seal were the 'Devil's Breath'. She knew to be careful with it. A drug often found in her native Columbia. It induced compliant behaviour in those unfortunate enough to inhale or inject it. Many rape victims complained that the last thing they remembered was having powder blown at them. Rohypnol was mild in comparison.

She checked her smartphone's map of Arundel and its environs before driving out of London, hitting ANPRs throughout the south west of the capital. She thought her new number plates were unknown. She wasn't speeding. She couldn't afford to be stopped by the police for any reason. She'd be in Arundel in a couple of hours.

Kelly had a scrolling map on her computer. As the Mercedes passed ANPR cameras, a symbol flashed up where it was and the map moved so the symbol was in the centre of the screen. It was obvious to Kelly that the Mercedes was en route to Arundel. She alerted a tired Vince.

Kelly rang Patrick's mobile number. There was no ring tone. Every fifteen minutes she rang it. The Telephone Unit Inspector and two of his officers were trying to locate the phone. They were liaising with all their contacts but without success. The only explanation, they concluded, was that the battery was out of the phone. No one could understand why. Kelly kept trying it.

The phone was lying on the floor of the Lexus. When Patrick had thrown his overnight bag onto the back seat, his mobile had fallen out. As it hit the floor, the battery flew out and under the passenger seat. He didn't hear it land or notice. His main concern was leaving London early. He had an urgent assignation.

The Trojan team's two carriers were hidden at the rear of Arundel Police Station in the car park. The station shut every night at 6pm promptly and the officer locked up and went home. Groves had got him back. The six man team were sitting in the darkness of the front counter waiting area, eating a Chinese meal. No lights meant the floor was littered with odd bits of rice, noodles, and meat.

As Kelly noted the progress of the Mercedes the DAC stepped out of his office. 'Is she nearly there yet?'

Kelly knew. 'About 10 miles away.'

The DAC had advocated a different course of action. 'It's a shame we couldn't be certain of her exact route. I'd have preferred CO19 doing a hard stop.'

Kelly had backed caution. 'Problem then is she could have a shootout and members of the public could get hit. Or she could take someone as a human shield.'

The DAC had been over-ruled. 'That was the commissioner's and chief constables' views. How's the surveillance team doing?'

Kelly was satisfied with all the arrangements. 'They are ready for her. So are CO19. Our only problem is, where the hell is Patrick?'

Kelly's computer pinged indicating the Mercedes had passed another ANPR. It was the last one before the roundabout at Crossbush where the road bore right towards the railway station. She called all the officers on an open Airwave radio channel. They were ready. Vince had put one of his officers at the junction of the A27 at The Causeway, which led into the heart of Arundel, anticipating the Mercedes would pass by. The officer was waiting. The surveillance team was waiting. Kelly was waiting with the DAC for an update. The CO19 officers were sitting in their carriers waiting.

Ten minutes elapsed. The Mercedes did not pass the officer on the outpost. It didn't appear near the house. None of the surveillance officers saw it. Another five minutes passed with still no sightings. The DAC was worried. Kelly didn't understand why it hadn't been seen near the house. Vince called the eyeball.

'Any sign yet?'

An officer with a clear view of the front of the house replied. 'No. No trace of the vehicle. No trace of any pedestrian movement.'

The DAC said to Kelly, 'Where the hell has it gone?'

Kelly didn't know. She considered what she knew as fact,

telling the DAC, 'The last camera was on the A27. The car should have turned right to go into Arundel passing the railway station and then the surveillance officer and the police station. The only other ways it could go would have been to turn left towards Littlehampton at Crossbush or keep on the A27 to Chichester. Which way has she gone?'

Larry Mortimore expressed his frustration. 'This is ridiculous. We need to find that car.'

•

John answered his door in Fulham and let Simon in. They both went into the lounge and John poured a glass of red wine for Simon as they made themselves comfy. There was no rush. Simon handed a USB stick to John who wrapped it in a tissue and put it on his small side table.

Simon's account was methodical. 'They met under the clock. I think everyone who arranges a meeting in Victoria Station meets under the clock. That's where I was standing. The man was late and rushed up to Marchant and kissed her. They spoke briefly about her work, and nothing about his. She told him there had been a few applications but didn't elaborate further. Then she asked him if he'd seen what had happened in Richmond. He confirmed he had. She said, "He was one of mine. I don't think he can be traced back to me. We had a good deal going." Then she spoke of him being one of two Russians from Columbia. She said, "The other one has her own agenda which was going to be the payday." I think they became worried at someone else standing close by and they moved off to the Grosvenor Hotel.'

John asked, 'Is the meeting on the USB?'

'Yes. Audio and video.'

'Did you get anything from the hotel?'

'Yes. There's a copy of his signature, Tristram Everdean, on the booking of room one hundred and six and his Visa card. I got some conversation from inside the room. One thing I picked up was him saying, "How much is here?" and her replying, "ten thousand pounds." They discussed Richmond and that she had sent him to sort out Brown. He said, "Can you control her?" I didn't hear her reply. If someone enhances the tape they'll pick up all of the conversation. She said something about a person called Derek who was starting to become a problem. I don't know who he is, but I think he may be in danger. Then they hit the bed.'

John inquired, 'And all that conversation is on the USB?'

'Yeah. Courtesy of a little gismo from Rocky.'

'Thanks for doing all that, Simon. How do you fancy a bit of bodyguarding?'

'I'm quiet at the moment so shouldn't be a problem. What's it all about?'

John told him the story about the murder of the supervisor and the Range Rover outside Kenny's HA. Then it's removal after Kenny mentioned it during a phone call. The fact it was blocked by the army intrigued Simon.

'So it looks like his phone is bugged. I'll take the usual gear and go over his house at the same time.'

John told him what was planned and that they expected some kind of backlash. Being a blocked vehicle by the army inferred to both John and Kenny a government agency.

Simon was cautious. Something didn't sound right to him, but he agreed to John's request. He drove home to Chichester where he lived with his girlfriend Alison Daines, now a DS in the Sussex Constabulary. All the way he thought about what John had said. Then a fanciful explanation slowly formulated in his head.

●

Patrick was in bed. Not his own bed but his neighbours' daughter's bed. He liked to get to Arundel early on a Friday because he knew her mum and dad caught the first flight of the day to Dubai. Eddie had an end of week supervisors' meeting while his wife revelled in the sun, surroundings and shopping. Then they'd catch the late flight home normally arriving just before midnight.

Lorraine and Patrick would spend the whole day together enjoying water sports on the river and sea at Littlehampton, then return to her bed to finish the perfect day. Lorraine was a busy estate agent but always tried to keep her diary free on Fridays. Today had been no different.

Patrick needed a shower and a change of clothes. He didn't want to push his luck and stay past 9pm. He had nearly been caught once when her mum and dad had got home earlier than expected. They knew him as a neighbour and didn't like him. Now he was saying goodbye. Lorraine opened the patio door and kissed him goodnight. He stepped onto her small balcony and gripped the glass partition on top of the dividing wall before swinging himself out over the river and round onto his own balcony. A method he'd perfected over a couple of years. His patio door was unlocked and he went inside.

He was worn out. It had been a great day up and down the river on jet skis and nearly an hour in bed with Lorraine. He decided to have an early night and shower in the morning. Climbing the stairs to the master bedroom that overlooked the river, he undressed in the dark throwing his clothes onto a chair and got into bed. He turned the television on. The eyeball outside saw the flickering lights reflecting in the second floor's other bedroom and alerted the team.

Vince was confused. The only way into the house was through the front door. No one had approached it. The rear of the house overlooked the river Arun and the foundations were sunk into the actual river. He concluded that it was a security feature with the television on a timer switch. He debated sending someone else to ring the doorbell. It was the only way he'd know for sure.

An older female detective sauntered up to the front door as if drunk. She lent on the doorbell for thirty seconds. Patrick was in bed and wasn't in the mood to get up, dress and go downstairs to open the door. He didn't move. If it was Lorraine she'd phone so he didn't care who it was. They'd leave soon enough. Then he wondered where his mobile phone was. He'd find it in the morning. Turning the television off, he fell fast asleep.

Vince and his entire team believed it was just a crude security device. They handed over to a new team just prior to 11pm. They were due to return at 8am the following day. CO19 settled down in their carriers to snatch a few hours' sleep. Several detectives from Sussex visited all the local hotels' car parks searching for the Mercedes. They missed it because it was parked out of sight in one of the staff parking bays behind the Crossbush Hotel.

Isabella was fast asleep in room six.

17TH DECEMBER 2011

At just past 1am Simon made a call to his dad.

'Simon, you have just woken your mother and she's not happy. This had better be good.'

'Hi, Dad. Something has happened and I want your help. When you were in the army you used to use different vehicles for different jobs. Did you have some kind of motor pool or workshops?'

'Yeah. An industrial unit in Wiltshire. They would get us what we wanted. You should know that.'

'We mainly used Range Rovers and Land Rovers. Our old stuff was either repaired, dumped or exchanged. Trouble is I didn't know who did what or where. Can you remember if they used to repair vehicles?'

'Yeah. They repaired anything for the army. Mainly specialist stuff. Trouble was they weren't very quick because it was usually armoured vehicles. Sometimes it would take nearly a year because they'd have to manufacture different parts.'

'Can you remember the address of the place?'

'No, but I'll send you a map with the location marked. Just be aware Simon, the security there is top notch.'

'I only need to check their work sheets for a particular vehicle.'

'I may be able to help you but not till tomorrow morning. Cancel that. Your mother has told me this morning is the appropriate phrase. Text me the details of it at 9.30am,' and he hung up.

42

17TH DECEMBER 2011
7AM

Rocky and Zina were in their workshop. They were checking all their equipment. They checked the overnight audio tape and found nothing new of note on Marchant's answer phone. The emails were all mainly innocuous messages from within the Foreign Office itself. One was from a known MI6 email address asking if the death of Gleb Kuznetsov had been noted as he was Russian.

Then there was an unusual email written in code. It had been sent by Tristram Everdean MP. They both looked at it and laughed. Rocky picked up a pencil and a piece of paper. The code was so simple, they couldn't understand why the sender had bothered. He wrote it down and gave it to Zina who deciphered it.

Chqdbsnq fbgp zmc gnld rdbqdszqx sn uhrhs
Rbnskzmc xzqc snczx qd jhkkhmf ne jtymdsrnu

She simply wrote the next letter in the alphabet beneath each cryptic letter in red ink. When she saw the z, there being no following letter, she recorded it as an a. It was probably the easiest code ever used.

Rocky phoned John and updated him with the overnight

information and told him about the coded email.

Checking the time, he and Zena went to the canteen for breakfast.

Isabella was helping herself to the buffet breakfast in the Crossbush hotel. She was considering her best course of action. She knew if everything went according to plan, she'd be a multimillionaire within days. A few businessmen noted her appearance with appreciation. Her trouser suit looked new and her court shoes were unmarked. She exuded confidence and class with a touch of menace. None felt assertive enough to approach her.

The officers from CO19 had sent one of their members to the drive-thru McDonald's, at Lyminster Road, Crossbush. Less than a quarter of a mile from the Crossbush Hotel. He'd consulted his list as he'd put the large order in. He was their best customer of the morning. They were now all back inside Arundel Police Station with the food scattered over the front counter. Tea and strong coffee was more their priority.

Patrick was just waking up. He was in no hurry to welcome the day and turned over. His breakfast would be later and out of a packet which he'd drown in milk.

Lorraine was up and washing her parents' breakfast dishes. They'd already left in a taxi to take them to the railway station for a day out in Southampton and an evening performance at the Mayflower Theatre. She'd tried to phone Patrick but was getting no reply. It didn't bother her. The walls were so thin that she'd hear when he was on the move and she'd knock on it three times. A code they'd used on many occasions.

Kelly was at her usual table in the canteen at New Scotland Yard eating a full English breakfast and reading a paper. The

DAC had stopped en route to the Yard at a greasy spoon for a couple of egg and bacon sandwiches. Now he was sitting at his desk enjoying them, ignorant of the egg dripping onto his tie. He remembered his time as a uniform PC when a tasty greasy breakfast was the norm before the day got going.

Vince was eating a cooked breakfast prepared for him by his wife. All his surveillance team officers were stocking up with breakfasts in one way or another and preparing flasks.

John was up, showered, dressed, breakfasted on two large croissants dunked in a bowl of coffee and was on his way to the Yard. He knew it was going to be a busy day.

Clive was taking his time over his breakfast. He was going to be picked up at 7.30am and he liked to savour what he ate. It was invariably a fruit-based breakfast that was extremely healthy. He'd already cycled ten miles on his exercise bike before having a shower and his first cup of coffee. His girlfriend was still slinging up 'Z's' and considered anyone who squeezed oranges a little strange.

Tabitha had settled for toast and marmite much to the disgust of her husband. She was already on the tube making her way to work. She always stood. Sitting on a seat would entail obnoxious substances being transferred to her expensive clothes. Her mind was wandering. Gleb Kuznetsov was going to have been her big payday when he split the money that he took from Chloe Mila's dead hands. Now she'd have to arrange to get it all from Chloe herself. Troubling her was how would she know when Mila would have the money and who could she trust to get it for her? She needed a new plan.

Detective Chief Superintendent Ashurst was already sitting behind her desk in Cobalt Square. Her Costa coffee was still too hot to drink. She watched the Kodak frame click from one image to another. Each one brought back memories. She rued her stupid idea of taking over from her husband. She had over a million in investments, a couple of hundred thousand hidden in an offshore savings account and just over fifty thousand in her bank account. Plus of course several properties which she owned outright. She was already wealthy and she'd wanted more. It had all gone so badly wrong. Now her daughter was in hospital and her son was in great peril. He still wasn't answering his phone. She had to rely on others. Something she'd never, ever done before. Pulling a sheet of paper towards her, she began to compose her letter of resignation.

Kenny helped his wife pack a suitcase. She understood his concern. Neither ate breakfast. Coffee was enough for each of them. Both preferred an early brunch. Ralph was eating his cereal and oblivious to the fact he was to stay with his grandparents for a few days.

Groves was already in Murray's old office at Chichester Police Station in Sussex. He'd not slept much during the night hoping for a call from the surveillance team to tell him they'd got Patrick. Or a call from the Sussex night duty CID who would tell him they'd found the Mercedes. He'd got neither. He was nibbling occasionally on a couple of Danish pastries as he considered all his options. His tactics overnight hadn't achieved anything. The new day was going to be stressful and he knew whatever he decided may affect peoples' lives. It didn't matter what happened as long as he made the correct decision and quickly. Being close to Arundel would, he hoped, help.

At 8am the cabbie walked into the Crossbush hotel. He called loudly, 'Cab for Chloe.'

Isabella replied, 'Me,' as she stood up and walked towards the door. She had a stylish raincoat on to protect her from the inclement weather and a matching rain hat. She was carrying a large over the shoulder bag. She wasn't going far. Just to Arundel town centre. She watched the cab drive away and then began to slowly walk about looking in the shop windows.

It was cloudy and overcast with a hint of rain. Ideal to see reflections in the glass of the windows. A lot of tourists were wandering about looking at flyers for the town and small paper street maps. The castle hadn't opened its gates yet so people were diving into small coffee shops and paying slightly higher prices for the privilege of a seat.

Delivery vehicles were struggling to park anywhere up the hill and were double parking. Cars were parked on both sides of the road instead of the car parks which were huge and less than five minutes' walk away. Isabella saw two people sitting in one of the cars as smoke lifted into the sky from the tail pipe. She walked past it. They both had their eyes closed, weren't talking and making no effort to get out.

She walked to the top of the hill and followed the road round towards the entrance to Arundel Castle cricket ground. Cars were parked on just one side of the road and in between a couple of four-by-fours she saw an old van with the driver taking what looked like a break. It was the same van and driver she'd seen at Cobalt Square.

Cutting down a cobbled street, she walked back on a different route to the café by the road bridge over the river

Arun. She walked to the counter and ordered a latte. There were no empty tables but one had an elderly lady sitting all by herself reading a paper.

'Do you mind if I join you, there are no empty tables?'

'Please. Take a seat. I hope you don't mind, but I do like to chat. Would it upset you?'

Isabella casually glanced around the café. No one appeared interested in her or looked out of place. 'Not at all. Do you live in Arundel?'

'Yes. I've lived here for over thirty years my dear. Such a beautiful town. We rely on tourists you know. I always say, stand in the middle of the bridge and you can see all the best bits of Arundel. You can see the castle in all its glory in one direction and then up the hill and the old main street in another. Then if you look south you see the rolling countryside towards Burpham and Crossbush. Of course you can see up and down the river as well. If you're into architecture, or just like me, a little nosey, look west along the river. You can see into the backs of all the different styles of houses with their foundations in the river.'

The old lady whittered on for a couple more minutes as Isabella drank her coffee. She watched a few of the patrons leaving and noticed the clouds were changing from white to a dirty grey. 'It was a treat speaking to you. I shall take your word and go to the bridge before it rains.'

'If you get to the castle have lunch in their restaurant. Some of the best food in Arundel. The Duke of Norfolk only has the best.'

Isabella got up. 'I'll bear it in mind,' and she left. No one followed her.

Lorraine banged on the connecting wall between the kitchens. Patrick was in his underpants getting a coffee. He didn't know Lorraine would have the house to herself. Walking onto his patio he saw her through the glass on top of the dividing wall. It didn't take him more than a minute to agree to her request. He put his coffee on the floor and swung himself around the dividing wall onto her patio and into her arms.

Isabella was in the middle of the bridge half a mile away with a monocular to an eye. She saw it all. She looked around for anyone else paying attention to the rear of the houses. No one. Thoughts rushed through her head. Why haven't they got anyone watching the back? Are they setting a trap? Why haven't they got someone protecting him? They must be watching the front of the house and don't know he's skipped over to next door?

She smiled to herself. He'd made it easy for her. She looked at the map and then 'street view' on her smartphone. There was a side entrance to the first house that led to its patio. Whoever was watching the front of Patrick's house couldn't see it. She could get onto the first house's patio, swing round onto the patio of Patrick's and then round onto the third patio and in through the open door. Then it would be easy. She just had to make sure none of the others plotted up in the area spotted her making her way there.

43

17TH DECEMBER 2011
10AM

Simon called his Dad, 'How did you get on?'

'I spoke to the workshop supervisor. He was just a grunt when I first went there. Now he is a major and practically running the place. Anyway, I told him the index number and he laughed. It was one of the backup vehicles for visiting military dignitaries. He said that it had been used on Salisbury Plain and had rolled and bent the chassis. That was close to a year ago. Because there was no hurry for the vehicle, they hadn't bothered repairing it yet. It was on their to do list.'

'Do they leave the vehicles outside to the elements or under cover?'

'Definitely undercover. They have a huge warehouse where they keep them pending repair.'

Simon suggested, 'So whoever cloned the vehicle must have been in the warehouse to see the index number?'

His father agreed with a proviso. 'Yeah. Or seen it when it was being used prior to its accident.'

From his dealings at Victoria and the Grosvenor Hotel, Simon knew that John was interested in Marchant. He took a chance. 'Could you ask if a person by the name of Tabitha Marchant has been there in the last year?'

'OK. Can't guarantee when I'll find out though.'

'As and when you can. Please just text me with any outcome.'

'I'll do my best.'

'Cheers, Dad. See you soon,' and they hung up.

Simon sent an email to John updating him.

John, Clive, Kelly and the DAC had a brief chat before going to see the commissioner. He had several comfy looking new chairs in his office. He welcomed them all in and offered them tea, coffee and biscuits. Each had their preferred refreshment.

'Well Larry, the gentleman I have asked to come has been delayed by about ten minutes. I'm sure he can assist you and your team with regards to this lady, Marchant.' He took a biscuit and looked at John and Clive in turn. Then smiling, he said, 'There are some things that senior officers can keep secret.'

John couldn't stop himself. Rocky had told him what the deciphered email had disclosed. 'I am sure I know who the two people are that are coming.'

The commissioner looked sternly at John, 'Well firstly, Mr Whiles, it's only one person, and it was arranged by me and me alone. Therefore, I would be surprised if you knew. Would you care to elaborate?'

John accepted the challenge. 'Well, I know it is the director of GCHQ who has driven down to London and is picking up the home secretary.'

They all looked at him as the commissioner put his cup down heavily on its saucer. 'How the hell did you know it was the director?'

John gave a half-hearted explanation. 'Someone sends information to me which disappears once I've read it. That's why I know the home secretary is coming with him.'

The phone rang and the commissioner snatched it up. He didn't speak, then hung up. He stared straight at John, 'Whoever your bloody informant is must be psychic. Both the director and home secretary are at the front desk and will be escorted here.'

Nothing else was said for the three minutes it took before the commissioner's staff officer knocked and walked straight in. He announced both people as everyone stood. Both shook hands with the commissioner who introduced all those present.

When the home secretary shook John's hand she said, 'I've heard about you from the chief constable of the West Midlands Constabulary.' The commissioner was stunned. He needed a quiet word with John and made a swift note in his diary.

Then he said, 'It may help if DC Whiles gives you an update with regards to the problem that has arisen. I feel that he has gained, somehow, more knowledge about the situation than the rest of us. The floor's yours, Mr Whiles.'

John went through the facts of how they came to speak to PC Brown who obviously lied to them and was murdered. How Brown sent information after his death regarding the person's phone number that he had been working for. Then how the Met had arrived at the number being registered to a Foreign Office account. Then John became hazy as to how he found out who the number belonged to.

The director cut into the narrative as he saw someone else's fingerprints at work. 'Mr Whiles, I have worked at GCHQ for the last twenty years in one capacity or another. I have learnt that the road is often, shall we say, Rocky. But find the right Boulder and things can become a lot clearer.'

All the others were lost but John knew what the director was telling him. 'You are correct with your analogy.' He took a sip of coffee and continued. 'My information is that Tabitha Marchant is selling visas for large amounts of money to certain people who would not normally be permitted entry to the UK. PC Brown's murderer, one Gleb Kuznetsov had one such visa. As you know, he is no longer a threat. However, a probable accomplice, Chloe Mila who has a passport with the exact same number arrived with him and has murdered three people. She is at present hunting a person in Arundel.'

The home secretary was a little put out. 'Can you prove all this?'

John was clear. 'I can. The problem I have is the evidence would not stand up in a court of law. How it was obtained would upset any judge.'

The director spoke, 'That wouldn't be an issue. It would not need to go before a court. There are other ways of dealing with it. Can you produce the evidence now?'

Clive undid a small silver case and produced the copies of the two passports which he handed to the home secretary. She passed them to the director. Then a small bundle of emails and he pointed out the relevant passages. Lastly, he produced a USB which he explained held taped conversations.

John said, 'There are more, but we considered these items to be the most serious.'

The director asked, 'Can I keep these?'

Clive replied, 'Certainly. I'll forward more should you need them.'

The home secretary was thinking before she said, 'How do these people know who to contact?'

John said, 'Some other information has come to my attention which is even more worrying. Tristram Everdean, who I believe you all know, is an MP and number two in the Foreign Office and is having an affair with Tabitha Marchant. It appears that he travels the world in his official capacity and meets many ambassadors and staff in different embassies. I can't prove if he passes on Marchant's details, but it is possible. I can prove he is aware of the visas for sale and is taking a cut.'

Clive handed over another USB.

The home secretary said, 'Please don't tell me you have intimate video footage?'

John smiled. 'Not quite.'

The director anticipated more. 'Is there anything else we should be aware of?'

John checked his watch and said, 'At midday a police officer is going to set in motion a series of events that I hope will prove one way or another that Tabitha Marchant is arranging to have people murdered.'

The commissioner looked at the DAC. 'Have you authorised this?'

The DAC lied, 'I am aware of what is going to happen. DC Whiles is organising it.'

The home secretary said, 'Are you suggesting a member of the Foreign Office senior staff is arranging to have British subjects and others killed? How can you prove it?'

'I would like to arrest her deputy, Derek Hodden, who I can prove was complicit in the murder of a drug addict at Heathrow. He's on video handing a bag to the victim which I believe contained the syringe and strychnine used to kill him. I believe his life is in danger as Marchant considers him a weak link. Once in custody I think he will tell us all about their nefarious activities.' John paused as he thought about Kenny. 'A senior police officer is going to update the PNC at midday with the intention of detaining the occupants of a vehicle using cloned plates. Once the vehicle's occupants are in custody, they will disclose who they are working for and what agency.'

The home secretary said, 'I understand the arrest of Hodden which is reasonable. As to the vehicle, I seem to have missed why it's being linked to Marchant?'

'I'm sorry,' said John, 'I didn't make it clear. A chief inspector at Heathrow had cause to speak to the CCTV supervisor of Terminal 5 about a security matter. Within a few hours the supervisor was murdered. Then the vehicle in question was seen outside the chief inspector's private address. As he made a phone call to check the vehicle on the PNC, it was quickly moved. The vehicle was using cloned plates that were blocked. We believe the vehicle's occupants are doing Marchant's bidding and are members of one of the security services. They would not wish to face a court.'

The director said, 'If what you're saying is true, it would appear there is a small cartel of people within government agencies engaged in criminal activities.'

John added, 'Of course, Tristram Everdean would come

within that category. How much he knows is debatable.'

The home secretary was annoyed. 'Leave him to me.'

The director interlocked his fingers and then extended his index fingers to touch the point of his chin. John could see he was formulating a response and waited. The commissioner was about to speak but realised everyone was waiting for the director. As he unfurled his fingers, he looked about.

'If I may be so bold, commissioner, I would like to comment. From what you have told us, Mr Whiles, you can prove and have established that Gleb Kuznetsov was PC Brown's murderer. The only slight fly in the ointment would be explaining how you found out his identity. As both men will be subjects of a coroner's inquest, I would not expect that to be much of a problem. With reference to Chloe Mila, you don't have the same problem with identification. As she can obviously be identified by the airline's manifest.'

Clive jotted a note on a piece of paper resting on the top of his case.

The director paused before continuing, 'Then we come to Tabitha Marchant and Tristram Everdean. These two fall within my remit, and Home Secretary, yours. Although both seem to have broken English laws, I would appreciate commissioner, your patience in pursuing them. I believe we would be able to provide evidence that they would find hard to refute. As Mr Whiles suggests, I think it would prove productive if Derek Hodden was arrested and questioned. As to the cloned vehicle, I should be interested to hear when the occupants are detained. One of my colleagues would obviously also like to speak to them.'

The commissioner said, 'Providing you keep Larry

updated, I see no problem in delaying our investigation into them. Would you have a time limit in mind?'

The director considered the possibility of a time frame. He knew he couldn't commit to one. 'No. It would really be decided by what we can discover and when.'

John said, 'I would hope that Hodden might expedite your enquiries. While Marchant is a free agent, she could pose a substantial risk to the lives of some people. She seems to have unfettered access to other agencies and information. That included knowing that both of you are here today.'

The director looked shocked, 'I don't know how she found that out. I spoke only to the commissioner. The home secretary only agreed to come when I mentioned it in this morning's briefing.'

Clive said, 'If I can assist. I'm sure you wrote in your diary about this meeting and I'm sure you told the home secretary this morning albeit via a secure link. Marchant's informant was Everdean. As he's in the Foreign Office, someone must have told him. It appears you have a leak!'

The home secretary looked at the director. 'This is getting worse.' She looked at John, 'Can you prove she knew we were coming here?'

Clive opened his case and handed her a copy of Everdean's original encrypted email. 'This was from Everdean, and this is the deciphered copy.'

The home secretary looked at them both before passing them to the director. She shook her head in disbelief. Sitting back in her chair she said, 'This is a tremendous breach of security. As you know, I have a security detail who really should know about this.'

Clive compounded her thoughts. 'If someone saw the director's diary, they wouldn't have known you were coming, so that rules that out.' He turned to the director, 'Did you tell your driver beforehand that you were going to pick up the home secretary?'

The director freely answered, 'No. I told him when we crossed the M25. So he couldn't have told anyone without me knowing.'

Clive stated what they all realised, 'That's him ruled out. That really implies the leak is someone within the Home Office.'

The commissioner saw what was coming. 'Home secretary, you made the decision to come here this morning. Therefore you wouldn't have marked your diary. Your call with the director was encrypted. That leaves just a couple of possibilities. Direct members of your office staff who may have overheard you or your security detail. It's easy enough to change your security officers without arousing suspicion. I will arrange that. As to your office staff, that is something you will need to sort out.'

She looked at the director, 'I'm going to need your help.'

'You'll have it, minister.'

44

17TH DECEMBER 2011
10.30AM

Isabella was waiting for a cloud burst. As soon as it started spitting, she turned her collar up and opened her brolly. Keeping her head down she started to walk slowly towards Tarrant Wharf. The rain became constant and then started to get heavier. She quickened her pace. No one would take note of someone trying to keep dry as they made their way home.

In River Road there was a new-looking BMW with a man and a woman sitting in it. She scurried past them and didn't elicit more than a casual glance. They could hardly see through the rain splattered windows. As she approached the junction with Tarrant Wharf, she kept tight to the building prior to the first of the three town houses. Then she walked down the side access to the patio of number one. She paused.

No one was following her. She'd seen that old van again, parked in a bay. It was at least a hundred yards further along Tarrant Wharf. Her map had been wrong. She knew if she could see the van, they could see her. She lowered her brolly and put it on the floor and waited a full five minutes with her back to the wall. Her little knuckleduster gripped tightly in her right hand. No one approached her and she was satisfied. They were obviously only watching the front door of the middle house. Moving to the side of the patio door she took a peek through the glass. An empty room.

She walked past to the dividing wall and putting her bag on her back with the strap over her head, she swung round onto Patrick's patio. She used the same method she'd seen Patrick use. She didn't hesitate but walked to the next dividing wall and swung around that. Now she was where she wanted to be. Outside number five. Stepping to the side of the patio door she quickly glanced inside. The room was empty.

Isabella tried the door. It slid silently open and she stepped quietly inside. She could hear Patrick and Lorraine two floors above. She opened her bag and took out a packet of 'Devil's Breath'. She checked her pocket for her small knuckleduster. Slowly, looking where she was stepping she climbed the stairs. Outside the bedroom door she stopped and took a quick glance in. They wouldn't see her until it was too late.

She quickly walked in. Lorraine was naked and on top of Patrick in the large double bed. Isabella tapped her on the shoulder and she turned round in a panic expecting to see her parents. Isabella blew the powder into her face and put her hand over her mouth and nose. Lorraine breathed the powder deep into her lungs. Groaning, she collapsed forward onto Patrick who was in rapture.

He had no idea what was happening. Isabella waited a few seconds before pushing Lorraine off Patrick who opened his eyes. She hit him in the face. 'Make any sound and I'll hit you harder.'

Patrick saw a petite woman who he thought he could handle. He started to sit up. 'Stay where you are. I need some answers to some questions.'

'What have you done to Lorraine?'

'She'll be all right shortly. It's you I have come to see.'

'I don't know who you are, but you can get out before I call the police,' and he started to sit up.

Isabella had her knuckleduster in her hand and hit him hard just beneath his heart. He gasped for breath. She hit him on his nose that broke in protest. Patrick collapsed back down with his hands on his face. His eyes were watering and small drops of blood were slipping from his nose.

'I'll tell you who I am. I am Isabella Posda. Daughter of the recently deceased Jesús Posda. You control a large amount of our money that should have been sent to Columbia. I have come to collect it.'

Patrick didn't know Jesús had a daughter. He didn't know he was dead. 'How do I know you aren't lying?'

'You are aware of the death of Kristoffer Svendsen. He tried to lie to me. Your sister is currently in hospital in a coma. Do you want to join one of them?'

Patrick was becoming frightened. He knew all about the death of his godfather. He'd heard that the killer was a woman. He didn't know anything about his sister but wasn't going to take a chance. He suddenly felt vulnerable. He was stark naked in front of this violent woman. With one hand, he tried to cover his embarrassment while his other hand nursed his nose.

'I didn't know Jesús was dead. I was going to send the money next week, I swear it.'

Two members of CO19 crept down the passage to the first house's patio. They found the umbrella lying on the floor. One whispered on his open radio what they'd found. The

Inspector instructed them to cover the patio and door.

The surveillance officer in the van confirmed he'd seen no one go to the first house's front door. Just the one person slip down the side alley. To all intents and purposes it looked to him as though the house was unoccupied. The inspector in charge of the firearms team conferred with Groves. Neither could understand why the woman would go along the alley to the side of the first house.

Groves called the detective in the van, 'Can you see any movement in the target property?'

'Negative.'

He called the armed officers on the patio, 'Could she have got to the target property from the patio?'

One of them replied, 'There is a four-foot high wall with an additional two-foot high glass screen on top of it separating the patios. There's no way she could have climbed over it.'

Grove's didn't understand why she would go to the first house. He called the inspector. 'Could there be a way from inside the house to the target property?'

'I'd think it highly unlikely but it's a dubious possibility.'

'The only way I think we can be sure is if you split your team with some entering the first house at the same time as some enter the target property. Vince has a key now to the target property so that should help.'

'I don't like doing that because it makes us more vulnerable. But to be honest, I think it's the only way.'

He instructed one of the officers on the patio to return to the front door. Calling Vince he asked him to make his way with the key to the target property's front door. He could only afford to send two officers to the target address and he and two others to the first house where he considered the female was likely to be. He had to leave his single officer covering the back. He didn't like it.

Vince quietly inserted the key into the lock and gently turned it. The door opened two inches and one of the other officers checked it wasn't booby-trapped. They pushed it wide open and covered the hall. At the first house's front door the inspector waited. When he heard they had the door open at number three, he nodded to the officer with the door bosher. The door splintered with a resounding crash, as both groups of officers stormed into the respective houses.

They were all shouting, 'Armed police. Show yourselves with your hands on your heads.'

Isabella and Patrick heard the commotion. She could see Patrick was considering shouting for help. She hit him hard in his testicles. He doubled up in pain. His breathing became rapid as he gasped for air. She found another 'Devil's Breath' from her bag and blew some of the contents into his face. She didn't bother covering his face, his fast deep breathing ensured he got a fair dose. He slowly passed out.

Isabella went into the bathroom and washed her hands. She didn't want to get any of the drugs into her lungs. Noise was coming through the walls from Patrick's house as the armed officers conducted their search. Walking back into the bedroom she saw Lorraine was sitting up. She started to prepare a syringe and then a thought occurred to her. The 'Devil's Breath' would ensure she would do her bidding.

'Stand up. I have a job for you.' Lorraine couldn't resist.

The officers were relieved. They hadn't found anyone.

They'd all known the woman was likely to have been a formidable opponent. Now they all regrouped by the broken front door to the first house. A discussion ensued as to where the woman had gone. Then they got an answer.

A naked woman approached them. Every man looked at her. On the patio overlooking the river, both Isabella and Patrick swung round onto his balcony. Then they slipped into his house. Isabella was ready just in case there were police still in there. Her timing was impeccable.

She heard Lorraine outside keep shouting. 'Where's my umbrella?' When one of them tried to put a coat around her she just shrugged it off. The rain poured down. The whole incident was becoming a debacle. An ambulance was summoned.

Groves called Vince, 'Did your man see where she came from?'

'No. He moved away when CO19 went in.'

Groves swore under his breath. He knew any advantage they had was now lost. His head swam. Where the hell did she come from? Was it the same woman who went down the side of the house? She wanted her umbrella and they'd found one. It implies it was likely the same woman. Why hadn't she been found during the search? There had to be an explanation, but what was it? He swore again but loudly.

Patrick sat on his bed. He answered all Isabella's questions. She took his keys to the Safe Deposit Centre. He reeled off several code numbers that she committed to memory. Then she fathomed her payday could be even bigger. More questions elicited answers that needed to be written down. She marvelled at how much information Patrick had committed to heart. His illegal dealings stretched to numerous other enterprises by players other than her own family. For sixteen minutes the questions and answers continued. She wasn't going half-cocked this time.

Groves drove to Arundel Police Station to have a quick debrief with the surveillance officers and the CO19 officers. A lone uniformed police officer stood outside the broken front door of the first house. The building contractor who was to repair it was en route from Brighton. The PC cursed the rain. He cursed the contractor. He cursed the officer who'd broken the door. He cursed his duty officer who'd sent him there. He cursed his life as the general dogsbody.

Isabella was in Patrick's kitchen on the first floor which overlooked the street. She heard a noisy engine outside and watched a large van manoeuvring by the entrance to the first house. The young, uniformed PC was directing the driver. It didn't really bother her. All those that could cause her problems had left. Checking the fridge she created a salad and sat down to eat it. Patrick was still sitting on his bed in a stupor. She'd deal with him before she left.

Isabella considered a cab to take her back to the Crossbush hotel to pick up her things and her Mercedes. No way could she get one to pull up outside Patrick's house. She knew it could be tricky to arrange for one to pick her up slightly away from the house. Cabbies would think she'd do a runner and would be reluctant to respond. Beneath the window she'd noticed the Lexus parked on the drive. A lot quicker and more private than a cab. She'd use that. Finishing her meal, she climbed the stairs.

Patrick had his eyes closed. She slapped him and he opened

his eyes. He'd told her so much. Criminals throughout the UK had secret deposit boxes in his depository. What they held could be worth millions. His godfather had helped spread the word that he was a safe pair of hands. Well, not any more.

She prepared a syringe. Under no circumstances could she afford to let him speak to the authorities. If they knew what she was planning, they could stop her or prevent it. The security box containing the Posda cash had been her primary endeavour. Now she knew her family weren't the only ones with a secret box. Patrick had told her of nine more. What they held could amount to a treasure trove and no one could tell the police about their ill-gotten gains being stolen. The needle slid easily into a vein. The excessive amount of the drug would eventually kill him. Shame she didn't have any strychnine.

She walked out of the front door. When she got into the Lexus, she adjusted the seat and started to reverse out of the drive. The PC gave her a casual glance as he spoke to the contractor. The rain had become incessant and he was in no mood for niceties. She clipped a raised flower bed.

'Stupid bloody woman. Big car that she can't drive.' Then he watched in amazement as she drove off without checking the damage. 'More money than sense.' Something triggered in his brain. It was strange. He moved away from the contractor and radioed his duty officer who'd sent him to the insecure house.

He listened to the officer and walked through the station to where Groves was holding his debriefing. 'Excuse me, can I interrupt for a second?'

'Yes? How can I help?'

The duty officer relayed what the uniform PC had told him. He was nearly knocked over as everyone scrambled without being told. The surveillance officers ran from the station to their vehicles parked in roads well away and out of sight. CO19 officers ran to their carriers in the yard. Groves walked to the front of the station in time to see the Lexus driving past on its way to the Crossbush Hotel. Isabella saw him show recognition and realised her Mercedes was no longer an option.

He grabbed his radio from his pocket and realised he'd turned it off prior to the debriefing. Fiddling with the buttons he managed to turn it on. He updated all the officers on what he'd seen. The CO19 carriers exited the yard at speed. They were just two minutes behind the Lexus, but it was much too late. Isabella was pulling into a staff parking bay next to her Mercedes.

Vince needed to know more. He parked on the drive to Patrick's house. Calling to the PC he said, 'If I'm not out in five minutes get backup.' He opened the front door and extended his Asp. He was back out in less than three. He called Groves.

'I need an ambulance urgently to the target address. I've found a man who I believe is Patrick with a needle in his arm. He looks like he's dying.'

45

17TH DECEMBER 2011
NOON

Kenny contacted his deputy and updated the ANPR. He'd welcomed Simon who'd gone through his house holding a little silver box with red, orange and green lights. The green one stayed illuminated all the time. Simon was relieved. There were no bugs. As to the phone, he couldn't be so certain. His equipment that he plugged into the incoming phone socket was inconclusive.

The first hit on an ANPR was in less than ten minutes. The Range Rover was moving in Victoria in London. They both knew it was close to all government buildings and the intelligence agencies. Kenny knew there were more ANPR cameras closer together in Central London than anywhere else in the UK. There were more armed officers in and around that area than anywhere else in the country. It was only a matter of time before the Range Rover was going to be seen by one of them. It hit another camera in Parliament Square. That's when a police armed response vehicle latched onto it.

The information room inspector authorised the deployment of firearms. An officer in the police car unlocked the security device holding their Heckler and Koch semi-automatic rifles and the two passengers checked the weapons. The Range Rover moved onto the Victoria Embankment with the red police car close behind it. The occupants in the Range Rover saw it behind them and knew the red colour meant the occupants had access to a lot more powerful firearms than they were carrying.

The radio chatter increased as the pursuers kept up a commentary. They reported the passenger was looking back towards them and was using a mobile phone. Then a report that the vehicle had suddenly accelerated. It began swerving past the more law-abiding car drivers as other police vehicles began closing in on it. It was just a matter of time.

As the Range Rover approached Blackfriars Bridge, it was hemmed in by three police cars and forced to a halt. Officers approached cautiously with their firearms raised and pointing at the occupants of the vehicle. An officer demanded loudly they showed their hands and interlock their fingers above their heads. The two in the Range Rover knew the score and waited for the inevitable.

The doors were gingerly opened and both the driver and passenger were hauled from the vehicle and handcuffed. Each was searched and a firearm was removed from each man before they were placed into a police van. It was a much more uncomfortable ride from Central London to Heathrow Police Station than it would have been in the Range Rover.

John was with Clive and Kelly in the DAC's office. They were discussing Marchant when a phone rang. Kelly picked it up quickly and said, 'I'll put you on the speaker phone so John and Clive can hear you.'

Groves gave them the blow-by-blow account of the incidents in and around the address in Tarrant Wharf. Then he described Patrick's medical condition. He had been stabilised in St Richard's Hospital. He confirmed the prognosis was not certain and asked that Glynnis Ashurst be informed. The three in the office looked at each other. None wanted the unenviable task.

Kelly knocked on the inner office door and waited. The DAC opened it, 'I know when there's a problem. You normally knock and walk in, you don't wait. What's happened?'

He listened. 'I really suppose it's down to me to tell her. I've already had a call from the commissioner. He's received her papers of resignation. I'll call her,' and he stepped back into his office and shut the door.

Kenny called John. 'Hi John. There's two in custody with the Range Rover on way to Heathrow. Do you want to come over?'

'Yeah, I'll be there shortly with Clive. That's a great result. Do you know if they have said anything yet?'

'Nothing so far. Just for your info, we have their mobiles. May be some help.'

'I'll see you soon,' and they hung up.

John called the director of GCHQ. 'Good afternoon, sir. Two men have been arrested in the Range Rover with the cloned plates. Both were tooled up. They are on their way to Heathrow. Do you want one of your operatives to attend?'

'Good afternoon, Mr Whiles. That was swift work. It's not even half past twelve. I'll have someone there within half an hour. It will be interesting to hear what they have to say.'

'I'll speak to your man later as to how you may want us to proceed.'

'Thank you. By the way, please pass on my regards to Rocky.'

'I will do. Goodbye,' and John hung up. 'Come on Clive, we're off to Heathrow. I'll keep you briefed, Kelly,' and he walked out of the office towards the stairs with Clive trying to catch him up.

Simon heard his phone ping and checked it. His dad had had a reply. The text was concise. *She was there in February regarding security vehicles for the Foreign Office minister who was hosting an official delegation from Saudi.*

Simon phoned John. He explained the system of armoured vehicle repairs and how some vehicles were left for long periods of time. Then he told him about the Range Rover and the reason it was blocked on the PNC. Nothing to do with the security services. Just the fact it was used as a secure backup vehicle. John was grateful. It explained where the false plates had come from. Simon kept the best till last.

'I caused some enquiries to be made with the depot. I took the liberty of mentioning Tabitha Marchant's name. I gathered from the Victoria meet that she was a person of interest to you. In February this year she was at the depot regarding something else. She could easily have seen the Range Rover in the holding workshop.'

'Brilliant. That explains even more. We're on our way to Heathrow. We'll see you soon.'

•

Marchant swore loudly several times. She'd told the men to format their phones. She thought hard. Could they have done it in time? What's on them that could lead anyone back to her? Where the hell is that idiot Derek? Can I put everything down to him? He'd spill the beans. I've got to get rid of him, Tristram. I've got to tell him. She picked up a phone.

'Can I speak to Tristram Everdean please? It's Tabitha Marchant calling on an internal line.'

'I'm sorry, Mrs Marchant. Mr Everdean was summoned to the Home Office. He's been incommunicado for several hours. I'll ask him to call you on his return.'

'Yes. If you would please. It's rather urgent.' Tabitha was worried. Her best two men had been arrested and she didn't know why or where they were. She yelled for her secretary.

'Have you seen Derek this morning?'

'Yes. He came in at 8ish this morning. A lady was waiting for him and they left together.'

'Do you know who she was?'

'Yes. She introduced herself as Katrina Parke. Something in the MOD Police. She had full clearance. I heard Derek check before he went out with her.'

'Do you know why he didn't tell me?'

'I'm sorry, I wasn't privy to that.'

'Thank you. Please shut the door on your way out.'

As her door closed, she rang Derek's mobile. It went to answer phone. She rang Tristram's mobile. That went to answer phone as well. She shouted in anger. 'What the hell is happening. Why can't someone tell me?'

She checked her official handbook of government departments' phone numbers. Picking one, she rang it.

'MOD Police control room. Can I help you?'

'Yes. I am ringing from the Foreign Office on behalf of Tristram Everdean MP. I am trying to contact Katrina Parke who is, I believe a member of your force.'

'And you are please?'

Tabitha hesitated. Should she slam the phone down or take a chance? 'I'm Tabitha Marchant,' and she gave her extension number.

'I have been instructed that any queries about Miss Parke should be addressed to the deputy assistant commissioner of the Metropolitan Police at New Scotland Yard. I have his phone number should you need it.'

'No thank you. I have it,' and she hung up.

She put her head in her hands. She couldn't help herself from shouting, 'What the fuck is happening?'

Derek was pondering the same as he ate what the Metropolitan Police considered a main lunch time meal. A cheese and pickle sandwich on dry bread presented on a paper plate. No chair to sit on or table to put the plate on in a cell, just a thin mattress on a wooden bench they called a bed. The custody officer handed him a cup of tea that looked like mud in a polystyrene cup. Then he slammed the cell door shut. Derek had been thinking all morning. He wasn't going to spend any more of his life than he had to where someone was going to slam a cell door on him. Whatever they wanted to know he would tell them.

On his arrival at the Home Office, Tristram Everdean was met at the front door by the home secretary's PPS who looked grim. Tristram thought, so would I if I was meeting the person who was likely to take over my job. He chuckled to himself. He was in a buoyant mood. He'd waited a couple of years for a promotion, and he thought this was going to be it. The Home Office was a definite step up from the Foreign Office. He was told to turn his mobile phone off and place it in a secure cage.

Two plain clothes security officers accompanied them to the minister's office. Tristram was impressed with the security. When he and the PPS entered the office he noted they remained outside the door. The home secretary was behind her desk and a man he did not know sat to one side. There was a chair in front of her desk which he concluded was for him.

'Good morning, minister,' and he strode forward with his hand outstretched.

The minister ignored his hand and said, 'Please take a seat. This gentleman and I wish to ask you some questions. Depending on how you answer them will affect your future. The Prime Minister is fully aware of what we wish to discuss.'

Tristram smiled. It was some kind of job interview. He tried to turn on the charm. 'Certainly, minister. I'm sure I can answer anything you wish.'

'How long have you and Tabitha Marchant been having an affair?'

Tristram's smile vanished. He blustered. What could he say? 'Several years. I didn't know it was common knowledge.'

'How long have you been taking money in exchange for visas for foreign nationals to have unfettered access to the UK?'

Tristram panicked. 'Minister, what are you saying?'

'I'm saying you are corrupt. With Marchant you've been selling visas for large amounts of money. We want to hear your side of the story.'

Tristram was seriously panicking. He could feel sweat under his arms. What could he say? They obviously knew, but how much?

Sebastian said, 'Perhaps I can help you start. Tell us how you passed on the details of Marchant to people around the world?'

Tristram couldn't speak. He was dumbfounded. How much did they know?

The Minister said, 'For goodness sake. You're a criminal. You have the chance now to tell us everything. You don't have long, I've a busy schedule this morning.'

Tristram knew his career had gone down the tubes in less than five minutes. Could he keep out of prison? There was only one thing for it, he started his story and he was going to blame it all on Marchant. He told them when he'd first gone to the Foreign Office, he'd met Marchant who seduced him and told him how they could make a lot of money.

He claimed she'd told him to make approaches to people in embassies around the world and soon they started to contact her. He didn't know any details about Marchant's transactions, but took a few pounds for each visa she authorised. Then he explained she started to blackmail him into arranging her promotion to senior level. He whined she was doing things that he didn't know about. Carefully, he snuck a glance towards Sebastian. He was sitting still and listening intently to what he was saying. The minister was studying him. Now Tristram thought he was getting the upper hand. He was wrong.

Sebastian said, 'Well, Mr Everdean, I've heard a lot of rubbish in my day and you are full of it. I know for a fact that you recently took a payment of ten thousand pounds from Marchant. I know one of the people you and she enabled to enter the UK murdered a policeman and in turn was lawfully killed. I know another person is currently wanted for three murders, committed most likely at your behest, who has also critically injured several more people. You are incapable of telling the truth. I think we have no alternative but to bring in the police.'

'No! Please don't.'

The minister got up and went to her door and opened it. 'He's all yours officers. Take him away and lock him up for ever.'

The two officers from the MOD walked in and one of them said, 'Mr Everdean. I am arresting you for conspiracy to murder and malfeasance in a public office,' and then he cautioned him. Tristram could hardly stand as he was handcuffed.

46

17TH DECEMBER 2011
1PM

Isabella was walking into the hotel when the CO19 carriers raced past. She watched them go to the roundabout where they disappeared from view. In her room, she changed clothes and packed her case. It would be a simple matter to get another car. As she walked into the bar she saw several groups of men. Some heads turned. She wanted a single man who was unlikely to be missed straight away.

She spotted him. A man was sitting at a table by himself with a glass of beer in front of him and he was reading a paper. As he was holding the paper she could see he had a wedding ring. He was at least ten years older than her, but it wasn't a problem. He hadn't seen her. She walked next to the table and appeared to stumble and start to fall. Grabbing the table, the beer glass shot onto the floor. He wasn't very quick but she allowed him to catch her.

She was profuse with her thanks and quickly struck up a conversation with him. When she told him she had to get back to her room but thought she'd twisted her ankle, it was a forgone conclusion that he'd help her. As her room door opened she let him walk slightly in front of her. A swift blow to the side of his neck caused him to fall forward onto the bed.

He was unconscious for only a few seconds, but long enough for Isabella to handcuff him to the metal headboard support and stick a piece of masking tape over his mouth. She found his car keys in a trouser pocket. They proudly bore a tag on the fob indicating a Mini Cooper. As she left her room she picked up her case and put the 'Do Not Disturb' sign on the door.

There was only one Mini Cooper in the car park and its indicators all flashed when she pressed the fob. She was soon driving along the A27 on her way back to London and the Queensgate Safe Deposit Centre. She was safe and soon to become a multimillionaire. The radio was on loud and she felt good.

•

Kenny and his deputy were in an interview room at Heathrow ready to interview one of the men from the Range Rover with the cloned plates. He had a lawyer who spoke first.

'My clients wish to point out they have diplomatic immunity and as a result demand to be released. Can you please check the diplomatic list to confirm this?'

Kenny expected some sort of shenanigans by the lawyer and had forestalled the question. 'We have and the result is negative. We have also checked with the Turkish Embassy and they have no knowledge of either one. Now are you ready for your clients to be interviewed?'

The lawyer requested a few minutes' private consultation. Then he said, 'My clients will answer any of your questions.'

After the preliminary legal necessities, the first interview commenced and the man was forthright in his answers. He explained how he came to have a false passport from Turkey and a visa from Marchant. Then how they stole a Range Rover and were told by her what index plates to use. He went on to say how they were told to use burner phones if they needed to speak to her and they only did the occasional job for her. They were mainly to intimidate and threaten people into making a payment. She in turn would leave money for them in a bin in Regent's Park. He had never actually met or seen her.

Kenny asked, 'Why were you outside the address in Windsor?'

'She'd asked us to tell the man in the house to stop his enquiry.'

'And how were you going to do that?'

'Probably break his legs.'

'Did you know he was a policeman?'

The man looked shocked, 'No. We keep well away from the police.'

Kenny asked, 'Why did you leave without doing that?'

The man answered, 'She told us to.'

'Did you know what the enquiry was about?'

'No. She didn't tell us.'

'How do you make a living in this country?'

The man looked at his lawyer who just nodded gently.

'We work for whoever is willing to pay us.'

'What exactly is it you do for these people?' asked Kenny.

After a short pause, 'We act as enforcers.'

'When you were being pursued, it was noted you were

using a mobile phone. Who were you talking to?'

'Tabitha Marchant. We told her what was happening and she told us to format our phones. That's why we didn't stop straight away. It gave us the time we needed.'

The second man corroborated the first's account. Then at the conclusion, Kenny prepared the charges they were to face. Both men knew their tenure in the UK was up. After serving time in prison they would be deported.

John and Clive joined Simon and Kenny in his office. They discussed the ramifications of the interview relating to Marchant.

John said, 'We need to confirm if Tristram Everdean has ever been to Turkey? Then he can be asked who he spoke to there.'

Kenny said, 'I'll sort that out.'

John looked at Simon. 'We may need a statement at a later date from the army about Marchant being at the workshop. It's unlikely at the moment. Do you think it would be a problem?'

'No, not at all.'

John said to Kenny, 'I'd like to conduct the interview of Hodden. I appreciate that the murder team here would like to speak to him re the delivery of the bag to the junkie. I could cover that but there are a lot more serious events to cover. Can you sort that out for us?'

'Buy me and Simon lunch, and I'll see what I can sort out.'

'Done. See you in the canteen.'

Marchant was on the phone to her contacts who she thought could help her. They were hearing rumours that people around her were being arrested and wanted her off the phone as quickly as possible. None wanted to be tarred with the same brush. She knew something was afoot and it was going to be only a matter of time.

She started to write names on a piece of paper and added small side notes.

Scrivener. Derek knows.

Tristram. Derek probably knows.

Brown. Derek might have heard.

Supervisor. Derek must suspect.

Gleb. Derek knows.

Mila. Derek knows.

The Turks. Derek knows.

She picked up a burner phone from her desk and dialled. 'Yes?' a voice answered on the other end.

'I need a job done urgently.'

'I'm busy for a few hours.'

'Fifty grand.'

The voice on the phone was firm, 'I'm still busy for a few hours.'

Tabitha was getting desperate. 'You owe me.'

'I'll call you when I'm available.'

'Wait. Can I meet you?'

'No. I've told you I'm busy,' and the phone cut off.

Marchant slammed her phone down and swore.

Rocky heard it all and saw a lot. He'd got the number she dialled and knew John would need to know.

'Hi, John. Can you talk?'

'Yes. I'm in a canteen.'

'I think the lady is looking to eliminate Derek Hodden. She rang a mobile but the woman the other end wasn't interested. Even when she offered her fifty grand. She said she was busy for a few hours. Do you want her mobile number?'

'Too right, go ahead,' and he jotted the number down. 'Cheers Rocky.'

'It looks like the lady is starting to panic. She's been calling lots of numbers and is trying to find where people are. I've recorded everything for you and when you're back in Reigate, I'll download everything to you.'

They hung up and John called Kelly.

'Hi, Kelly. I think I've got a mobile number for Mila.'

'Brilliant. Give me the number and I'll get it tracked. I've had Groves on the line, they've lost her. He thinks she's up to something involving Patrick Ashurst.'

John told her the number and hung up. He casually mentioned what Kelly had said to Clive who looked horrified.

'Jesus John. "Pat" on our video. She was after his phone number from Svendsen. Remember when we were in Ashurst's office we saw the two pictures of her kids.'

'What about them?'

'Patrick was outside a building with a plaque on the wall. It was for a safe deposit centre. Do you think she's on her way there?'

John called Groves. He told him what Clive thought.

He agreed to check Patrick's property for keys. Then he called Kelly. All concurred it was a long shot but all they had. Kelly updated the DAC who called the commissioner.

'Good afternoon, commissioner, I hope I'm not disturbing you but something has come up.'

'Larry, I've just got a pot of coffee; do you want to come to my office. It's a lot more secure nowadays to speak face to face.'

'I'll be with you in three minutes.'

The DAC told the commissioner about the arrests of Derek Hodden and Tristram Everdean. He glossed over the arrests of the Turks.

'I presume you are fully briefed about the incident in Sussex?'

'Yes. The chief constable was on the phone to me not long ago. Seems we messed up big time. Two people seriously ill in hospital, and one of them is critical. I understand the woman evaded capture. Not our finest hour.'

'The person who is critically ill is Patrick Ashurst.'

'My God, Larry. She's only got two kids and they are both in hospital. Have you told her about Patrick?'

'Yes. She took it badly.'

'I can understand that.'

'Two matters have come to my attention that I wanted to run past you. A mobile phone number has come into our possession which we believe belongs to Chloe Mila. This is currently being tracked and appears to be heading towards London. The main bone of contention is Patrick Ashurst's occupation.'

'And that is?'

'He is the manager of a safe deposit centre in Queensgate. DCI Groves has established he has no keys at his house in Arundel or with him in hospital. Therefore it's possible Mila has got them. She may be on her way there to rob it.'

The commissioner poured himself a coffee. He lifted the pot towards the DAC. 'Please.' He poured another cup full and passed it to him. They sat in silence sipping their drinks. The commissioner was considering what he'd been told. It had been decades since a major depository had been raided successfully.

'Tell me Larry, I seem to remember the last time a safe deposit centre in London was robbed was in the eighties and that was in Knightsbridge, not far from Queensgate.'

'I think you're right.'

'How did DCI Groves come to this conclusion?'

'It came from DC Lavington. When he was in DCS Ashurst's office he noticed a picture on her desk of Patrick in front of a wall plaque stating it was a safe deposit centre.'

'The sharp eyes of a proficient detective. Mark my words Larry, that man will go far. The question now though is what are we going to do about it?'

47

17TH DECEMBER 2011
3PM

Derek sat upright in his chair in the interview room. His trousers felt dangerously loose without his braces and he felt improperly dressed without his tie. Why the police had taken them had eluded him. He'd originally asked for a solicitor but had quickly dispensed with his services when the man had told him not to answer any questions other than the words, 'No comment.'

This was his opportunity to let them know exactly what Marchant had been doing and the fact he had no choice but to do what she'd asked of him. She was his line manager and a senior officer in the Foreign Office. What she ordered was done. He had a modern history degree yet didn't remember it had been a defence put forward during the Nuremberg trials. It had not been an accepted argument.

The formalities were complied with and John began the questions as Katrina Parke sat passively by his side. He asked about Derek's background and how he'd joined the Civil Service. Then about several speedy promotions which took him to the Foreign Office and then to Tabitha Marchant's office.

'How did you come to work solely for Marchant?'

Derek unashamedly answered, 'She seemed to pick me out

from the crowd. I think she recognised my talent.'

Then John started to probe deeper as to what he knew Marchant was doing. Derek readily accepted he knew she was issuing visas to various people for money. He stated she kept a stamping machine in a locked drawer.

'How do you know that?'

'I've seen her using it a couple of times. It's a genuine machine that stamps and prints a visa into a passport. She keeps it secure. She doesn't want anyone else knowing about it.'

'Whose passports does she stamp?'

'She gets passports sent to her in the post or even delivered to the reception desk by embassy couriers. They come from different countries worldwide.'

John was incredulous, 'How do these people know to contact her?'

Derek did not hold back. 'Something to do with Tristram Everdean but I don't know.'

'How much does she charge for a visa?'

'It depends on who they are and what she thinks they would be willing to pay. I've heard her talking of five thousand pounds. But I'm sure she charges a lot more.'

'How much does she give you?'

'She gives me two thousand five hundred pounds a month to post them to wherever they need to go. It's a perk of the job.'

John declared, 'You realise that it's illegal?'

Derek seemed extremely blasé, 'I know she shouldn't be doing it, but that's down to her. I was doing what I was told. She gives me the money for expenses. Taxis and postage.

Buying cheap mobiles. That sort of thing.'

'That's a lot of expenses.'

'At first I tried to give her back what I didn't spend but she told me to keep it. I didn't object. It came in handy.'

'So after these expenses, how much do you normally have left a month?'

'About two thousand pounds.'

John was amazed how much money was passing through Derek's hands. 'On top of your pay?'

Derek didn't seem perturbed. 'Yes.'

'Why do you buy cheap mobiles for her?'

'She uses them to speak to people who want the visas. It's a form of security. She only uses the same phone to speak to each person. Once she has completed the transaction and got the money, she destroys them.'

'Mr Hodden, you can't be so naïve as to believe what you were doing wasn't illegal. Why didn't you report it?'

'That's all very well. If I tried to report it, she would get to hear of it. Any member of the Foreign Office would be entitled to see any complaint made against them. I couldn't tell Tristram Everdean because he was having an affair with her. The minister doesn't concern himself with complaints. If Marchant wants, she can have people eliminated. I did not want to become one of them.'

'You could have gone to the police.'

'Oh no! She has contacts there. She'd know within hours.'

John had picked up on his previous remark. 'What do you mean when you say she can have people eliminated?'

Derek didn't appear worried and said, 'She can order people to be killed.' John looked at Katrina.

'Do you know that for a fact?'

'Just recently, I had to go into her office and I overheard part of a conversation where she was instructing someone to kill a CCTV operator at Heathrow. Then a day later I read about it in the papers.'

'Who was she asking to do this?'

Derek paused as he thought what to say. It was obvious to John he was considering lying. 'I think it was someone who owed her a favour.'

'Was it someone whose passport she'd stamped?'

Reluctantly he answered, 'Yes.'

'A woman by any chance called Chloe Mila?'

Derek knew the name. He was starting to worry. He couldn't understand how the police knew. 'That name sounds familiar.'

'Mr Hodden, please don't lie. I am aware that you delivered a bag to Mila at Heathrow on the 28th of November. You handed it to an intermediary who was murdered. Where did you get that bag from?'

'Tabitha gave it to me. I swear it. She told me where to meet a person and what he'd say. I was to give him the bag and confirm he knew who to hand it to. I didn't know what was in it.'

'Please think carefully before you answer my next question. How many other people can Marchant call upon to commit murder on her behalf?'

Derek looked straight at John. 'I can't be sure, but I'd estimate at least half a dozen. I don't know names so please don't ask. There is a man in MI6, she calls him 'B'. He is someone quite powerful and she finds it amusing that he is one above 'C'. I think he asks her to arrange for people to be killed or disappear. She doesn't seem to have any problems organising it. I thought she was authorised to arrange that sort of thing.'

John seemed incredulous that Derek believed what he was saying. 'Murder is a crime. People in this country can't authorise the killing of another. You must know that?'

'She is so high up in the Foreign Office that I thought she could.'

John lent back in his chair. He looked at Katrina Parke. She was still watching Hodden closely. It was obvious that she was struggling to believe how stupid Hodden appeared to be. John continued to ask questions and Hodden continued to answer. The more he asked the more he drew the conclusion that Marchant had realised how stupid he was and used him as a skivvy.

When John had finished, he settled back as Katrina started to ask questions. She was more interested in the procedures adapted and changed by Marchant and Everdean and the collusion of MI6. Then during an answer, Hodden explained how they would sometimes watch live feeds of surveillance operations being conducted by MI6 around the world. John's ears pricked up.

Katrina asked, 'How often did you watch the live feeds?'

'Perhaps three or four a month. Tabitha told me once she could learn a lot from them.'

'Did they know you were watching in MI6?'

'Not all the time. She could somehow dial into them without anyone knowing. Someone must have told her when they were being shown. Probably 'B'. Some were fascinating to watch.'

Katrina was fascinated and asked, 'What sort of operations did you watch?'

Derek was happy talking freely. 'When people were trying to buy things. Nuclear secrets, that sort of thing from foreign agents. The films could always be used later for blackmail. Well, that's what Tabitha told me. Then when people were being watched to check they weren't up to no good. Really exciting stuff. It was mainly mundane rubbish when very little happened. Tabitha seemed to enjoy them more. God knows why. They'd have a video of a restaurant or club where there was a meeting going on. They were boring but Tabitha loved to see who was there. We even watched a funeral service last month which practically sent me to sleep. Some drugs cartel in Columbia where the top man had been shot. Who cared? Even Mila was half asleep most of the time.'

Katrina looked at John. Hodden was oblivious. 'Did Tabitha ever record what you watched?'

'Sometimes. She never kept anything for long. I suppose if she wanted to see anything again she'd just get a copy from MI6.'

Katrina continued to ask questions and Hodden held nothing back.

At the conclusion of Parke's questions, John asked, 'Do you remember seeing Mila at the funeral?'

Derek hadn't remembered what he'd said. He didn't want to have any connections to do with the woman. He thought it was a trick question thrown in at the end of the interview to see what he would say. 'I'm sorry. I can't recall ever seeing her.'

John wrapped the interview up, and Hodden was returned to a cell.

He said to Parke, 'Can you get hold of the video from whatever funeral he was talking about?'

'I'll speak to the director. The problem will be: who do we trust in 6? It could be the person he calls 'B'. I'll come back to you on this.'

48

17TH DECEMBER 2011
6PM

Isabella walked up Queensgate. She found the Safe Deposit Centre at the junction with Cromwell Road overlooking the Natural History Museum. The front door which faced onto Queensgate was securely shut and looked to her as if it was made of steel. The windows had stout iron bars across them. The plaque on the wall displaying what the premises were and a phone number was highly polished. There were several cameras high up, focused on the front of the premises and a CCTV camera entry system on the front door.

She stood outside and lit a cigarette. It afforded her plenty of time to look about. People scurried past her hoping to get to shelter before the next shower of rain and paid her no heed. The street lights were all blazing and with the headlights of passing vehicles it seemed nearly as bright as the middle of the day. Houses across the road overlooked the entrance to the premises and could conceal any number of watchers.

Isabella was wearing her raincoat with the collar turned up and her hat pulled slightly forward. She was sure that her picture must be well circulated and didn't want to make it easy for anyone to spot her. Checking her watch as though waiting for someone who was late, she continued to nonchalantly pivot around as she scoured the surrounding area for anyone looking out of place.

There were cars parked both sides of Queensgate but nothing in Cromwell Road which was the main arterial road to the west. Isabella watched as the traffic lights at the junction changed and several cars ran the red lights. Then others waiting for the green took off as though at a Grand Prix start. It appeared to be a normal evening.

She sensed movement at the door and spun round to see a middle-aged smartly dressed woman standing in the doorway. The woman lit a cigarette as she held the door open with her body. Isabella watched her. The woman looked about and then back inside the premises as a phone rang within. She flicked her barely smoked cigarette into the road and went back inside shutting the door behind her. Isabella assumed the woman to be a receptionist.

She thought if there was anyone else in the building she would have allowed the front door to shut. Then when she'd finished her cigarette she'd have rung the door entry system to be allowed back in. Also, anyone else inside would have answered the ringing phone. The woman had to be alone inside the premises. It was going to be easier than she thought.

She made a phone call that was answered on the second ring. A woman answered as she'd expected.

'Hello. Can I help you?'

'Good evening. My name is Chloe Mila and I am a security advisor to Patrick Ashurst.'

'Good evening Ms Mila. Mr Ashurst has never mentioned you in the past.'

'He has asked me to conduct a spot security check on the premises in Queensgate this evening.'

'I will await his authority before I can permit you entry to these premises. Should you arrive unannounced I will inform the police. If you are aware of what these premises are, you will be aware of security protocols that are in place.'

'I am fully aware of what the premises are and I would expect you to inform the police. However, Patrick has given me the keys to the front door. I shall attend at 11pm and as I enter I will expect you to activate the hold-up alarm. I shall deactivate it with the current code. Does that meet your requirements?'

'That is acceptable although I would have expected Mr Ashurst to have had the courtesy to have informed me of his intentions beforehand.'

'Without wishing to be rude: it wouldn't have been a spot check then would it?'

'I will expect you at 11pm,' and the woman hung up.

Isabella hung up and waited. She slipped the battery into Patrick's phone that she'd found in the Lexus. It played half a dozen bars of 'The Sorcerer's Apprentice' before switching automatically to answer phone. She waited a little longer and there was a loud ping indicating a new text message. She checked it and smiled.

'Mr Ashurst, I have just been contacted by a female called Chloe Mila who claims to be your security advisor. She states you have asked her to conduct a security spot check. I hope you have authorised this. I shall activate the hold-up alarm when she enters the premises. I would appreciate in future that you inform me of your intentions as to security matters.

I await your response. Tina.'

Isabella typed the agreed security code; *The sky is blue and the sea is green.* Then she briefly typed, *Sorry Tina, forgot to tell you. Chloe is OK. Pat.* The message was sent. It was going to be so easy.

Isabella walked to the Old Brompton Road and into the first respectable looking restaurant. There was no rush. She ate well and had half a bottle of a decent red wine. As the time marched on, the restaurant filled with boisterous punters. When she paid her bill she saw the time was approaching 10pm. It was less than a five minute stroll back to the stolen Mini to collect her case and then another five to the Safe Deposit Centre.

It paid to be cautious. She stood twenty yards from the front door of the safe deposit centre and lit a cigarette. Her empty suitcase stood at her side with the handle extended. Again she casually turned about looking for the unusual. A few more minutes wouldn't hurt. Most of the commuters had got home or wherever it was they had been rushing to. There were a few new parked cars but she couldn't see any that were occupied.

She ambled up to the front door and lit a fresh cigarette from the burning embers of the previous one. Patrick had told her the middle lock had to be turned first. If not, it disabled the top and bottom ones for four hours. The door was heavy and she pushed it open. Once inside the hallway she let the door swing shut and tapped the code into the keypad. Everything was going like clockwork.

The receptionist had watched her arrive on the CCTV monitors and then personally as she entered the building.

Isabella saw the metal grill across the entrance to the stairs down to the strong room in the basement. The stairs leading to the first and second floor offices were free of encumbrances. At the end of the hallway in an open plan office the receptionist sat behind a huge mahogany desk watching her every move.

'Ms Mila, I presume. An hour early.'

'Have you activated the hold-up alarm?'

'You're the security advisor. You should know.'

Isabella stepped around the desk and saw the button on the floor had been depressed. She picked up the phone from the desk and dialled a number.

'Security control, please state your code number?'

Isabella reeled off a ten digit number.

'Your alarm has been activated; we are contacting the police.'

'I'm sorry. Please cancel them. It was set off in error,' and she gave a different code number.

'We'll cancel them now. Thank you,' and the phone hung up.

Isabella sat down in a padded armchair facing the desk and looked around the room. The opulent wall paper to one wall complimented the wooden panelling on the other three. Large pictures in guilt frames hung tastefully about. The plush carpets were deep enough to hide a mouse should one have ever ventured into the building. The chromium backed computer screen sat upon a stand slightly to one side of the ornate desk. It's images unable to be seen by anyone other than the receptionist. It was an office meant to impress.

The receptionist glanced at Isabella's suitcase and then the computer monitor on the desk. It's multiple split screens displayed images from every camera including the room they were in. They were duplicated on monitors in every office upstairs. Seven members of CO19 were watching one in a second floor office where the room's camera had been disabled. They were not moving or making a sound.

Isabella explained that she was there to confirm the security was adequate. She claimed, as if in passing that Patrick had asked her to remove some items from the vault and take them to him. Hence her suitcase. The receptionist seemed agreeable which surprised Isabella. She expected at least a little suspicion or even reluctance to adhere to the request. But all Tina asked her to do was extinguish her cigarette.

A small ornate glass ashtray was on the desk. It had the butts of four cigarettes in it. Isabella stubbed out her cigarette and wondered why. Such a silly thing to ask. Would a rich client be asked to stub out a cigarette? Highly unlikely. Isabella was starting to get edgy. She had to remain focused on the prize sitting in a box downstairs.

Standing, she told Tina that she wanted to go into the vault. Walking to the secure gate she entered Patrick's code into the pad to open the first lock. She turned to watch Tina press the release for the second lock. The metal gate swung slowly open and was caught by the retaining latch which held it. Isabella carried her case down the stairs followed by the receptionist.

The final hurdle was in front of her. A huge six-foot thick circular steel door. The penultimate code number she'd recalled awaited. Her slightly shaking finger punched it into the key pad. As if on greased rollers, the door slid silently to one side. Tina pointed a key fob at a receiver inside the vault and pressed it. She told Isabella that all the sensors and cameras were deactivated within the vault. Isabella wanted to run inside but contained her excitement.

As Tina returned to her office, Isabella went to box number fifty and inserted a key. Opening it she pressed a button inside. A hidden door six feet high and four feet wide, with dummy boxes on the front, opened. There were ten large safe deposit boxes exposed behind it. Patrick had told her these were for wealthy people, mainly criminals to hide their wares. She put her trolley case on the table and opened it. Then she removed her shoe and took out a piece of paper with the list of code numbers for the other nine boxes. If any of the holders of those boxes had been aware that Patrick was able to open their boxes so easily, they'd have taken their business elsewhere.

Her first priority was to empty the Posda family's box. Tapping in the code she slid the large box out till it locked in position. She opened the lid and looked inside. Her heart fluttered. There were piles of fifty pound notes. But more to her liking were piles of bearer bonds. Isabella estimated there was approximately five million in currency and thirty million in bonds. She left the cash where it was for the time being and transferred all the bonds to her case.

A loaded Glock 17 handgun and two spare magazines were propped up at the back of the box. She quickly checked the weapon and slipped it into her inside coat pocket. One never knew when it would come in useful. Her case was hardly a third full. She checked the weight to be sure she could lift it back up the stairs. Clothing would weigh more.

The next box she opened was practically empty except for dozens of uncut diamonds and some jewellery all wrapped in velvet. It went into her case. She moved from one box to another. Bonds being her favoured items, although nearly all the boxes contained bundles of cash. She put some into her case but realised too much would make the case unwieldly.

Then a thought occurred to her. She grabbed all the cash from every box and put it into the Posda family box. It boosted the amount by millions of pounds. If she was clever, she could come back for it later with her emptied case. Isabella knew you could never have enough. It didn't take her long to secure each box and then shut the disguised door.

As she exited through the steel door she broke a beam and the round door started to close as she began to climb the stairs. She heard a bell ring and a voice said, 'Tina, it's Lorenzo. Where are you? What are you doing? Let me in.'

Tina replied, 'Sorry. I can't let you in at the moment.'

'Why not? I've got to deposit the takings.'

'I have a client here.'

'It's never stopped you before.'

Isabella got to the top of the stairs and put her case down. Something wasn't right. There was a noise coming from upstairs. She ran into the reception room and saw Tina standing behind the desk looking at the computer monitor. As she passed it she saw movement on the screen. Pulling the gun from her coat pocket she aimed it at Tina's head.

49

17TH DECEMBER 2011
11PM

Isabella knew she'd walked into a trap. She told the receptionist to turn round and then took hold of her around her neck with one arm and placed the barrel of the gun against the side of her head. She clung tightly to her using her as a shield. The woman was bigger than Isabella who hid easily behind her.

The first armed officer arrived in the entrance pointing a Heckler and Koch semi-automatic rifle towards her. He couldn't fire without hitting the receptionist and Isabella knew it.

Someone behind him called out, 'Armed police.'

Isabella said, 'Put your weapons down and back away.'

'We can't do that. I would suggest you place your weapon down and surrender. You are trapped here.'

'I beg to differ. You cannot fire without killing Tina, or whatever her name is. I can fire at you and I hope you believe me when I tell you I'm an ace markswoman. Just because you have body armour doesn't stop me seriously wounding you.'

All the other six members of CO19 were in a line behind him along the narrow corridor. None could help him. If he was shot and fell, they'd have to climb over him. Then of course she could probably do the same to the next man. They all knew she held all the cards.

The voice from behind him spoke, 'OK lady. You win. Leave the woman alone and we'll give you free passage.'

'No. I want to see you all going up the stairs to the second floor and into an office where you can be seen on the CCTV. Then I'm going out of the front door. Any deviation and the lady here dies. Do you understand?'

'OK. Right lads. Back up. My man at the door will reverse all the way. I don't want you taking a pot shot at his back.'

'I don't think you trust me.'

'Too damn right lady.'

Isabella wasn't sure she trusted the armed men. They didn't seem too concerned she'd get away. Was there something they knew? Was there someone outside? She watched them retreat up the stairs and into an office. They gathered around the monitor in the room.

She yelled out, 'And shut the door.' Isabella watched them for a couple of minutes and saw they were obviously watching her. Seven of them. Armed personnel normally worked in pairs. Now she thought there had to be one outside. A serious problem. Was he a sniper in a house opposite or alone on the pavement? She feared the sniper.

How was she going to get away with her loot? If she took her case the receptionist might make a move and she'd be vulnerable. She knew she could prevent those inside following her but she would still be a target. Slowly a plan formed in her mind, but it was risky.

Isabella marched the receptionist quickly in front of her along the hallway. At her case she commanded her to wheel it in front of them. The firearms officers knew she couldn't see the monitor from the hallway. On the second floor, they opened the office door and one stole out to the landing at the top of the stairs. He couldn't see down to the hallway and relied on what he was being told via an earpiece.

Isabella ordered the receptionist to tap in the code to open the front door. Lorenzo was still outside becoming ever more frustrated that he wasn't being allowed in. He was leaning on the door and nearly lost his balance as it opened inwards under his body weight. He was confronted by Isabella pointing a gun at him.

'Step away one yard or I will shoot you. I am not here to rob you.'

Lorenzo was no fool and did as he was told. He knew if he lost the money he was carrying his life would be worthless. His boss would accept no excuses. Both Isabella and Tina stepped out of the front door letting it close behind them. They heard the racket of the men inside running down the stairs.

The sniper fifty yards away across the road and one floor up could not see Isabella clearly as Lorenzo was in his way. He cursed to himself. His colleagues had reached the hall as the door slammed shut. None were privy to the code which would open the door.

Isabella waited. Two minutes passed and then she saw what she was waiting for. A lorry stopped at the traffic lights for vehicles travelling south in Queensgate. She got ready.

She spoke to Lorenzo, 'Slow that lorry down when it gets level with us. I don't care how you do it but slow it down. Or I'll shoot you.'

As the lights changed, the lorry trundled forward. It

crossed Cromwell Road towards her. Faster than walking pace. Lorenzo stepped off the pavement into the road. The lorry braked hard to avoid hitting him. Then with a blaring horn and a foul mouthed tirade from the driver, it slowly drove round him and on towards Old Brompton Road. Isabella ran along the pavement trying to keep it between her and the houses opposite.

She heard the crack of a rifle firing and the sound of a bullet hitting the pavement a few feet from her. Both Lorenzo and Tina stood by the front door and watched Isabella running along the pavement pulling her trolley case behind her. She didn't hear any more gun fire.

The sniper hadn't enough room to adjust his position. He'd anticipated an easy shot, if need be, as she exited the safe deposit centre. Now he was trying to get a bead on a fast moving target with obstructions in his way. He had missed his chance and was cursing loudly.

Tina started to shout the code number to the men inside. The noise of traffic and solidity of the door made it practically impossible to hear. When they eventually heard and tried to punch in the number, their fingers in Kevlar gloves kept hitting several buttons at once. They were locked in until one could wrench his gloves off.

Isabella was already past Old Brompton Road and at the stolen Mini. She threw her case onto the back seat and started the car. She knew she had to drive normally so as not to draw attention to herself. Joining the busy traffic on Old Brompton Road, she saw several of the armed police running along the pavement.

She reached the junction with South Kensington

underground station and the car spluttered and slowed. Pushing the accelerator to the floor it picked up a little speed before coughing and spluttering again. Isabella looked at the dials. The car was out of petrol. She hadn't filled it up at all and the trip from Sussex had emptied the tank. She guided it to the side of the road.

Isabella got out of the car and pulled her case out after her. A passing bus driver shouted at her rudely pointing out she was blocking a lane of traffic. She couldn't care less. She walked into the underground station. There were people coming up from the platforms and others trying to buy tickets and go down the stairs to the platforms. It was chaos as the underground was shortly to stop running.

She knew the police would soon be flooding the area looking for her. An abandoned vehicle outside an underground station would focus their search. Isabella saw a sign showing the way to the museums via an underground passage. A uniformed man was standing by the gate at the entrance to it.

'No need to run love. You can't go in. The tunnel shut at 10pm. This bloody gate has jammed so I'm stopping people going down.'

'I need to go down there. I got delayed.'

The man looked at her pulling her suitcase and said, 'Just this once. Go on then,' and he let her pass. 'There's a guy at the other end who'll let you out.'

She muttered her thanks and walked into the tunnel. It ran for about fifty yards and then turned at a right angle to go about half a mile to the Science museum. Isabella heard the gate behind her rattling as the man cursing aloud, pushed and pulled at it. She smiled. The police wouldn't be following her now.

She didn't know where the tunnel ended but hoped it was far enough away where police wouldn't be looking for her. She'd grab a taxi and head for the Savoy. They definitely wouldn't be looking for her there.

A third of the way along the tunnel she heard voices and a radio echo from the far end. They had beaten her to it. An exit tunnel to the Natural History Museum was on her left and she darted into it before anyone would see her. She had to adapt. Lighting a cigarette she followed the short tunnel to the exit stairs leading up to the museum. The exit gate was shut and locked with a padlock. She picked the lock easily and stepped into the museum's gardens.

There was a huge ice rink in front of her and a carousel further on. Christmas was a profitable time of year for the museum. People from all over London came to skate while their kids played on the carousel. Now it was closed and deserted.

The security guard in the office within the main building saw her on one of his monitors as she walked around the edge of the ice rink. He radioed to his two colleagues who were patrolling within the museum and they made their way to a small door, rarely used, leading to the gardens. As they approached Isabella, neither expected her reaction. Before a word had been spoken she'd hit one so hard on the side of his face using her knuckleduster she knew he'd be unconscious for a long time.

She kicked the other so severely in his testicles that he couldn't stand and was struggling for breath. His radio had tumbled to the floor and she picked it up. It was obvious which button she had to press.

'If you call the police, I shall kill one of your colleagues. Do I make myself clear?'

A voice came over the radio, 'I won't call them, are they all right? Can I call an ambulance?'

'They'll survive. They don't need any medical help.'

The one whose groin was tender was getting his breath back but was in agony. He tentatively got to his feet. He was struggling to get words out.

'You can walk. You are going to lead me to your security office or suffer the consequences.'

He started to hobble cautiously towards the door, holding his groin, followed by Isabella. They went into the building through the small door which she pulled shut behind her. In the open plan office by the ornate main entrance to the museum, they joined the chief security officer. He was seated behind his desk and they both sat down as Isabella lit a cigarette.

'You can't smoke inside the museum.'

'Well I'm going to,' and she blew smoke out through her nose. 'I am going to stay here for an hour and then I shall leave. Please don't underestimate me or you might suffer. Have you a normal radio?'

'Yes.'

'Please put it on. It will help pass the time.'

50

17TH DECEMBER 2011
MIDNIGHT

John, Clive, Kelly and the DAC were in the office. They'd listened to the farce unfolding in the safe deposit centre over the Airwave radio system. Then the escape from the building. Kelly mobilised everyone she could think off to try and find Chloe. An officer phoned her with the details of the abandoned Mini. It didn't take her long using the PNC to establish the owners details.

She rang the phone number she'd found for the owner. It took her only a few minutes to establish from his wife that the owner should be in the Crossbush Hotel in West Sussex. Alarm bells started ringing. An urgent call to Groves sent him and Shackleton rushing to the hotel. The man hadn't been seen since the morning. The urgency brought the manager from his bed with a pass key to his room.

Opening it they all entered. There was no trace of the vehicle's owner. Shackleton went back to the reception area and spoke to the young man behind the desk. Describing Chloe, the man instantly knew who he was talking about. He'd seen her when she'd arrived and made no bones about the fact he fancied the woman. Then he disclosed he'd let her leave her Mercedes in the staff parking area.

Shackleton ran out to where the staff parking was and

found both the Mercedes and Patrick's Lexus. He ran back in to find Groves and the manager. They moved along the corridor to Chloe's room. Still on the door was the 'Do Not Disturb' sign. They went into the room and found the bound man fast asleep.

The call to Kelly was swift. Now they knew for certain what car she'd used. John couldn't help thinking that as soon as they got close she found a way out. They were playing catch up all the time. Negative reports were being radioed and phoned in to the office. With each one, John became more despondent.

The CCTV on the tube had been checked. She hadn't gone down there. The local taxi drivers on the stand hadn't seen or taken her anywhere. All the restaurants that were still open were being checked. Roads were being searched. All were starting to believe she may have hijacked a passing vehicle. John was sure she was hiding somewhere in the area. He needed to be there.

With Clive, they hurried to his parked Vauxhall in Strutton Ground. John drove swiftly to Harrington Gardens and parked across from the tube station and the abandoned car. There were uniform and plain clothes officers rushing about. It was clear to all in the area that something serious was happening.

An elderly man dressed for the elements was being pulled along by his barking dog. It was the biggest Alsatian Clive had ever seen and he was reduced to fits of laughter as the man kept shouting at it to slow down. As the man drew level with them, he glared at Clive who tried to keep a straight face as the dog started to sniff one of the Vauxhall's rear wheels.

'Are you with them?' and he waved in the general direction of a few uniformed officers.

'Yes I am. Is there a problem?'

'They run away from me as soon as they see Buster here eyeing them up. Shit scared of a little dog. There's a guy in the gardens of the History Museum lying on the ground at the back of the ice rink. I think he might be dead. Can you tell them for me?'

John ran the short distance to where the officers were. Less than thirty yards and he was out of breath. He told them what the man had just said and started to make his way to the museum with Clive. He called Kelly with the information. Crossing the Cromwell Road even late at night was fraught with danger and took them a few minutes. They were joined by two of the CO19 officers.

Looking over the five feet high railings they could see a person lying on the ground. The railings were too high to climb and were spiked to keep people out. The consensus was that they should throw the lightest and fittest over them and that was Clive. He wasn't so sure it was the best idea but was overruled. The two CO19 officers lifted him until he could stand on one of their shoulders. John held him steady and he was able to put a foot on the railings between the spikes.

Clive wobbled precariously before eventually managing to jump over them, landing in a heap on the grass. He breathed a sigh of relief that he hadn't become impaled or seriously injured. He ran the few yards to where the man was lying on the ground. It took him seconds to realise the man needed medical help and he called for an ambulance. The security guard in the office saw Clive moving via the CCTV. Isabella didn't notice.

John realised something was wrong. He could see that there were a couple of CCTV security cameras which would have shown the unconscious man. Yet no one had summoned help. He called Clive to get back to the railings for his own safety. Then he called for all the CO19 officers to assemble and they discussed how to proceed.

They needed a ladder to get over the railings quickly. The paramedics would need it as well. John called Kelly and explained what was wanted and she called the fire brigade. It was agreed they would meet an officer outside the Victoria and Albert Museum. Speed was now of the essence. The ambulance and fire brigade arrived at the same time.

In less than two minutes there was a ladder against the railings and one ready on the pavement to be placed on the garden side of them. CO19 were going over first and would jump down from the top. Once they were all in the gardens the fire brigade were to place the ladder the other side and assist the paramedics over. How they were going to extract the injured man was still debateable.

The firearms officers all got into the gardens without problems and were seen by the security officer on his CCTV screen. He needed to distract Isabella, who had lit another cigarette, from checking the monitor.

'I need the loo.'

'Where is it?'

'Just over there,' and he pointed behind Isabella.

She turned to look, facing away from the screen. 'Where's your phone?'

'Here,' and he produced it from a pocket.

'Leave it on the desk. Any funny business and your friend here will be the first to suffer.'

'OK. I get the message,' and he walked to the toilet door. He flung it open so it banged as it hit the wall and Isabella watched him. When he exited he saw she was still looking in his direction and away from the screen. As slowly as he could he walked back to his chair. He sat down and casually glanced at his screen and saw the two paramedics tending his colleague. There was no trace of the group of men he'd seen running across the garden earlier. Two were concealed close to the railings protecting the medics.

The rest had found the small door which Isabella had closed but hadn't locked. All had slipped quietly inside the building and were advancing gingerly towards the distant sound of the music coming from the radio. Then a soft chink of metal touching more metal. One of the men's carabiners holding his gas cannister had swung and touched a metal display stand. They all froze.

Isabella lit the penultimate cigarette in the packet with her lighter. She pulled the belt tighter on her coat and stuffed her hands deep into the pockets as though she was feeling the cold. Neither guard heard a thing. The firearms officers continued their chary advance and their leader signalled three of them to circle further around and approach in a pincer movement. It was going well.

Isabella stood up and moved to the side and behind a wall of the entrance to the open-plan office. In the dim night light of the museum's displays she spotted the silhouettes of the three moving around. She took two cherry bombs from her pocket. Putting the fuses of them to the cigarette end she counted four seconds and tossed them towards the three men. She stuck her fingers in her ears and shut her eyes.

Two seconds later they exploded between the men. The effects were immediately devastating. All suffered hearing and visual problems and were completely disorientated. It would take them at least fifteen to thirty minutes to recover sufficiently to use a firearm competently. One was unconscious and two of them suffered slight shrapnel injuries to their lower legs. They all carried at least one stun grenade which didn't have the same destructive capacity as Isabella's cherry bombs. She'd incapacitated three men with ease.

She knew there had to be more and kept tucked behind the wall. The two security guards had thrown themselves to the floor as the explosion reverberated around the exhibits. Several glass cases shattered and rare exhibits fell to the floor. Some of the more delicate ones broke as others rolled about becoming obstacles in their own right.

The remaining three officers fanned out not wishing to present themselves as an easy target for any more of her bombs. They'd seen the flash of the explosion and heard the din and knew she was a dangerous foe. Their ears were ringing from the noise over forty yards away. A radio call from the sergeant to his three colleagues went unanswered. It was going to be pointless trying to arrest her and hard to neutralise her.

The group's leader threw a stun grenade more in anger than in anticipation towards the entrance of the security office. It hit the floor and bounced once before rolling towards Isabella. She stepped towards it and kicked it back towards him. He hadn't considered the time delay in his effort to disable her before it took to explode. He was felled by his own grenade's incapacitating qualities.

Isabella spotted one man trying to creep around a large crustacean displayed on a plinth. She knew it was pointless trying to shoot him in the head or torso because of his body armour. He paused a second too long and left a leg in view. Isabella fired three aimed rounds at it. The first clipped the edge of some armoured leg shield and tore a gouge across his thigh. The next hit him just below a knee guard shattering his tibia and the last hit the top of his boot, glancing off it into the tendons of his foot. He fell over knocking the exhibit from the plinth which smashed onto the floor sending shards in all directions.

She yelled out, 'You have a chance. You are alone now. You can withdraw or I may end up killing you.' She stole a swift glance and was sure there were two shadows moving some distance apart. A trick of the light. She knew there was only one man left.

The remaining officer said nothing, knowing to do so would give his location away.

'Suit yourself,' and she scoured the shadows amongst the exhibits. He was well hidden. She smiled to herself. She'd got the upper hand yet again. Now all she had to work out was how to get past him. A bullet whizzed past her making her jump backwards. She'd seen the muzzle flash. She'd one cherry bomb left.

There was a prehistoric skeleton of a large flying bird suspended from the ceiling by two wires above where the muzzle flash had been. The display below, and where the man was concealed, showed the birds potential food sources. She needed the skeleton to fall but how? She couldn't shoot the restraining wires because no one was that good a shot, and she didn't believe the cherry bomb was powerful enough to break them.

She wasn't sure what would happen. The explosion might not even rock it. She lit the fuse with her lighter and threw the cherry bomb underarm high in the air towards the skeleton. The officer watched it arch upwards and followed it's trajectory. He was still looking up as it exploded. The flash caused him to lose vision as black floaters were all that he could see before passing out. The skeleton swayed back and forth but held.

Isabella cursed. It had been rather a forlorn hope but worth a go. She didn't know the man had been rendered unconscious from the blast and was no longer a threat. Listening intently, trying to tune out the distracting sounds of the radio still playing in the office, she thought she could still hear him moving about.

A shadow moved and she fired a rapid four rounds in its direction. It was nothing. The swaying skeleton was shifting shadows all around the exhibition area. Twice more she fired at the shadows. The man behind a large display case was considering his options. If he fired she would know where he was and he knew everyone else was out of the fray. If he spoke she would know roughly where he was. He had to ask for assistance via his radio and take a chance.

He peeked round from his hiding place to try and see where Isabella was. No sign of her. He slipped his borrowed gun into his anorak pocket to free up his hands and to use his radio. Then he felt something pressing in his neck and he knew exactly where she was.

'Drop that radio. Who the hell are you? What are you doing in here?'

Clive realised he had a chance, 'I'm part of the museum security staff. My radio wasn't working. I've been upstairs and heard the racket so came down stairs and walked into this.'

Isabella pushed him away from her and looked at him as he turned round to face her. An unarmed big black man without any body armour or even looking like a policeman. He was dressed all in black with a coat on and ridiculous red trainers. 'Why aren't you in uniform?'

'I work alone upstairs so can wear what I like.'

'How do I get out of this place?'

'They can let you out,' and he waved towards the open-plan office. 'They keep the keys.'

Isabella turned to look towards the two guards still prone on the floor and she put her gun into a pocket. She called to them, 'You can get up now. I need to leave,' and she started to walk towards them.

She heard Clive moving behind her and she spun round. He was pointing a gun at her which was shaking about in his hand. Slowly she put her hand back into her pocket. She was taking a risk. Watching his gun shaking about so much she believed he'd probably miss her even at close range. It was obvious to her he wasn't used to firing a gun.

'Who are you?'

'Police. Do not try anything or I'll be forced to shoot you.'

'I don't think so,' and she started to slowly withdraw her gun.

Clive watched it clear her pocket and start to lift with the barrel towards him. He'd never fired a gun in his life, but he liked films and he'd seen how they did it. He supported his gun hand and crouched slightly. The gun steadied. He didn't even know if there was a safety catch. The firearms officer who'd handed him the gun when they entered hadn't said. He started to panic. Would the gun fire?

Isabella smiled. She had nearly brought her own gun to bear and he was good as dead.

The noise was deafening in the large gallery. Clive just kept pulling the trigger. Bullet after bullet. Some hit Isabella and others flew past her and into the museum. Glass cases smashed and exhibits were destroyed but Clive didn't hear them. Isabella's gun dropped from her hand. She was propelled backwards by the force of the bullets. Only five hit her and eleven missed. Clive only stopped pulling the trigger when the gun was empty. Isabella was dead.

51

18TH DECEMBER 2011
1AM

John scrambled over the railings and into the building. The paramedics were calling for more ambulances as the fire brigade were building a metal platform over the railings. It was chaos. Clive was sitting on the floor looking at Isabella's lifeless body. He couldn't take his eyes from her. He was in serious shock and being tended to by a medic.

The two CO19 officers who'd protected the paramedics and were uninjured were trying to assist their colleagues. The DAC was at the door to the museum waiting for someone to open it and let him in. Uniform officers were being stationed around the gardens to deter onlookers who seemed to gather even in the middle of the night.

Inside the museum the security staff were calling the museum's directors and supervisors. The damage was extensive and the museum was likely to be closed for several days with great loss of revenue. The police were slowly putting their investigation together and had sealed off the whole gallery and office. A police technician had attended and was downloading all the CCTV from the museum.

John spoke to the DAC. He'd recovered Isabella's suitcase. They both knew what she had in it. A secret camera, independent of the safe deposit centre's security, had been planted by the police in the vault. It had recorded all Isabella's actions and each code number she punched in. It would take days to go through all the bonds and trace their criminal owners. Patrick would have little choice but to help, when, and if, he recovered. At least nine serious criminals were going to have a lot to answer for.

The DAC and John had limited knowledge about the proceeds of crime legislation but knew what would happen. The police would seize everything in the suitcase and all the cash still in the Posda family safe. The house in Clabon Mews would be sequestered and then probably sold. Government coffers would benefit by untold millions.

•

Tabitha Marchant was woken by her mobile phone ringing. Her bedside clock was showing 3.07am. Her alarm had been set for 4am. At least two hours before she expected a knock on her door by the police. Plenty of time to be out of the house and put her plan into operation.

She listened as the person at the other end explained what had happened. She sat up as the details of the incident were relayed. It had taken her a long time to get to sleep worrying about those around her. Now she had even more to worry about. Explaining to her husband there was a problem at work, she hurriedly dressed and went to see Curly before going to her office.

The security officer on the front door of the Foreign Office waved her in. As soon as she entered the lift, he called an emergency number. He informed the person of her arrival.

The director of GCHQ was woken and told. Then the home secretary was woken and told. Katrina Parke was woken and told. Her husband, Sebastian woke and listened in to the call.

The planned morning arrest of Tabitha Marchant was unfolding rapidly. They all needed to know what she was up to at that time of night. Rocky was in bed studying a manual about laser guidance when a text pinged its arrival. He looked at the message and laughed. The director had texted him directly with a phone number requesting an urgent call.

'Good morning, sir. I'm impressed you found this number. Were you using the hack I taught you many moons ago?'

'Hello, Rocky. I certainly was. You never called me sir before.'

'That's because I worked for you. Now I don't I'm a lot more respectful.' Both men laughed. 'This must be urgent at this time of night? What can I do for you?'

'I was at a meeting the other day with the Met commissioner, home secretary and a few others including John Whiles. I thought I saw your fingerprints on some information so I decided I'd give you a private call. Totally off the record. I have a problem regarding a woman by the name of Tabitha Marchant. She has suddenly gone to her office at this ridiculous time of night and I need to know why. She was going to be arrested later this morning. I have discovered there has been a shooting this evening and the police have killed Chloe Mila. I believe both these names are known to you?'

'It is possible I've heard them before.'

'Would you be able to task your: shall we say "informant", to see if they could establish what she is up to?'

'I'll ask them as soon as I can and call you back.'

'Thanks Rocky. I owe you,' and they hung up.

Rocky went to his lab and checked his equipment. He could see Marchant sitting behind her desk. The recording machine showed she'd made several calls and he downloaded them to a single file. Then he checked the numbers she'd dialled. Several embassies abroad and a couple of local calls. He watched her go to a large grey safe and dial in the combination. There were three large shelves and on each were stacks of money in different denominations.

Marchant ignored most of it and Rocky watched the film of her take out five large bundles of Euros in high value notes and put them on her desk. She slammed the safe door and spun the dial. He listened to the phone call she made and watched her stuff her bag with the money. Her other bag was padlocked which he thought strange. The money would be a lot safer in it. Time he concluded was paramount. She was running.

Rocky called the director, 'She's going to Biggin Hill. She has just phoned someone she addressed as 'B' and asked him for help. It's a number she's called before and he is someone in 6. I have the name of Barrington. Don't know if it's a last or given name though. I think I should let DC Whiles know. Perhaps he could stop her?'

'Yes. Could you do that please Rocky? I'll see what I can put in motion just in case. I'll find out who this Barrington is and I'll let you know.'

Rocky called John and updated him. He updated the DAC. He called IR. They called the local police who dispatched a car with two officers to intercept Marchant when she arrived. It was going to be a simple arrest. Or that's what they all thought.

The director called Sebastian. He explained the predicament of trying to establish who Barrington was. 'Whoever he is, I want him dealt with. He's an embarrassment to 6. It's your old department. It might be the person that Thérèse Posda was trying to tell you about. I'll call 'C' and tell him you're going to be there shortly. Once you establish who he is, I'll leave it up to you what happens.'

Sebastian understood.

Marchant had seen the writing on the wall. The police were closing in on her. Derek was missing and she'd worked out he had to be under arrest somewhere. She hadn't been able to silence him in time and she knew he'd probably row for shore. Tristram was missing as well. He'd keep quiet. If he didn't, he'd be locked up for a long time. Her two Turkish enforcers had disappeared. They could drop her in it if they talked. She'd paid them well in the past so she hoped they would stay quiet. Both Kuznetsov and Mila had been killed by the police and any chance of seeing any money from them had evaporated.

How the police had got onto her and her associates was her main concern. They seemed to have homed in on them rather easily. She knew people had probably talked but the police shouldn't have been able to prove anything against her. It should have all fallen into Derek's lap. That's why she had picked him as her deputy. He was stupid enough not to see that he would be the patsy if it all went wrong. The only problem was she'd failed to shut him up permanently. Something wasn't right.

Before she'd gone to sleep, she came to the conclusion she was under surveillance. Somehow they must have bugged her office. The police wouldn't have been allowed to do it which left the security services. Box 500 would be the most likely. Who would authorise it though? The minister? It had to be. Tristram would have told her if he'd known. How else could they have got to Mila and Kuznetsov? It looked like they had got into her computer. They must have colluded with the police. At least they hadn't got into her burner phones.

Now she was in her element. 'Catch me if you can' ran through her mind. A few obscure phone calls to some embassies might muddy the water. Let them see all the Euros if they had video. A simple clue for anyone. A call to 'B' asking for help with a plane from Biggin Hill to France. Another easy clue to follow. Tabitha didn't care if they found 'B'. He could look after himself.

She ran down the stairs and out of the front of the building. A cruising black cab stopped. Just a couple of miles and she got out. As soon as it was out of sight she hailed another. A few more miles and she swapped once more. Tabitha was deposited at the entrance to the airport. She knew the police would be able to track her as she wanted but they would be too late. Elstree airport was deserted except for a comatose security officer and a scruffy middle-aged Polish man stinking of booze who was expecting her.

Katrina Parke wasn't far behind. She didn't trust Tabitha one inch. The security officer told her that Tabitha had got into a taxi right outside the front doors of the Foreign Office. She quickly found the first cabbie. When he told her where he'd dropped her off, she knew that she had laid a false trail.

She was heading north away from Biggin Hill. The second cabbie was more elusive. He was taking way too long to find.

Katrina opened her laptop and studied a map. She drew an imaginary line from the Foreign Office through to where the cabbie had dropped Tabitha. Then she extended it and checked the map either side of her line.

There was a small airport landing strip marked. Elstree. Katrina dropped the laptop and gunned her small Ford Fiesta. It was still a long way off.

The Pole led Tabitha to a small Piper Cherokee single engine plane.

'Where's your luggage?'

'I've only got this,' and she handed him the locked bag which he flung into the rear of the plane. 'This is an emergency flight. I've got to get to Brussels as quickly as possible.'

'Money up front as agreed. Five thousand Euros.'

Tabitha gave him a small bundle. 'I've got a slight request. I'm a very nervous flyer especially in little planes. Can you take off and then land so I can watch from the ground to make sure you can do it? An extra grand.'

'You've got yourself a deal.'

Tabitha gave him the money. The man struggled into the cockpit. 'Five minutes, straight up and straight down.' The drink was clouding his mind but the money was an easy incentive.

Tabitha walked away as the plane started up and taxied to the single runway. She had used the man several times before but only to bring people into the country. She knew him to be a drunk who would do anything for a few grand.

As the plane lifted off the tarmac, Tabitha smiled. She watched it climb up and away from the ground and then begin to slowly bank for its return. She pressed the button on the fob that Curly had supplied with the bag. There was a loud explosion and the plane was engulfed in flames as it broke up in mid-air. Burning debris landed on buildings setting some on fire.

The security guard ran out of his small sentry box to see some of the falling debris. He didn't see Tabitha slip out past his security box and walk off towards the main road. She didn't hurry. It was nearly a mile and a half before she would be able to find a cruising cab. The gathering crescendo of sirens converging around the airport caused her to smile.

She happily said out loud, 'Sort that lot out.'

52

18TH DECEMBER 2011
5AM

Zena watched the video replay of Marchant in her office. She wasn't sure. She watched it through again. Rocky was starting to worry.

'She's being obvious. Making sure that the Euros can be seen before putting them into her bag. Why not straight from the safe into her bag. Blatantly talking about Biggin Hill. Silly calls to embassies. I think she's worked out that she's being watched and is laying a false trail.'

Rocky agreed. 'I'd better let DC Whiles know.'

He phoned John who was back in the DAC's office chatting to Kelly and the DAC. They were all concerned for Clive who was struggling to come to terms with what he'd done. One of the Met's psychologists and a welfare officer had been called from their beds. They were with him in a private ward at St Thomas's Hospital.

The call from Rocky explained a lot. There had been no contact with Marchant at Biggin Hill. The reports of an unauthorised flight taking off and then the plane exploding at Elstree looked ominous. Timing would have been about right for Marchant to have been there. Why would a little private plane be taking off at that time of night? To get her out of the country? John didn't think so. He considered it was likely to be a red herring and said so. He pulled up an ordnance survey map of the area on a computer. It told him nothing.

Kelly asked, 'What would you do in her position?'

'I'd go somewhere obscure where we don't have an extradition agreement. Brazil is a good favourite. Nice climate and surroundings. It was good enough for the train robbers. Her money could easily be changed.'

'A light plane would be no good. You need an airliner.'

'Of course! Heathrow. We'd easily get her back from Europe. You wouldn't get a flight out of Luton to South America. Must be Heathrow. We need to alert SB.'

The DAC said, 'We're guessing Brazil, but it could be anywhere.'

Kelly snatched up her phone and checked a number in her book. She got a sleepy reply from the SB duty officer. When the DAC was mentioned he snapped into gear. An image of Marchant pinged into his email inbox. He alerted all his team at each terminal. Now it was wait and see.

All three went to the canteen and managed to get breakfast. The welfare officer joined them and said Clive would be over his shock soon. A small piece of good news.

Back in the office they sat and waited. The DAC spoke to the director of GCHQ and the home secretary. Barrington Webster had easily been identified by Sebastian as he was the only one in MI6 with that as a given name. They all agreed that he should be arrested by the Met. John relished the prospect of interviewing him with Clive when he was up to it.

Sebastian could play dirty to. He'd got Barrington's

personnel file and found his home phone number. Pulling out of his jacket pocket a burner phone he called the home number shown.

'Barrington here. How can I help you?'

'I suggest you don't go into work today. That's if you don't want to be arrested. Marchant is on the run and Tristram Everdean and Derek Hodden are spilling their guts. The police and "C" know all about you and your dodgy deals and are waiting for you.'

Before Barrington could respond, Sebastian hung up. The burner phone would be in pieces within the hour.

Barrington panicked. He'd thought the call earlier from Marchant about getting a plane from Biggin Hill sounded strange. Now it was making sense. She was running. He had a family. Could he just up and run as well leaving his family behind? No, of course he couldn't. But then if he was arrested and sent to prison, he wouldn't see his family other than at visiting times. And then only if they deemed to visit. What should he do?

Sebastian didn't care. He hoped he'd run. It was always easier to get rid of someone who was in hiding. No one missed them. It was a lot harder to arrange a suicide in a prison cell. Not impossible: just harder.

Katrina Parke got to Elstree as the emergency services were in full swing. She quickly established that a light plane that had taken off unexpectedly during the night without authority had exploded in mid-air. No one could tell her how many or who were on board. She smelt a rat. She knew something wasn't right. A phone conversation followed with the director. He in turn called the DAC.

Information flowed both ways. The director explained what had happened at Elstree and that it appeared Marchant had been heading in that direction. The DAC said that it was his view that she was laying false trails and would likely head to Heathrow. The director concurred and updated Katrina Parke.

She made her way as fast as she could to the airport. Kenny was woken and alerted the DCI in charge of the MIT at Heathrow. By 7am there were over fifty people scouring the airport for Marchant. Katrina guessed it had to be Terminal 3. International flights mainly to North and South America. She was banking on Marchant going to South America where she could disappear. Terminal 5 was mainly British Airways and as Marchant would know, could easily be monitored.

Marchant came up from the underground into Terminal 3. She made her way to a ticket desk and stood patiently waiting for the sales woman to finish a phone call. Two officers saw her and called the duty officer. Patrolling armed officers were summoned to attend and arrest her. Katrina Parke sprinted from her position to the desk. She stood shoulder to shoulder with Marchant for less than fifteen seconds.

She placed a small tablet on the desk top in front of her. 'Within a minute you are going to be arrested. You will be held for the rest of your life in a military facility. No contact with the outside world. A rat in a cage to be experimented upon. What life is that? This pill will stop all that.'

Marchant looked around and saw uniform policemen with guns approaching. Parke moved away from her. Tabitha picked up the pill. But then she hesitated.

'Police. Open your hands and interlock your fingers above your head.'

She hesitated. The two police officers pointed their guns at her. 'Do as I say.'

Marchant didn't want to die. She didn't want to be shot. She didn't want to take the pill. What frightened her the most was being locked up for the rest of her life. What sort of life was that? She saw one take out a Taser. She knew it was now or never. She put the pill in her mouth and swallowed it.

The Taser hit her in the middle of the chest and she fell to the ground. The two armed officers moved cautiously forward and one handcuffed her. He needn't have bothered, she was dead.

The irony had flitted through her brain as she died. The arrival of Mila at Heathrow had been the beginning of her downfall.

Katrina Parke sent a short text message to the director. *She took the tablet.*

EPILOGUE

6TH JANUARY 2012
NOON

It was 12 noon and the entire murder teams from Heathrow and Reigate were gathering for a delayed Christmas lunch at the Burford Bridge Hotel in Mickleham. Vince and his surveillance team, the Telephone Unit officers along with the CO19 firearms officers were also in attendance. The chief constables of Sussex and Surrey with DAC Larry Mortimore, DCI Sylvester and Chief Inspector Kenny were invited guests. The hotel had laid on a traditional Christmas meal with customary decorations. Alcohol was flowing freely and the noise was gradually increasing as it was consumed.

At the conclusion of the meal, the chief constable of Surrey stood to address everyone. He banged an empty wine bottle on the table for attention.

'I'd like to thank all of you here today for your work in relation to solving the two murders at Heathrow and the two murders here in Surrey. Unfortunately, we are unable to put the culprits before a court of law, but that was their choice when they took on CO19. I'd like to just update you with the current situation.' He drained his glass which was immediately topped up by an attentive member of the hotel staff.

'I have been informed by the commissioner of the Met that he conducted a review of all officers who joined the police from within the Foreign Office. It amounted to five officers. One we all know is in custody pending trial. PC Brown happened to be one. The other two are being interviewed as to any connection with Marchant. As to Marchant herself, the director of GCHQ and his security team are trawling through all her emails, texts and phone calls to establish who she permitted entry to the country and who she arranged to be killed. Her bank balance was probably more than everyone's here put together. That, along with the proceeds from the safety deposit centre and the sequestration of the house in Chelsea will go to the Treasury and keep the country going for about an hour.'

Laughter erupted around the room as he quaffed his wine.

'At present, Tristram Everdean MP and Marchant's deputy Derek Hodden are being extremely cooperative, presumably to keep their prison sentences to a minimum. I am also told that Barrington Webster, who was something quite high up in one of our security services was assisting investigators as to his involvement with Marchant. Unfortunately, he decided to take the cowards way out and has committed suicide.' He glanced at some notes.

An unsolicited comment of 'Shame,' was easily heard.

'A lot of you aren't aware that Chief Superintendent Ashurst has resigned from the Met. The less said about that the better. Her children are both in hospital recovering from their encounter with the woman we all knew as Chloe Mila. Enquiries made by the director of GCHQ on our behalf have revealed that her true name was Isabella Posda. She was the daughter of a renowned Columbian drug lord who recently met his end by a bullet.'

Someone from the middle of the room said loudly, 'Life can be a bitch.' The majority laughed because they didn't care.

'To continue. We are still trying to establish what Gleb Kuznetsov's real name was. It looks like that will remain a mystery.' His glass was topped up and he swallowed a mouthful. 'As you probably know the inquest was formally opened and adjourned in relation to him. The coroner was asked by our lawyers if we could release the film of the encounter with CO19 and he had no objections. It will be put to all the networks by Scotland Yard's Press Bureau tomorrow evening in time for the early news bulletins.'

Loud applause greeted the news.

'Now ladies and gentlemen, we come to some information that was given to me today from the home secretary via the DAC. It appeared that she had a mole in her security team. This came to light during the investigation. For those of you who are still sober, you may have spotted that I only referred to four of the five officers who joined the police from the Foreign Office. The fifth was on her team and reporting back to Tristram Everdean. That officer is now in a similar position to PC Scrivener.' He paused for a few seconds.

Several derogatory terms were called out.

He continued, 'The home secretary was told about this afternoon's little sojourn and handed us a personally signed piece of paper that I shall give to the hotel. Its common name is a cheque. It is from her personal account to the value of two and a half thousand pounds. This will just about cover half of the alcohol consumed.'

Several cheered and a loud voice shouted, 'I'll vote for her.'

'I think that about covers everything.' He looked at the DAC and the chief constable of Sussex. 'Have either of you anything to add?'

They both shook their heads. 'In that case, carry on. The hotel is providing rooms for those who want them. I must tell you all. Please don't drive from here today. The police are real bastards here in Surrey.'

GLOSSARY

POLICE RANKS REFERRED TO:

PC	Police Constable
WPC	Woman Police Constable
DC	Detective Constable
PS	Police Sergeant
DS	Detective Sergeant
Insp.	Inspector
DCI	Detective Chief Inspector
Supt.	Superintendent
Ch. Supt.	Chief Superintendent
DAC	Deputy Assistant Commissioner

ABBREVIATIONS USED:

Airwave	Police Radio System
ANPR	Automatic Number Plate Reader
Asp	Modern Extendable Baton
Black Rat	Traffic Officer
Box 500	MI5
C	Head of MI6
CO	Commissioner's Office: aka New Scotland Yard
CO19	Firearms Unit

CODEC	Computer Programme
Church	Customs and Excise
CPS	Crown Prosecution Service
CRO	Criminal Records Office
Door Bosher	Hand Held Battering Ram
FME	Force Medical Examiner
GCHQ	Government Communications Headquarters
HA	Home Address
HOLMES	Home Office Large Major Enquiry System
India '9 9'	Call sign of Police Helicopter
IPCC	Independent Police Complaints Commission
IR	Information Room at New Scotland Yard
JTAC	Joint Terrorism Analysis Centre
MIT	Major Investigation Team
MOD	Ministry of Defence
MP	Member of Parliament
Plasticuffs	Thin Plastic Handcuffs
PM	Post Mortem
PNC	Police National Computer
PoLSA	Police Search Advisor
PPS	Parliamentary Private Secretary
RO	Registered Owner
SAS	Special Air Service
SB	Special Branch
SBS	Special Boat Service
SIO	Senior Investigating Officer
SIS	Secret Intelligence Service (MI6)
SOCO	Scenes of Crimes Officer
The Job	Metropolitan Police Publication
The Met	Metropolitan Police

The Yard	New Scotland Yard
Trojan	Specialist Firearms Officers
TSG	Tactical Support Group
USB	Universal Serial Bus (Storage Device)
'4 2'	Surveillance Motorcyclist
5	MI5
6	MI6